PRAISE FOR CLAIRE DOUGLAS

AND

The Girls Who Disappeared

"Thrillingly tense and twisty."

—B. A. Paris, author of *The Therapist*

"Twisty, exciting yet so very real."

—Gillian McAllister, author of *Wrong Place, Wrong Time*

"Clever and terrifically compelling, I think *The Girls Who Disappeared* might be my new favorite Claire Douglas novel!"

—Sarah Pearse, author of *The Retreat*

"Claire is a mistress at weaving the reader into a web of domestic deceit."

—Jane Corry, author of *The Dead Ex*

"Moody, menacing, and gothic, *The Girls Who Disappeared* is a chillingly atmospheric thriller."

—J. P. Delaney, author of *My Darling Daughter*

THE GIRLS WHO DISAPPEARED

ALSO BY CLAIRE DOUGLAS

THE GIRLS WHO
DISAPPEARED

a novel

CLAIRE DOUGLAS

HARPER

NEW YORK • LONDON • TORONTO • SYDNEY

HARPER

Originally published in Great Britain in 2022 by Penguin Random House UK.

THE GIRLS WHO DISAPPEARED. Copyright © 2022 by Claire Douglas. All rights reserved. Printed in the United States of America. No part of this book may be used or reproduced in any manner whatsoever without written permission except in the case of brief quotations embodied in critical articles and reviews. For information, address HarperCollins Publishers, 195 Broadway, New York, NY 10007.

HarperCollins books may be purchased for educational, business, or sales promotional use. For information, please email the Special Markets Department at SPsales@harpercollins.com.

FIRST US EDITION

Library of Congress Cataloging-in-Publication Data has been applied for.

ISBN 978-0-06-327741-0 (pbk.)

23 24 25 26 27 LBC 5 4 3 2 1

For my readers

THE GIRLS WHO DISAPPEARED

The Accident

November 1998

THEY WERE SINGING. THEY WERE DRUNK. THEY WERE happy. That was what Olivia recalled most, afterwards. How happy her friends had been.

Sally was in the front. She always was. She said the back seat made her nauseous. And, as Olivia's best friend, it was the natural place for her to be. Sally was chattering away about Mal, a boy she fancied who'd finally asked her out, not that this surprised Olivia. Men always gravitated towards Sally, with her huge dark eyes and bubbly nature – including Olivia's own boyfriend, Wesley. It was still a bone of contention between them, a subject that was now off-limits to preserve their friendship.

Sally's voice was high, excitable and a little slurred as she recalled the moment Mal had bought her a Diamond White. Olivia was finding it hard to hear her over the radio and the rain that was getting louder and heavier by the minute.

Tamzin and Katie were in the back, mascara smudged below their eyes, their glittery crop tops poking through their not-warm-enough coats, smelling of booze and perfume. They arms were wrapped around each other's necks, acting as though they were still at Ritzy's as they crooned along to 'Two Become One' by the Spice Girls.

Olivia's heart sank. They'd promised they wouldn't drink too much tonight. It had been Tamzin who'd goaded the others. Olivia had noticed her at the bar ordering double shots and flicking her long, peroxide-blonde hair over her slim shoulders, obviously hoping one of her many admirers would pay. And they usually did. Hers was a different type of beauty from Sally's: brasher and more in your face with her colourful Wonderbras and skirts that barely covered her arse.

It hadn't been raining as Olivia had headed out to pick up her friends earlier that evening. And it had only started to drizzle as they left the nightclub ten minutes ago. But now the downpour was so heavy that Olivia was finding it increasingly difficult to see the road ahead. Rain gathered in rivulets either side of her windscreen nearly obscuring her vision, despite her wipers being on max. The road stretched out in front of them, dark and all-encompassing as though they were travelling through space. Even on main beam it wasn't enough to cut through the mist that was beginning to hover above the ground like dry ice.

As it was Olivia's turn to drive she'd only sipped one glass of wine all evening. But now she felt it burn the back of her throat, hot and acidic, as her little Peugeot 205 was buffeted by the strong winds. She wasn't a nervous driver usually but she'd only passed her test a few months ago. And tonight felt different. She hated this road at the best of times. The Devil's Corridor cut straight through the forest, and the tall beech and fir trees that reared up on either side made the road feel oppressive. Further on were the famous standing stones, and then their little town wrapped around it, a tourist trap full of mystical shops and tearooms.

The drumming of the rain drowned the music, splashing onto the tarmac like darts shot from the sky. Olivia clutched the steering wheel tightly, knuckles white. The rain was now so loud that the others stopped singing abruptly and Sally dialled up the radio.

'Turn it down,' snapped Olivia, and Sally did as she asked without complaint. It was too dark to see her expression, but Olivia knew she'd offended her friend. She experienced a twinge of regret: she hated upsetting Sally.

'What a night!' exclaimed Katie, leaning forwards, gripping Olivia's headrest. 'Look at that rain.'

'Can you sit back?' Olivia's voice was unusually curt. Katie was the eldest and the leader of the group and didn't like to be told what to do. Olivia couldn't see her face but she imagined her rolling her eyes at Tamzin. Nevertheless she heard her flop back against the headrest. They weren't wearing their seatbelts.

'I hope I hear from Mal tomorrow,' Sally piped up, in an attempt to break the tension, but she sounded more subdued now. 'He said he would phone and – Shit! WATCH OUT!'

Someone was standing in the middle of the road.

It all happened so suddenly: Olivia slammed on her brakes and swerved. The car skidded and spun around, the wheels clipping the bank, causing it to flip over, metal scraping against tarmac as it landed on its roof, eventually coming to a grinding halt in a ditch. Olivia could hear the screams of her friends as pain ripped through her legs. And then she blacked out.

* * *

When she came round the car was the right way up. Her clock flashed amber in the darkness: 01:10. How long had she been out? There was a deathly silence. No sounds from her friends. Her heart hammered as she remembered. *Oh, God, oh, God. Are they okay? Are they injured? Did I hit the person in the road?*

Olivia tried to move but yelled in pain. One of her legs was pinned beneath the steering-wheel column, which had crumpled downwards, trapping her. 'Sally?' She turned towards the passenger seat. It was empty. Where was Sally? She tried to look behind her, craning her neck towards the back seat, expecting to see Katie and Tamzin, dreading that they might be dead, but they weren't there. Panic welled within her as realization hit.

She was alone in the car.

Had they gone to get help? But they were in the middle of nowhere and Katie had a mobile, a pink Nokia. She was so proud of it. She had the best job out of the four of them: an assistant pharmacist. One of them would have used that to call the police or an ambulance. Their bags were gone too. There was nothing in the car to suggest they'd ever been there. But they wouldn't have just left her. One of them would have stayed. Sally, definitely. Her best mate.

Olivia started trembling uncontrollably as pain and fear gripped her, turning her insides to ice as she remembered how the accident had happened: the figure in the road, which was now empty, stretching into the seemingly dark void.

Who had it been?

And where had her friends gone?

Day One

1

Jenna

THE DEVIL'S CORRIDOR IS AN APT NAME FOR THIS LONG, STRAIGHT A-road that leads to the market town of Stafferbury in Wiltshire. Over the years there have been reports of many strange happenings: unexplained accidents, apparent suicides, sightings of hooded figures and the sound of a child crying in the dead of night. But none more mysterious than the Olivia Rutherford case twenty years ago this week. Three young women disappeared from a crashed car and haven't been seen since . . .

I pause the recording on my phone as I take in my surroundings. There is definitely something eerie about this road. It looks as though it's been built straight through a forest and all I can see at either side are thickets of tall, dense evergreen trees that reach towards the bruise-coloured sky and the swollen black clouds. So far I haven't spotted any houses or buildings along here. I could be somewhere Scandinavian rather than the depths of Wiltshire. I've been parked on the verge for the last ten minutes and only two cars have gone by.

A presence in my peripheral vision makes me jolt. A man is peering in at me through the passenger window and my heart races. He must have come from the forest. He looks early fifties, maybe a little older: craggy face, a bushy beard, shaggy grey eyebrows beneath a fisherman's hat. His shoulders are rounded under a long waxed overcoat that reaches mid-calf. He's holding the lead of a white whippet-type dog with three legs and a brown patch over its left eye. The dog stares soulfully at me. I reach down for the mace in my handbag and place it on the seat beside me, hidden by my thigh.

The man makes a rolling motion with his hands. I lower the window just a fraction and keep my finger on the button. The smell of pine and unwashed clothes hits me.

'Can I help you?'

'I was going to ask you the same,' he calls, in a thick West Country accent. 'Have you broken down? You shouldn't pull up here. It ain't safe to be on this road all alone, like.' He has a missing front tooth.

Thunder rolls overhead, a low beastly growl that adds to my unease.

'I was . . .' I hesitate. Perhaps it's best he doesn't know I'm a journalist yet. 'I'm just on my way to Stafferbury.'

'Are you lost?'

'No. I pulled over to do . . . something.' I'm aware I sound vague.

'Right.' He frowns, his suspicious gaze sweeping over my modern Audi Q5 before landing back on me. His eyes are very dark, almost black. 'Well, Stafferbury is just another two miles or so down this road. You can't miss it.'

'That's great, thanks.'

I quickly close my window to discourage any more questions, my hands trembling as I slide the gearstick into drive. I pull away from the grass verge so quickly the tyres screech. From my rear-view mirror I see him standing there, his dog sitting at his feet, staring after my retreating car.

I'm feeling a little less rattled as I arrive in Stafferbury. The town is just how I imagined it would be. Just like the black-and-white photographs I've pored over before driving more than two hundred miles to get here from Manchester. It's hardly changed since the late 1890s and, of course, the standing stones are even older. I notice them first. They are in the adjourning boggy-looking field to my right, set five metres apart in a semicircle, large and ugly, like a set of uneven teeth. They don't seem to be in any particular formation, not like Stonehenge. Even from here I can see that a film of green algae has formed over them, like plaque.

A family in brightly coloured raincoats, the kids in funky wellies with a small dog in tow, clamber over the stile into the field where the stones are. I wonder what Finn would think of it here. As an image of my floppy-haired ten-year-old son swims in my mind I feel a pang of longing so strong it's painful. Since the separation from his dad I'm used to being away from him – I have no choice now that we share custody. But I hate it. It feels like part of me is missing.

The high street is set in a horseshoe shape with a war memorial separating the two roads, and in addition to the one I've just driven down there is another heading away from the town, snaking between two medieval-looking buildings with an ominous-sounding pub, The Raven, on the corner. Its sign – a big black bird with sinister beady eyes set against a grey sky – gives me the creeps. From my satnav, that road leads to the back-streets and countryside beyond.

I'm staying in the forest in a cabin that looked beautiful and modern on the website. I'd wanted to see the high street before heading to my accommodation so had deliberately missed the turning from the Devil's Corridor, and now I go back on myself. I continue through the town, which has been dressed up for Christmas, taking in the little boutiques selling mystical ornaments, jewellery and incense, a café in one of the Tudor buildings called Bea's Tearoom, a few clothes shops sporting tie-dye T-shirts and fringed skirts, and a place called Madame Tovey's – she professes (according to the large sign outside, complete with a tarot card illustration) to be able to tell your fortune. It's a cute town, small and quaint, with its Tudor buildings, cobbled streets and Christmas lights twinkling at leaded windows. I can see why tourists are attracted to it, but there is an air of the rundown about it. It's like Avebury's poor relation. Maybe it's more bustling in the summer, I think charitably. It is a cold November Monday, after all, with only a few people about.

As if on cue the rain comes, fast and furious, drumming loudly on my roof. I notice a young couple dart into a nearby shop, holding hands and giggling, and I experience a tug of envy. Gavin and I were like that once. I drive around the war memorial, the stones now on my left, as I head out of the high street and onto the sinister-sounding Devil's Corridor once more. There is a dirt track that forks off, no more than half a mile from the field of standing stones, which will take me further into the forest. As I turn down it, I wonder if it's a little too remote. Perhaps I should have booked a B-and-B in the town.

After a few hundred yards I come to a purpose-built holiday cabin similar to the type you get at Center Parcs, surrounded by beech, pine and fir trees. I slow down to get a better look at the name on the front door. Fern. I'm staying in Bluebell, though I've no idea where that is. In the distance I think there are two or three more, but it's hard to see clearly with the rain battering my car and the phalanx of trees as deep as the eye can see. When I spoke to Jay Knapton, the owner, on the phone to make the booking, he'd explained that the complex wasn't fully built yet and that only half a dozen cabins were dotted through the forest at the moment. He had sounded impressed when I told him the reason I was visiting.

I drive on, my tyres sluicing through the wet mud. I hope the first cabin, Fern, is occupied, although it certainly looked empty. I don't like to think about being alone in the forest. I slow down as I approach the second cabin trying to catch the name on the grey front door. Bluebell. Relieved, I pull up on the driveway. It's only matting and turf underfoot, and as I step from the car my heel sinks into it. What was I thinking wearing heeled boots to come to a forest? Thank goodness I have my wellies in the car. I stand for a moment, looking up at the cabin, ignoring the rain seeping through my wool coat and soaking my hair. I'm besieged by the memories of our family holiday to Center Parcs last Christmas. Finn had been so excited – the house among the trees, he'd called it. My heart twists when I realize there may never be another family holiday with all three of us, or a Christmas Day spent all together. From now on, it will be Finn with either me or his dad – and in time Gavin's new partner. Because, of course, there's going to be a new girlfriend, if there isn't already. Why else would Gavin announce, late one night four months ago, that he needed 'space' from our fifteen-year marriage? And our nineteen-year relationship? Why else would he move into a studio flat near his office?

This is not the life I'd envisaged. This is not the future I want.

And I'm still bitter about it. I'm furious that the life I'd had, the life I'd loved, has been ripped away from me. That our little family unit has been broken up. This is not what I wanted for our son. For me. Sometimes I want to hurt Gavin so badly – to punish him, to stop him seeing our son – that it eats away at me. But I know that's selfish and unfair on Finn. I know that. I do. And I'd never do it. Yet this anger . . . I take a deep breath. Get it together, Jenna, I tell myself. I won't think about all that now. I won't wallow. I'm here to do a job. This is a career-changing opportunity for me and I can't let my emotional turmoil over Gavin mess it up.

I turn back towards my car, plipping open the boot to retrieve my large holdall. It weighs a tonne and I curse myself for packing too much stuff. It used to infuriate Gavin, who only ever needed the bare minimum. I like to pack for every eventuality and can't go anywhere without my heated tongs. There is a small porch, which I shelter under while I release the key from the coded safe on the wall as per the rental instructions. The hallway is warm and welcoming, with a coat rack, a padded bench and pull-out wicker boxes for shoes. I hang up my wet coat and perch on the bench to take off my boots.

The open-plan interior is even nicer than the photos suggest: white walls, wooden floors, which must be warm due to the underfloor heating, a modern orange L-shaped sofa, sheepskin rugs, snuggly blankets and cushions. There is a fabric deer head on the wall that has coloured fairy-lights entwined around its antlers, which Finn would love. The living area has an open fireplace with a stack of logs in a basket beside it, and beyond the sofa there is a small dining-table. A white high-gloss kitchen overlooking the front driveway leads off the living room. It has grey stone work-tops and an island with chrome-legged bar stools. I take in the gadgets: the fancy sound system that I'll never be able to get working but if Gavin was here he'd have on within minutes, the instant-boiling-water tap, the scary high-tech cooker and hob. I'm used to an old range. I wander back through the living room and along the hallway to the bedrooms. There is a master bedroom with an en-suite and next to it a twin room. I try not to think of Finn and what a kick he'd get out of this place as I dump my bag on the king-size bed.

I return to the living area and take my mobile from my bag. Then I snap a close-up of the deer's head to send to Finn, before opening the front door and taking a photo of the forest, grateful for the porch. The result is an atmospheric image of the woods and the rain, which softens the edges of the trees, the purple up-lighters through the branches giving the image some colour. I'll add this later to my Instagram page. It will help whet the appetite for when the podcast comes out.

It was my idea to make this podcast. As soon as the press release landed on my desk a few months ago I became obsessed with wanting to know everything about the case. And I was sur-prised to learn that, apart from reports of the late 1990s and early 2000s, it seems to have been largely forgotten. I'd remembered it as Olivia Rutherford's friends had been in their late teens, like me, when it happened and, as I stared down at that crumpled press release, I suddenly knew that I needed to cover this – and not just as a cursory three-paragraph article on the BBC website marking the twenty-year anniversary, but a proper in-depth investigation. Thankfully, my editor Layla at the Salford office agreed that it would be perfect for their new streaming service so I've been sent here to gather as much information and record as many interviews as I can. Layla will help me edit it into a six-part series when I return to Manchester. I'm excited about the new challenge as, even though I've been a reporter for seventeen years, I've never made or hosted a podcast before.

I close the door on the rain and go back into the kitchen, dropping my phone on the worktop, then stand at the sink looking out of the window at the forest, trying not to think how depressing as well as beautiful it is. I have a side view of the cabin opposite, set further into the trees, mostly obscured, apart from a right angle with a narrow rectangular window. There is a light on and the amber glow is comforting. I'm relieved that I won't be alone in the forest after all. It's not yet 4 p.m.

I pour myself a brew with the fancy boiling-water tap, grateful that the owner has provided milk, bread, butter and teabags, then sit at the table and get my paperwork out of my bag, spreading it in front of me. I've printed out old newspaper reports from November 1998 when the three girls went missing, and a photo of Olivia's smashed-up white Peugeot 205. It's a miracle anyone got out of it alive.

A dog barks, interrupting my thoughts, and I stand up to get a view from the window. I see a figure coming out of the cabin opposite with a big German Shepherd on a lead. It's hard to tell if it's a man or a woman, as they're wearing a coat with a peaked hood pulled up and tied under the chin but, whoever it is, they're tall. I move closer to the window, leaning across the sink to get a better look. The person stands for a second in the rain, looking towards my cabin. Then they turn right, taking a path further into the forest, the dog pulling at the lead.

I close the curtains, returning to my paperwork, ignoring the shadows that dance in the corners of the walls, determined not to dwell too much on the fact I'm alone in a place where spooky things seem to happen and people disappear.

2

Olivia

THE RAIN IS HEAVY, THRUMMING ON THE BACK OF OLIVIA'S waxed jacket as she bends over to pick out her pony's hoof. Her knee and calf ache. They always do in this weather. She knows the weight of Sabrina's leg will cause her own to buckle if she doesn't hurry up. The only light comes from the flickering bulb inside the stable, and it casts such a weak glow that she can barely see what she's doing. Not that she needs to. She can pick a hoof in her sleep.

Since the accident Olivia prefers the company of horses to people. Solid, dependable and comforting. They don't let you down, or judge you, or get angry with you, or nasty, or manipulative. They don't answer back or hurl cruel words at you, or trick you into doing something you aren't comfortable with. You know where you are with them. Since recovering from the accident, Olivia has surrounded herself with them, which was easy to do, considering her mother owns the town's only riding school and livery stables. She hasn't driven since that fateful night, but she can still ride horses. It's her only freedom.

She doesn't hear her mother crossing the yard until she's beside her, a frown on her face and a tangle of head-collars thrown over her shoulder. Olivia glances up, lowering Sabrina's leg.

'Are you okay, love? You look tired. Maybe call it a night?'

'I'm nearly done.'

'Okay. I'm finishing up here and then I'll put the jacket potatoes on. Are you seeing Wes later?' Her mother's greying bob is plastered to her head so she looks like a Lego character, and a raindrop is snaking down her face to hang off the tip of her nose.

'No, not tonight.'

'Great. We can catch up with *This Is Us*.' It's just what Olivia needs tonight. To snuggle up with comfort food and her favourite show. Perfect escapism. Her mother heads towards the tack room.

Sabrina neighs and blows out through her large nostrils, her breath clouding in front of her. Olivia buries her head in the animal's neck. She loves the smell of horses, the warm, wet, steamy scent of them. She leads the pony back into the stable and unclips her collar, quickly runs a brush over Sabrina's chestnut coat and throws a rug across her back. She wonders if her mother has remembered it's the anniversary on Wednesday.

Twenty years. She can hardly believe it. Sometimes it feels like yesterday. And at others it feels like a lifetime ago.

The yard looks dark and menacing now everybody's gone home. She should be used to it, but she's not. She never will be. The dark freaks her out, that's the truth of it. It always has. Maybe if she'd been less fearful, more courageous back in 1998, if she'd told the truth, her friends might still be here now.

The beam from her torch shines onto the rain-slicked concrete as she lets herself out of the stable. 'Goodnight, my precious,' she whispers, as she fastens the latch on the door while the wind whips at the corner of her jacket. She turns in the direction of the tack room. It's quiet, in darkness. Her mother must have gone back to the house. Olivia eyes the five-bar gate that separates the riding school from the house in trepidation. The security lights have gone out and only one window is lit up in the distance. The space between here and the house is dark and expansive and she shudders. The rain comes down heavier now, pelting onto the iron rooftops of the stable buildings, dancing a rhythmic tune. She pulls her hat firmly over her fair hair. *I do this every night*, she reminds herself (although more often than not her mother waits for her), and tonight is no different. It doesn't matter that it's the anniversary on Wednesday, or that, for weeks, she's felt this undercurrent of something she can't name rippling through the town. She says this over and over to herself as she hurries towards the gate as best she can even though she's limping on her left leg, the beam of her torch sweeping over the path ahead, illuminating the rain.

When she reaches the gate she pulls back the latch, lowering her torch as she does so. The gate crashes closed and suddenly someone is in front of her. A white face peering out of the darkness. Olivia screams and jumps back in fright.

'Liv, it's me, you idiot,' says a familiar voice. Wesley. It's just Wesley. Of course it is. He's holding a golfing umbrella and moves forwards so that she's under it too. 'You're soaked, you wally,' he says, wrapping a protective arm around her shoulders and squeezing her to him so tightly she can barely breathe. 'I knocked and your mum said you were still finishing up.'

'What are you doing here?' she shouts, above the rain. 'I thought we were having a night off.'

He guides her towards the house, buffeted by the wind and rain. 'I wanted to see you. Is that a crime?' His voice carries over the wind. 'What a fucking awful night.' She nods although he can't see her in the dark and she leans against him. Her head only reaches his shoulder and she finds his height and weight comforting, despite how firmly his arm is clamped around her waist. She realizes, with a sudden jolt of horror, that he's been holding her up for the past twenty years. She's surprised he still hangs around. Maybe their relationship – which has never moved beyond the dating stage even though they're in their late thirties – suits him. It must do, she supposes. She's thought about it a lot, alone in the bedroom of the house she grew up in. But she feels she's living a static kind of life, the kind of life she's lived ever since the accident, like she's been stuck, unable to move on, to move past it, to grow. So it's only natural her relationship with Wesley would be stunted too. She knows others think it strange that they have never married or even moved in together. But this is the life she deserves, she supposes, when she is here and her friends are not.

They don't speak until they've reached her mother's odd, mismatched pebbledash house. They fall into the glass lean-to that smells faintly of feet and rubber. A bare light bulb hangs above their heads as Wesley shuts the door against the noise of the wind and rain and Olivia's ears ring with the sudden silence.

'How's your leg?' he asks, as he closes his massive umbrella and shoves it in the corner. A spoke has come loose from the fabric.

She rubs her knee. It aches so much she wants to cry. 'I think I need my painkillers,' she replies. She perches on the wooden bench while he helps her take off her boots. She can do it herself but she knows he likes to feel useful. She was in a wheelchair for six months after the accident and Wesley had been her saviour, pushing her around the narrow streets of Stafferbury, fending off unwanted words and attention like a shield.

And he's still doing it.

He looks up, his blue eyes serious, and inclines his chin just a fraction, his jaw set. He bends down and takes her hands in his. 'I've spoken to Ralph,' he says, his voice sombre. 'And I came here to warn you.'

'Warn me?' She feels a flash of panic.

'There's a journalist sniffing around. Just remember what we've always agreed. Okay? No interviews.' When she doesn't say anything he adds, more harshly this time, 'I said, *okay?*' He clasps her hands even tighter so that she feels like an animal caught in a trap.

She nods, swallowing her cocktail of anxiety and doubts. 'Okay.'

3

Jenna

IT'S GONE MIDNIGHT AND I'VE BEEN SITTING AT THE
kitchen table for hours, poring over old articles and photographs
between cups of tea punctuated by the odd glass of warm wine
I brought down from Manchester. Gavin never liked it when I
drank too much, being teetotal himself. I eye my empty wine
glass. It doesn't matter now, does it? He's not here. I can drink
as much as I like. But the thought isn't a jubilant one. I sigh and
move away from me the documents I'd been leafing through.
A headline screams out at me: 'THE GIRLS WHO DIS-
APPEARED: WHATEVER HAPPENED TO THE
MISSING THREE?' It's a puff piece from about five years ago
disguised as investigative reporting, although most of the facts
look as though they've been cobbled together from articles that
came out at the time. I doubt the journalist who wrote it even
came to Stafferbury.

I push my reading glasses back onto my hair and rub my tired eyes. Earlier, after several failed attempts and a burnt fingertip, I was successful at lighting the fire and the crackle of the flames and the warmth had made me feel less alone somehow. But now it's died out and the room is cold and silent, apart from the rain throwing itself against the window panes. I wrap my cardigan further around myself and get up. I'll take a cup of tea to bed, I think, as I turn on the tap and fill another cup with boiling water. Gavin had wanted a Quooker when we renovated our kitchen two years ago. I'd said no, telling him I found the reassuring bubble of a kettle boiling comforting. I play that conversation back regularly wondering if things would have been different if I'd said yes to the sodding Quooker. If I'd been more pliable, less bossy. If I hadn't taken charge of that kitchen renovation, persuading him to go with the painted white Shaker-style cabinets and charcoal grey island even though I knew deep down he wanted something more contemporary.

I sigh heavily and peer between the thick moss-coloured curtains. The cabin opposite is in darkness. There is no comforting glow from the rectangular window poking through the trees any more, just the faint intermittent flicker of a solar light at the end of my drive and the purple hue of the uplighters in the trees opposite. The person I saw leaving there hours ago still hasn't returned, as far as I can tell. I feel totally alone in the forest. The thought chills me. I drop the curtain and move away from the window with my mug of tea. I want to go home to the Victorian semi in a leafy street in Manchester with the cherry blossom in the front garden and the hot-tapless kitchen that I love so much. I want my old life back with Gavin and Finn and being curled up in bed on a Sunday morning drinking coffee, the newspapers spread out on the duvet in front of us and Finn snuggled between us playing Minecraft on his iPad. I yearn for it so much my heart aches with longing. I thought we were happy.

I'd FaceTimed Finn earlier and even though Gavin hovered in the background, he didn't say hello to me or acknowledge me at all. He's moved back in to look after Finn while I'm away and the sight of him in the house where he belongs brought a lump to my throat.

I take my tea and do what I've been dreading all evening: I turn off all the lights and head for bed.

The air smells musty, as though the cabin has been closed up for months, which it probably has. I doubt there are many requests for bookings in November. I shrug off my cardigan and climb between the crisp white sheets, the satin eiderdown heavy across my legs. I'm glad I'm wearing my fleecy pyjamas. The king-size bed feels huge with just me in it. The headboard is one of those with lights built in and I keep mine on but I'm too tired to read. My mind is full of all the things I need to do tomorrow. I've got until Friday to gather as much content and information as I can for the podcast. Just four days. Although, right now, that feels like a lifetime. I close my eyes, thinking of Finn's little body snuggled up to mine. I know Finn will be missing me. Luckily Mum will be picking him up from school and looking after him until Gavin gets home from work, and I'll see him on Friday evening. The thought of that will keep me going this week.

My mind turns to Brenda, the detective I'm meeting in the morning. And then I need to try to pay a visit to Olivia. I want to get her unawares, but who knows if she'll talk to me? After the accident Olivia had been in hospital for months recovering from numerous operations on her leg to try to save it from amputation and had to have metal pins put into it. She's never given any interviews.

I turn over, pressing my face into the pillow. I need to sleep. I'm just drifting off when I hear a high-pitched scream. It's so loud and piercing that it rips right through my consciousness and I bolt upright in bed, my heart hammering, sweat breaking out all over my body.

What the fuck was that?

Another chilling scream, then silence, although I can hear the blood pounding in my ears. I climb out of bed and go to the window, pulling aside the curtains. Someone is standing just beyond my car, their hood pulled up so that it's impossible to see the face clearly. I think it's the same person I saw earlier with the dog. Should I call the police? I turn and grab my phone from the nightstand, but when I look back nobody is there.

4

Olivia

OLIVIA TURNS OVER IN BED, BLINKING IN THE DARKNESS, wondering what woke her. The room is cold, her mother rarely turns on the heating, and the single-paned window rattles in the wind. She can hear the far-off whinny and stamping of hoofs, which isn't unusual in a storm. She reaches across to snuggle up to Wesley and finds his side of the bed empty. He must be in the loo as it's still warm. She presses her face against the pillow and tries to go back to sleep. But she's awake now and she knows she'll continue to be so until Wesley returns. When the minutes tick by and he still hasn't come back she realizes she's going to have to find out where he's gone.

Slowly she puts her feet to the floor, wincing as the pain travels up the ankle of her left leg and into the knee. She limps to the door. The corridor is dark and empty – she always found it spooky as a child with its shady corners and creaky floorboards.

Her mother's bedroom is at the other end of the landing, and between their rooms are two others, one a bathroom, the other unused, a place for junk. The bathroom door is ajar, and from where she stands she can see that Wesley isn't there. Has he gone downstairs? Maybe he couldn't sleep but, even so, he wouldn't just wander around the house on his own: it's not his home. He's respectful like that, is Wesley. And as a result her mother loves him. Probably – she sometimes wonders – more than she does.

She eyes the stairs with a sense of dread. For nine months after the accident she'd slept in the dining room. But now, after years of physios and operations, she can live a normal life, most of the time. Physically at least, with the help of painkillers. But stairs, particularly at the end of a long day, can still play havoc with her knee. She's got used to living with the chronic pain. The accident had damaged her muscles and nerves, but the emotional pain was harder to deal with.

Survivor's guilt, her therapist had told her. She'd only managed five sessions before he'd started probing too deeply and she'd had to leave.

She peers down into the darkness. It doesn't sound like Wesley is there. He must have gone home. Why? Why would he just abandon her in the middle of the night, to go back to his depressing one-bedroom flat above Madame Tovey's, without even waking her up to say goodbye? He's never done that before. She recalls their conversation. They'd talked in bed in low whispers for nearly an hour so as not to wake her mum. Did she say something to offend him? Is he now in one of his moods? She knows from experience they can last for a week. He didn't seem angry or annoyed and she'd fallen asleep with his arms wrapped around her.

She turns and heads back to her room, slumping onto the

edge of her bed. Wesley is such a force of nature, so in control. They'd only been together a little over a month at the time of the accident, and afterwards she'd handed herself over to him gratefully, amazed that this wonderful man still wanted to be with her. Wanted to look after her. She'd fancied him for years at school with his thick dark hair and intense blue eyes, his confident stance. She'd put him on a pedestal, really, but he hadn't been interested in her then. It wasn't until after they'd left school and all the business with Sally was finally over that he'd turned his attentions to her. Now, as he's aged, she often thinks his confidence is more of the brash quality, the kind that, on occasion, makes her wince. But back then he was quirky, funny and popular at school, always hanging around in a large crowd, a lot of whom he's still friends with. He was a year above her and never knew she existed. It was Sally who had first caught his eye. Sally with her big doe eyes, her clear skin and her long, swishy chocolate brown hair that never frizzed in the rain, like hers did. Sally . . . Olivia squeezes her eyes shut, trying to push the thought of her best friend from her mind. She can't think of Sally now. Or teenage Wesley, or any of it. It's too painful, even after all these years.

Instead she turns her thoughts to her earlier conversation with Wesley. His insistence that she doesn't talk to this journalist, whoever she is. Not that he needs to convince her of that. What seems off, though, is why he seemed panicked at the idea that she would. He always said he wouldn't be interviewed either out of respect for her, but the way he was acting tonight and his air of desperation have made her wonder if maybe she isn't the only one with something to hide.

5

The Holiday of a Lifetime

STACE HATED THE HEAT. SHE HATED THE STICKINESS OF IT
*and the way it made her T-shirt and shorts cling to her body and her
stomach turn over, like she'd eaten something bad. It hit her like a
wall as soon as she got off the plane so that she felt she couldn't take
deep enough breaths. The others were excited, chattering away on
the drive from the airport to the villa, faces slick with sweat, dark
patches under the arms of Maggie's yellow T-shirt, Trevor with a
straw hat he wouldn't be seen dead in in England but that now sat
at a jaunty angle atop his curly head. Martin's ultra-pale skinny legs
protruded from khaki shorts. Legs she hadn't seen since school. She
couldn't bring herself to join in on the good-natured banter with the
driver of their minivan. She already knew she should never have
agreed to it. John-Paul had persuaded her.*

*'But we can't afford it,' she'd said, hoping that would be the end
to it when he first broached the subject. They were flat broke, that*

was the truth of the matter. Holidays to exotic far-flung places were for other people, not them. And that was fine. She was happy with their little life, their weekly outing to the local pub, their takeaways in front of the TV and their tiny rented flat above the launderette with the damp patch shaped like a butterfly on the ceiling above their bed.

But John-Paul wasn't like her. John-Paul was different. She'd known that the first time she'd met him eighteen months ago. He had been an out-of-towner – a stranger, an outsider – but that was what had attracted her to him. There was something of the exotic about him with his Spanish mother and his Catholic upbringing and his lust for travel. He had strayed into her life by accident, really, just 'blowing through town like tumbleweed', he'd said when she'd first met him. And she'd liked that, the poetic-ness of it. He was that kind of person, always talking in similes and analogies in his soulful voice with a hint of a Spanish accent. A wanderer, he'd said, but then they'd fallen in love and she'd convinced him to stay, and over time he'd stopped talking poetically or about his writing ambitions, instead swapping his tie-dye T-shirts for a data-inputting clerical role, but she could see it in his eyes sometimes, the wildness of him, like a beautiful caged animal that was desperate for escape.

So, when he told her his mate Derreck had moved to Thailand and got himself some cushy job and had invited them to stay in his five-bedroomed villa with river views, he had looked so desperate, so hopeful that she felt this was a compromise of sorts. 'We'd just need to find money for our flights, that's all,' he'd said, in the same pleading tone, his hands warm beneath hers. 'I've got a bit saved up. Imagine the romance. You'll love Thailand. It's one of the most amazing places. Bangkok is like nowhere else you've ever been.' Which wasn't hard to accept when she'd hardly been anywhere. But she'd relented, seduced by his stories of South East Asia. She'd go with him, she'd decided. That might curb his wanderlust, and bring them closer. Over the last six weeks, since John-Paul had lost his job, their relationship had deteriorated.

'And also Derreck asked if we wanted to bring some mates,' he'd said, his deep chestnut eyes lighting up. Straight away she knew which mates. Her crowd, who had subsequently become his crowd. The lads, as he called them, consisted of Griff, Trevor and Martin. And their other halves were Leonie, Hannah and Maggie respectively. She'd been at school with the girls and Martin, had known them for ever. They were like her family.

Of course they were excited: a chance for them to get away for two weeks from their dull jobs and the grey January English skies and the incessant rain. They couldn't pack their suitcases fast enough. And now here they were, on this 'holiday of a lifetime', as Leonie and Hannah kept calling it, their arms linked, reminding Stace of their fourteen-year-old selves at school.

There were so many different sensations Stace was experiencing on that journey to the villa, the heat being just one of them. The smells – a mixture of fish, vehicle fumes and something sweet – the noise of the tuk-tuks and the motorbikes and cars that zoomed past their minivan; the sights, the sun poking through a hazy blue sky and the multi-lane motorways, the smaller roads lined with market stalls, and barely dressed men leading elephants along the pavements. It was like nowhere she had ever been and she felt terrified. Maggie was pressing her nose to the glass and exclaiming in wonderment, 'There's an actual elephant in the street!' Or 'Are those Buddhist monks?'

By the time they pulled up in front of a gated complex Stace felt car sick. John-Paul looked like he felt the same. His enthusiasm had begun to wane before they'd even left the UK. At one point he'd asked her if perhaps they were making a mistake. But her friends were so excited there was no way Stace could let them down now.

'Wow,' said Martin, standing on the paved driveway in awe, his arm slung around Maggie's slim shoulders, his strawberry-blond hair standing up in peaks. Trevor removed his hat and used it to fan his thin face. Hannah jumped up and down in excitement and clapped her hands.

'Fuck! We're staying here!' she exclaimed. She often spoke in exclamation marks. Even Stace, feeling hot and sick as she was, couldn't help but be impressed with the sight that greeted them.

Before them stood three identical sparkling white villas, detached and evenly spaced, grand with their wedding-cake-esque pillars. Stace had never seen anywhere so beautiful and in that moment excitement flared in her belly. Maybe it wouldn't be that bad after all. 'Wow,' said Martin again, his mouth hanging open. 'I can't believe we're staying here.'

'How can his friend afford a place like this?' whispered Maggie, her dark hair piled on top of her head in a messy but stylish bun. Maggie had always been the glamorous one of the group. It had been a source of shock to all of them when she'd fallen for pale, lanky Martin.

'I bet he's a criminal,' said Griff, under his breath. Always the joker but as he said it Stace experienced a flash of panic. They knew nothing about this Derreck. John-Paul had been vague, said he'd met him travelling and they'd kept in touch and that he was a bit of a 'caballerete', whatever that meant. But she'd hardly heard John-Paul mention his name until the invite.

The front door of the middle villa suddenly opened and they all stopped in their tracks, falling silent. A tall, lean guy with *golden blond hair stood there, a cream fedora perched on his head, like he thought he was Robert Redford in* The Great Gatsby. *Behind him was a vast hallway of polished wood. He was wearing an open-necked shirt with the sleeves pushed up to the elbow, revealing tanned and muscular arms. There was a collective hush as they took in this Adonis figure and Stace noticed how Martin grabbed Maggie's hand firmly in his own freckled one.*

'Welcome to Chao Phraya Riverside Villas,' he said, with a sweep of his arm, like he was a Shakespearean actor in a play. And framed as he was between the white Roman-style pillars in front of the wedding-cake villa he could have been. 'I'm Derreck.'

Day Two

6

Jenna

I HARDLY SLEPT LAST NIGHT AFTER SEEING SOMEONE LURKING around outside. Maybe I've spent too long reading about all the weird things that have happened here and imagined the whole thing. This place is definitely eerie: the way the light falls between the trees, the remoteness of the cabins, the unnerving night-time silence only punctuated last night by some screaming, which I think must have been foxes. My rational mind says it's all down to nature, but another part is wondering if there might be some truth to these legends after all. I read that in 2012 two men spent all day searching for a baby they heard crying in the field of standing stones, but despite looking everywhere for it they never found the source, and there have been numerous reports of sightings of a hooded figure along the Devil's Corridor. It's hard to know what has become folklore and what is reality. But don't all myths stem from some semblance of fact?

* * *

I'm awake at 6 a.m. but my relief at making it through the night with no more interruptions is short-lived when I realize it's still dark. I get up anyway and sit at the kitchen table with a brew. I've got a few hours before I'm due at Brenda's. My eyes were so tired last night that I could barely focus on the information I gathered before arriving here. I pick up an old press cutting with a photo of the four girls: Katie, Olivia, Sally and Tamzin are sitting around a table in a pub garden on what looks like a summer evening at dusk, young in their 1990s fashion.

Olivia is pretty with a streaky blonde Rachel haircut and Sally is wearing a velvet choker and a crop top. Sally is a beauty, there's no getting away from it, hair so dark and sleek as to be almost black, with huge almond eyes and poreless skin. Tamzin is pretty in that bleached-blonde way, and Katie cute with a light brown bob and freckles. I put the photo down, then pick up another with the headline 'LOCAL ODDBALL ARRESTED'. I blanch at its insensitivity, pleased that at least some things have changed. There is a grainy photo of a dishevelled, bearded man on the front with his head down. The name Ralph Middleton pops out at me. There's something familiar about him and then I realize with a jolt he looks very much like the guy who spoke to me on the Devil's Corridor yesterday. According to the article, he was the one who found Olivia trapped in her car on the night of the accident and called the police. The piece doesn't really say much more than that he lived alone with a menagerie of animals and was considered 'odd' by the locals. I'll need to interview him for the podcast but I can't help feeling a rising anxiety at the thought of being alone with him.

At 7.30 a.m. I FaceTime Finn. I know Gavin probably thinks I'm being a control freak and has told me on more than one occasion that he can cope with Finn by himself, thank you very much. The 'I am more than capable: after all I do run a multi-national finance company' lecture I often get. But it's not just so I can make sure Finn remembers to take his packed lunch and brush his teeth: I miss him and want him to go to school knowing I'm thinking of him.

Finn answers with a yawn. His lovely sandy brown hair is tousled, the cowlick (so like Gavin's) is sticking up and he's still in his favourite Minecraft pyjamas. I ache to wrap my arms around him and bury my nose in his familiar biscuity smell.

'Good morning, handsome,' I say, while he groans and pulls a face at me, even though his green eyes twinkle. 'Did you sleep well?'

'Okay. I've got a maths test today.'

'Oh, no, that's not fun. Did Dad help you revise last night?'

He shakes his head. 'Nah. He was working.'

I feel a tug to my heart. 'Did Nanna pop over?' I'm so grateful my mum lives only a few streets away.

'Yes, but she's worse at maths than you are,' he jokes. It's a running theme in our house, my lack of maths skills. Gavin is the one who is good with numbers.

'I hope you didn't say that to Nanna.' I laugh. 'And are you looking after Rolo?' Rolo is our black-and-white cat, the size of a small pig.

I make a mental note to call Mum later and ask about Gavin. My pride won't allow me to ask him when the space he so desperately needed from me will have been enough. Or if he still loves me or sees a future in our marriage. So, even though I want to scream and rage at him and demand answers, I'm doing my best to be the mature one. For now.

From somewhere out of shot I hear Gavin's voice calling Finn for breakfast. 'Yep, Rolo's fine. Don't worry about him. Gotta go,' he says.

'Love you, little man,' I say, blowing him kisses.

'Love you too, Mum,' he replies, and my heart feels like it's being crushed. It was always Mummy until fairly recently.

Finn moves from the screen but he hasn't exited FaceTime so I have a view of his messy bedroom and the Harry Potter Lego constructions he's displayed proudly on his shelf. I'm about to turn off my screen when I hear something else and I freeze.

It sounds like the unfamiliar laugh of a woman.

7

BRENDA HAWTHORN LIVES IN A PEBBLEDASH BUNGALOW ON top of a hill overlooking Stafferbury. I push my way through the wooden gate that's nestled between two thick rose bushes that I imagine to be glorious in the summer but are now just thorny and ugly. The rain has stopped and a wintry sunlight spills onto the pavement, refracting in the puddles and causing me to squint. I should have brought my sunglasses. Despite the sun it is cold with a bitter wind and I'm grateful for my bobble hat. I can't stop thinking about that woman's laugh. Why was there a woman in my house?

Brenda opens the door after my first knock. I tower over her stocky frame. She's around seventy and has a no-nonsense look about her in her sensible plaid skirt, a cream polo-neck jumper and no makeup. She has on delicate gold pear-drop earrings, which seem at odds with the rest of her attire. Her face is weath-ered and slightly tanned, and her eyes crinkle warmly behind black-framed glasses.

'Jenna, nice to meet you,' she says, thrusting out her hand and shaking mine vigorously. 'Come in, come in.' I step over the threshold into her warm hallway just as a shaggy dog trots towards me and pushes my leg with its nose. 'Don't mind Seamus. He loves people, don't you, boy?'

I bend down to stroke his wiry head. 'What breed is he?' I ask, more out of politeness than anything else. I'm a cat person.

'Oh, he's a mix of all sorts. He's got some kind of sheepdog in him, I know that much.'

I follow Brenda into a compact kitchen that fans out into a garden room. 'This is lovely,' I say, as I notice the views. From here I can see the church spire and the rooftops of Stafferbury. The house has an air of solitude and I suspect she lives alone. I make myself comfortable in one of the wicker armchairs by the window and open the phone app my editor recommended. Brenda looks slightly horrified as I plug in my external microphone. 'You don't mind if I record you?' I give her what I hope is a reassuring smile.

'Sure,' she says, sounding anything but. 'So you're making a podcast? I'm not really *au fait* with all this technology nonsense.' I'm tempted to tell her that neither am I and this is all new for me. But I decide against it. I don't want her thinking I'm unprofessional and backing out.

She lowers herself carefully into the armchair opposite, wincing slightly. 'Hip problems,' she explains, and indicates the spread of croissants and other pastries on the glass coffee-table. 'Help yourself. Coffee?'

I ask for black, no sugar, and she leans forwards to pour me a cup. I'm itching to help her but I don't want to offend her. So instead I busy myself setting up my phone and camera on a little tripod on the table. I tested it before I left home yesterday and it picks up sound surprisingly well. I make sure to angle the microphone towards where she's sitting.

'Thank you for seeing me,' I say, as Brenda pushes a coffee cup in my direction. 'I know we spoke on the phone but it's lovely to meet you in person.'

'Likewise.' She smiles, settling back in her chair and sipping her drink. I glance around the room. There are no photographs of children or grandkids, no wedding pictures, no clue as to what kind of life she leads. The bungalow is small, simple, with beautiful views and a pretty garden, but it seems cut off somehow with its high position over the town's rooftops. She's making an effort not to look at the mini-tripod in front of her, instead fixing her eyes on me. 'It's such an interesting and perplexing case. It's one of my career regrets that I hadn't managed to crack it before I retired. It was literally as if those three girls just disappeared into thin air.'

'Can you give me your recollection of exactly what happened that night?'

She takes a sip of her coffee and smacks her lips together. 'Well, a nine-nine-nine call was received at around one twenty p.m.,' she says confidently, and I'm impressed she remembers the details so well. She must have worked on hundreds of cases, yet this is obviously the one that keeps her awake at night. The riddle she's never been able to solve. 'The call was made by a local man called Ralph Middleton. He claims he arrived at the scene after the car had crashed and only eighteen-year-old Olivia Rutherford, the driver, was in the wreck. She had to be cut free by paramedics. At that point we had no reason to believe there had been anyone else in the car.'

'Right,' I say, taking an almond croissant and ripping into it. 'When did you realize that Olivia's friends had been in the car too?'

'A colleague of mine received a phone call the next day from Sally Thorne's father to say his daughter hadn't come home.'

The croissant suddenly turns to cardboard in my mouth as I think of Finn and fast forward to his future teenager self, how frantic I would be if he didn't come home after a night out. My wonderful, warm, funny, sensitive son. It's painful as I swallow.

'By then precious hours had been lost,' continues Brenda, her face wistful. 'Hours when we could have been looking for them. But in the confusion nobody twigged that the girls had been in the car with Olivia. Tamzin's parents thought she was staying with friends as it wasn't unheard of for her to stay out all night. She was a bit of a good-time girl by all accounts.'

'So when did the police discover that all three girls were missing?'

'Not until later that day when we interviewed Olivia in the hospital. By this time Mr Thorne had rung Tamzin Cole's and Katie Burke's parents and worked out that all three of them hadn't been seen since leaving home the night before. At first they assumed they'd all gone off somewhere together, maybe another friend's house, until they rang Olivia's mother and she told them about the accident.'

'And then Olivia told you they'd been in the car when she crashed?'

Brenda nods, her face grave. 'By the time we got to speak to

Olivia it was nearly six p.m. as she'd been in theatre most of that day with doctors trying to save her leg.'

I grimace.

She sips her coffee and looks thoughtful. 'And then, of course, everyone began to panic.'

'God, how awful.' I reach for my mug.

'I still thought maybe they were all together somewhere. But it was out of character for Sally in particular to go off radar. They weren't tearaways or problem kids. They all had jobs, lived at home, came from decent families. Sally Thorne seemed to have it all. She was beautiful, popular and clever. She was having a year out before taking up her university place at York, working as a temp with Tamzin. She would have been the first in her family to go to university. They were understandably proud.'

I feel a swell of sadness for Sally and her family in that moment.

'And the others?'

Brenda reaches over for a pastry. 'Well,' she says, tearing the pain au chocolat with her fingers. She seems to have forgotten about my mobile with its intrusive tripod and microphone and is no longer eyeing it with distrust. 'Katie was the eldest. She worked at the pharmacy in town. Apparently she was sensible, trustworthy. And then there was Tamzin . . .' She sighs, and I lean forward expectantly.

'Oh, yes?'

'She'd been sacked from two jobs for returning to the office tipsy after her lunch hour. And then there was some . . .' she pauses to swallow her pastry '. . . unfortunate business with the money.'

'The money?'

'Yes. Tamzin's last job, before she disappeared, was with a firm of solicitors in town. After the girls went missing Lloyd Groves, who owned the firm, came to us to say the petty cash had gone.'

'How much?'

'A couple of hundred pounds.'

'Not really enough to run away with,' I muse.

'I suppose it depends on how desperate they were. Or what they'd planned. The money was never found.'

'And did Olivia Rutherford know anything about the missing money?'

'She says not, but . . . I don't know. I think that girl has been lying from the beginning.' She pulls a face. 'I always got the sense Olivia was hiding something.'

This is interesting. 'You think Olivia knew more about the money and her friends' disappearance than she let on?'

Brenda leans forward to put her empty plate on the coffee-table. 'I definitely think she knew something – something she's never told us.'

'If Tamzin and the others took the money to run off some-where, then why? And why not take Olivia with them?'

'One theory floated at the time was that Olivia was so badly injured in the crash they had no choice but to leave without her.'

'Wouldn't they have aborted the plan?'

She brushes crumbs from her skirt and shakes her head. 'It depends how desperate they were to get away. But I don't think that's what happened. Their bank accounts were untouched. They have never contacted their families. No.' She takes off her glasses and uses the hem of her jumper to clean them. 'I think something bad must have happened to them.'

And despite the warm room a chill runs down my spine. 'I read that Ralph Middleton was a suspect?'

'Yes. He's a strange fellow, a loner. But I always thought he was harmless. Still, we had to bring him in because he had found the car after the accident and rung the ambulance. He did save Olivia's life. She was in a bad way.'

'That was the only reason he was a suspect?'

'No. It was also the way he acted when we first interviewed him. Very twitchy. He kept changing his story. First he said he was out in the forest at that time of night walking his dog, and then because he couldn't sleep. He lived – well, still lives – in a caravan in the forest. Not far from where your cabin is, actually. So it is plausible he was up at that time and wandering the forest with his dog. But, well, he intimated that he saw something strange at the scene . . .'

'Like what?'

'A bright light. He then started going on about alien abduction. I think he was high that night – he is said to smoke a lot of wacky baccy. A few days later he changed his statement and said he'd been mistaken about the bright light. And then a witness came forward.'

I sip my coffee, not taking my eyes off her.

'Someone reported seeing a man believed to be Ralph with a young girl fitting Tamzin's description around ten a.m. on the morning after the accident. We brought Ralph back in for questioning but he said it had been his friend Jade Marlow, a known petty criminal and drug addict who, at the time, was in her early twenties.'

'And did she back up his story?'

Brenda nods sagely. 'But she would, I expect, and knowing her, for the right fee. She looked nothing like Tamzin apart from the blonde hair. Anyway, after the accident Ralph and Olivia became closer. He would visit her all the time and when she got better she would often go to his caravan and hang out there. But, of course, people began to talk. Thought perhaps the two of them had been in it together. But you know how people like to gossip.'

I make a mental calculation of Ralph's age. He's got to be at least in his fifties now which would make him in his thirties back then.

'What else do you know about Ralph? Has he ever been married?'

'Nope. Never married and has always lived alone with his animals.'

I pause to drain the rest of my coffee, then place my cup on the table. 'And were there any other suspects?'

She picks a crumb of pastry from her lip. 'Yes. Wesley Tucker.'

'Who's he?'

'Olivia's boyfriend.'

I can't hide my shock. 'Olivia's boyfriend was a suspect? Why?'

'Some say he had a fixation on Sally Thorne before he started going out with Olivia. According to reports from her parents, he'd made a bit of a nuisance of himself, bombarding her with messages, leaving notes outside her house and sending her flowers and presents. You know the type? Doesn't like taking no for an answer. He'd been in the same class as Katie at school and there had been no love lost between them either, let's put it that way. According to her friends and family, she made no bones about how much she disliked him. And two days before the accident a witness reported seeing him and Tamzin Cole arguing in the street.'

'Did you ever find out what about?'

'He said it was about Olivia. Apparently Tamzin didn't approve.' She pushes her glasses back onto her nose and offers me another croissant and I take a chocolate one this time.

'I wonder why Olivia would want to go out with someone who had so obviously been hung up on her friend,' I say, breaking up my croissant.

'Yes, we found that odd too. But they're still together all these years later.'

'What? They're married?'

Brenda shakes her head. Her hair doesn't move. 'No. They never got married. Olivia still lives at home helping her mum run the riding stables. And Wesley lives in a studio flat above Madame Tovey's. But they're still a couple.'

'Wow.' This is a surprise. Olivia is around my age and she still lives at home. In a town where it sounds like she's viewed with suspicion. 'Why would she want to stay?'

Brenda shrugs. 'It's not that unusual. A lot of folk stay in this town.' She chuckles. 'Me included. Stafferbury born and bred. I doubt I'll leave now.' She casts her eye around her conservatory. 'It suits me here. I'm bedded in, a bit like the weeds in my back garden.' She twinkles at me. I realize I like her. I like the solidness of her, the no-nonsense attitude. She reminds me of my mum.

'But did you ever seriously think Wesley Tucker had anything to do with it?'

'We couldn't prove anything about him or Ralph Middleton. And there are a lot of folk around here who believe that this town is cursed. Olivia Rutherford's friends aren't the first to disappear from here. Over two hundred years ago a similar thing happened – if you can believe the reports.'

'What? Really?'

'Three local farm girls went missing back in 1750 or something. I think it was believed they were sacrificed. The stones can attract cults and paganists. Especially back then.' She folds her arms. 'Not that I know much about the history of the stones although historians do think they were built in line with the sun and moon, and that human sacrifices were made there. The night the girls disappeared, apparently the sun and moon were in the right alignment with the stones.'

I suddenly feel sick, remembering the film *The Wicker Man* I saw years ago with Gavin mainly because he had a teenage crush on Britt Ekland. 'You don't believe they were sacrificed, though, do you?'

'No, of course not.' She rolls her eyes. 'There was another thing . . . about Olivia's accident.'

'What was that?'

'Well, in a statement from her hospital bed Olivia said she'd thought she was being followed in the days leading up to the accident.'

'What?' This hasn't been in any press cutting I've read. 'Did you find out who?'

'No, I'm afraid not. It was followed up, of course, but nobody fitting the description was ever found. The best thing to do would be to speak to my colleague, DS Dale Crawford.'

'Okay.' I reach forward and turn off the recording. 'Would he be willing to speak to me?'

'Sure. He's great, is Dale. He was only a young whippersnapper when I was in the force twelve or so years ago, but he's around your age now and specializes in cold cases. A bit of a hot shot. He rang me last week to tell me that his team will be picking up the Olivia Rutherford case again.'

'Why is that? Has there been some new information?'

She eyes me without speaking for several seconds, and then says, 'I think it's best you speak to him about it.' She bends down to pat Seamus who's collapsed at her feet, his chin resting on one of her moccasin slippers. And then she stands up. I do the same, gathering up my equipment, then follow her to the front door, my mind whirling.

As we pass the side table in the hallway she stops to pick up a card and presses it into my hand. DS Crawford's contact details. 'Dale is brilliant,' she says, as she opens the door and I step out into the cold air. 'But he's a police officer at the end of the day. There might be things he won't be willing to share. So if you have any questions after speaking to him don't hesitate to ring me, okay? I'm happy to tell you anything you need to know from when I was covering the case. Also, I'll dig out some of my old paperwork. On the QT like. I did end up photocopying some statements, though Dale wouldn't approve. These days everything is done much more by the book.' Her eyes glint with naughtiness and I can't help but laugh. Then she grows serious again. 'And don't be fobbed off, Jenna. Because I don't doubt for a second that someone in this town knows what's happened to those girls and has kept quiet about it for twenty years. It's time to spook them into revealing themselves.'

8

Olivia

OLIVIA WHEELS THE PILE OF HORSE MANURE ONTO THE dung heap and watches as the steam rises into the grey skies. She used to stand in it during the winter when she was a teenager to keep her feet warm. She's mucked out three of the horses already, between trying to get hold of Wesley. And each time it goes straight to voicemail.

After waking to find him gone last night she'd eventually fallen into a fitful and restless sleep. When her alarm went off at 6 a.m. and she saw the bed beside her still empty the strange unhappy feeling settled itself around her, as though she was being suffocated by her heavy duvet, making her doubts resurface as to what he's hiding. He's been so distant these last few months. Longer, really, if she's honest with herself. Maybe it's been a gradual thing over the years, the gentle eroding of their love, like seawater over a pebble, but in the beginning he was so attentive to her. She relied on him emotionally and physically. He was the one who carried her from her bed to the wheelchair when she had to sleep downstairs, camping in a sleeping bag on the floor just in case she needed to go to the loo in the night. He was the one who sat with her, holding her when she woke terrified from a nightmare, imagining that she was still trapped in the car. She can't even pinpoint the exact moment it changed. But it seems the stronger she gets the weaker their relationship becomes.

She'd mentioned her worries over breakfast. Her mother was busy flitting about the kitchen in that hyperactive way she had when Olivia plonked herself at the table.

'Do you want eggs?' she'd asked, when Olivia admitted she was worried about Wesley. Eggs, it seemed, were the answer to everything: lack of energy, depressed thoughts, missing boyfriend.

'No, thanks, I can't face eggs this morning,' Olivia replied, her stomach a choppy sea of unhappiness.

'Oh, he'll be okay,' her mum said dismissively, scooping a poached egg onto Olivia's plate ignoring her refusal. 'He's a grown man. Wesley's always struck me as a very independent soul. You can't pin a man like that down, love, and don't even try.'

She'd never known her mother to have a boyfriend, even though she suspected she must have. When Olivia was a child her mother would sometimes leave her with her grandparents to go away for the odd weekend. Olivia often wondered if she had been meeting a man. But even if she had her mother wouldn't tell her. But that was her all over. She liked to compartmentalize her life.

'Do you not want me to get married? Don't you want grandkids?'

Her mum had scoffed, pushing her thick fringe away from

her face. She'd stopped dyeing it years ago, back in her late forties, and let the grey take over. It suited her and brought out the silver in her eyes, softening the creases in her skin, giving her cheeks an almost violet hue. 'It's your life, sweetheart. You know I'm not a baby person, anyway. I much prefer horses.'

'Great, thanks.'

Her mum let out a bark of laughter. 'Oh, don't be so sensitive. I love *you*, of course.' She clapped Olivia on the back, much like she would the neck of a beloved horse. She might not be the most maternal of mothers but Olivia knows her mum would do anything for her. It had always been just the two of them and as a result they were close. 'You don't want to be getting married either, believe me. That's where the trouble starts,' she'd finished ominously. Not that she would know, never having been married herself. When her mother found out she was pregnant, back in 1980, the father had wanted nothing to do with either of them. Olivia had been brought up in this house with the help of her grandparents, sadly both having passed away within months of each other when she was fourteen and the only grandchild, her mum having no brothers or sisters.

What if Wesley's finally left me? she thinks now, staring at the screen on her mobile, willing his number to flash up. What if he's finally seen the light? Seen that she isn't worthy of him? Someone as large as life, as technicolour as he is should be with someone equally so. Someone like Sally had been. Not her, not dull cardboard-cut-out Olivia, with her half-life and her hollow heart. She's been waiting twenty years for him to leave her. There was that time, a couple of years ago, when she'd thought he might. He had seemed so distant, making excuses not to see her as often, and when he did he acted like a man with the weight of the world on his shoulders. It had lasted a few months but then he'd reverted to his old self.

She often wonders where this neediness, this reliance on Wesley comes from. Was it growing up without a father? She knows Wesley's not perfect – she's realized that as the years rolled by. He's loud, bossy, a bit controlling, and sulks for hours, days even, if she doesn't do as he wants. Once when she told him she was too tired for sex he didn't speak to her for three days. But he can also be so loving and attentive, making her feel like the most important person in the world. And that he's always on her side. That nothing is too much trouble. If she rang him to say she was stranded she knew he'd come and pick her up, no matter what time of day or night it was. He's always made her feel protected, her first and only boyfriend. Being with him is like slipping on her favourite fleecy dressing-gown and she worries that if she takes it off she'll be cold and naked and vulnerable.

She checks her watch. It's eleven o'clock. He'll be at work. He's had the same job since she's known him, at the bank in the next town.

Her thoughts are interrupted by the sound of tyres crunching over gravel and she looks up. Her mum has gone to pick up some horse feed and the riding instructor, Mel, isn't due in until 2 p.m. for the first lesson of the day. So who could it be? She leaves the wheelbarrow where it is and heads to the little office at the front of the stables just in case someone has come in from the street to book a lesson. During the weekend local kids help out at the stables because of their love for the horses. But during the week it's usually only her and her mum. Mel arrives for lessons and to look after her own horse, Fargo, but that's where her duties end. Olivia will take experienced riders for hacks, usually on a Sunday, but the teaching is left to Mel.

She doesn't recognize the silver Audi or the tall, attractive woman who strolls confidently through the iron gate, her red hair flowing from beneath a forest-green bobble hat. She's an out-of-towner – that's immediately obvious from her smart wool coat and her heeled boots under well-cut trousers. All in black apart from the hat. When the woman reaches the office she hesitates as though wondering if she should step inside. It's no more than a glorified shed, set just in front of the stables, and is sparsely furnished, apart from a metal cabinet in the corner and, facing the door, a solitary desk containing the riding school diary. Wesley is always on at them to computerize their diary. But Olivia and her mother are technophobic, no matter how many times Wesley tries to mansplain it to them. In the end he'd given up.

'You can come in,' says Olivia, smiling as the woman hovers uncertainly on the threshold. 'Are you here to book a lesson?' She goes to the desk and leans over the chair to flick open the diary to today's date.

'No. No, thank you,' the woman replies, looking panicked at the idea. She steps into the office. She has an accent. Northern. Olivia likes the sound of it. It's warm and friendly and instantly puts her at ease.

'Oh . . . then how can I help?'

'Are you Olivia Rutherford?'

And then it hits her. Of course. How stupid of her not to realize straight away. The journalist. The one Wesley had warned her about. And now she's here, in Olivia's private space, and she doesn't know how to handle it without her mum or Wesley.

Coldness settles over her and she juts out her chin, folding her arms across her padded jacket to protect herself. 'And who's asking?'

'My name's Jenna Halliday. I'm making a podcast for the BBC on the events that happened here twenty years ago. I know you've never spoken to the press before but this is a bit different, being a podcast, and I was hoping you'd want to be part of it because . . .' But Olivia finds it hard to concentrate on the rest of Jenna Halliday's words, drowned as they are in the pounding noise inside her head. Something about wanting to get 'your side of the story across', and how an exclusive interview with her would 'put off other journalists who might show up'. Olivia has heard it all before. She's never spoken to the press about the accident. Not then and definitely not now.

Olivia shakes her head and places her hands over her ears, without thinking or caring that she might look infantile or rude. 'No. No. No. NO.'

Jenna stops speaking, her features softening. She lifts a hand towards Olivia and then, seeming to think better of it, lowers it. Her eyes are very green, Olivia notices. The colour of the gooseberries that grow in her mother's garden. The gooseberries that she hasn't touched since they made her vomit all night when she was five.

'I'm sorry,' says Jenna, gently, and Olivia notices a blush to the other woman's cheeks. 'I didn't mean to upset you. It must be so traumatic still, never knowing what happened.'

'And yet you decided to come and speak to me anyway?' Olivia pushes her shoulders back, although it doesn't matter how straight she stands: she'll never be as tall or as elegant or as self-assured as this woman. This Jenna Halliday, who has probably gone through life getting exactly what – and who – she wants.

Jenna looks down at the floor and when she lifts her head Olivia is surprised to see her expression is open. Authentic. 'I felt it was only right to give you a chance to tell your side of the story. Considering the podcast is about your friends' disappearance.'

'My side of the story?' Olivia can feel a whoosh of heat to her throat, rising to her face. 'It's not a *story*. It's not fodder for the entertainment of others. This . . .' she inhales deeply, trying to control her emotions '. . . this is my life.'

'I understand.'

'How?' Olivia tries to stare down this woman, this intruder. 'Since when do journalists ever truly understand? Has this happened to you?'

'Well, no, but –'

'Well, then, don't talk crap. It's insincere.'

'I'm sorry. I can't even imagine what you've been going through.'

Olivia feels tears prick her eyes. How to even begin?

Jenna assesses her calmly but with compassion and it makes Olivia feel conflicted. She wants to hate this woman. She wants to blame her for all of it. For the accident and the years afterwards, her ongoing pain both physical and emotional. How she feels alienated in her own town because of what happened. How people still regard her with suspicion, gossip about her, or are openly hostile so that all she wants to do is hide away. Yet this woman doesn't seem like all the other journalists she's met in the past. She seems warmer, almost empathetic, actually willing to listen to Olivia. But no. She promised Wesley. She can't go back on that.

Jenna reaches into her bag and extracts a card. 'I'll go now but if you change your mind here are my details.' She hands the card to Olivia, who takes it and tosses it onto the desk as though it were a piece of litter. 'I'm in town until Friday.'

There are a few beats of awkward silence. And then, at last, Jenna gives a small smile before she turns and walks out of the office, with a swish of her fine copper mane, reminding Olivia of the chestnut stallion they used to have at the stables.

Olivia breathes a sigh of relief, her legs shaking. She slumps down onto a wheely-chair, a burning sensation at the back of her throat.

Wesley is right. There is no way she can talk to this woman. No way.

Because she knows if she starts to talk, she might never stop.

9

Jenna

I'M NOT SURPRISED OLIVIA HAS DECIDED AGAINST BEING IN-
terviewed. It's what I'd expected. But I won't give up. There has to
be a way to break down her barriers. I just need to find it. What
I am surprised about, however, is how small and sad she seemed.
She spoke to me with such passion and feeling, as though her
emotions were just below the surface, like a swimmer about to
break through the waves. The opposite of me, the scuba-diving
variety, who will do anything to hide how I'm truly feeling.

Like when Gavin told me late one night as we were getting
ready for bed that he was moving out. I'd been sitting at my
dressing-table, taking off my makeup, and I could see his reflection in my mirror, bare-chested as he hung up his shirt, and it
had crossed my mind that we hadn't had sex for a few months,
which was unusual for us. But we'd both been so busy, me with
my new job at the BBC and him as CFO, that we hadn't had

much time for each other. So I had gone to him, shedding my pyjamas as I walked suggestively over to him and reached up to kiss him. But to my horror he pushed me away. 'I'm sorry, Jenna, I can't do this.' *Jenna*. Not Beauty, his pet name for me. In that moment I felt anything but. Then he broke it to me that he needed space from our marriage. And the whole time I sat on the edge of the bed, humiliation washing over me while he packed a bag, fighting back tears, trying to remain calm when I felt like I'd been punched in the gut. I wanted to howl and beg him to stay. If I'd shown half the passion Olivia just had, would I have saved my marriage?

As I'm getting into the car an old Land Rover with *Stafferbury Riding School and Livery Yard* emblazoned down the side pulls up beside me and a woman in her early sixties steps out. She's tall and strong-looking. Attractive, in a weather-worn, outdoorsy kind of way. I can tell straight away she's Olivia's mum. The similarity is startling: the same deep-set grey eyes, the same sharp nose, pointed chin and high cheekbones. The same defensive expression. She strides in front of my car carrying a large bag of horse feed, turning in my direction, her eyes glinting. I'm expecting her to come to my window, and my heart quickens in anticipation, my mind turning over the well-worn phrases I usually use. Instead she walks away from me towards the five-bar gate. I consider getting out of the car to talk to her, but I sense she'll be even more closed than her daughter.

As I reverse, I notice Mrs Rutherford watching me, her hand on the gate latch, the bag at her feet. Maybe the rumour mill is already at full grind and she knows who I am. I can still see her in my rear-view mirror as I pull out onto a winding lane that leads me towards the high street. I'm distracted and take a hairpin bend too fast, nearly veering into a BMW coming the other way down the lane.

I apply the brakes, my breathing slowing along with the car. The BMW driver is around my age with a shock of dark hair and he mouths, 'Fucking idiot,' at me as he passes. I drive on towards the high street. Just before the field of standing stones a lane leads to a National Trust car park. I park, then head along the path that runs parallel to the stones and cross to the rank of shops and cafés, my breath fogging out in front of me. I tug my bobble hat further over my ears, coldness seeping into the fabric of my clothes. As I'm walking I ring the number Brenda gave me for DS Crawford. It goes straight to voicemail and I leave a short message, explaining who I am and where I got his number. I drop my mobile into my pocket and pause outside an attractive Tudor building with Bea's Tearoom in white flowery writing hanging from an old-fashioned black sign. A chalk board on the pavement indicates that the tearoom is upstairs. It looks like a good place to get coffee and gather my thoughts. I also plan to write down some notes from Brenda's interview that I'd like to follow up with DS Crawford.

I climb the narrow stairs and am out of breath by the time I reach the top. An open doorway leads into a cosy room with ceiling beams and a floor with a slight incline. The carpet is red and faded to rose pink in places and the waitresses (I note they are all women) are wearing old-fashioned black uniforms with white frilly aprons and matching hats. A tourist trap, I imagine. Two arched leaded windows look out over the high street and the standing stones in the distance.

'Can I help you?' says a young girl, who can't be older than eighteen. She looks faintly embarrassed by her get-up, making me wonder if she's new.

'Do you have a table free?' It's a silly question when only one is occupied, by an older couple who aren't speaking to each other. The woman is watching me and not even trying to hide it.

'Just for yourself?'

'Yes. Please.' It doesn't faze me, eating alone. My life as a journalist has always been solitary. Especially in the early days when I worked for a press agency and spent many hours door-stepping celebrities or politicians, then had to file the story over the phone. I'd huddle up on a kerb somewhere, or a hidden corner of the street, and furiously write out the first paragraph so that I didn't stumble over my words when reciting them to the short-tempered editor at the other end of the line.

She leads me to a table next to the window and takes my order. When she's gone I glance around the room. It's not very big, with only half a dozen tables and, apart from me, just the older couple sipping tea from fine-boned china cups. The woman has platinum-blonde hair and a thin, anxious expression and she keeps glancing at me. I smile at her, but she averts her eyes, her face frosty. Charming. Word must have spread that I'm here. I open my notebook half-heartedly, trying my best not to feel uncomfortable. I survey the uneven walls with their thick paint, cracked in places, and the mahogany tables and chairs. Someone has put up bunting along the counter where pink and yellow iced cupcakes are piled high on pretty bone-china cake stands. I imagine this place is heaving during the summer months with tourists hoping to soak up the quaintness.

I pick up my pen and scribble *Olivia said she was being fol-*

lowed, then underline 'followed' three times. I wonder why this wasn't in the press. Brenda said nothing came of it. Unless . . . I chew the end of my pen Unless the police didn't believe Olivia? I take my phone out my pocket and place it on the table. No call back from DS Crawford yet. I'm itching to speak to him.

'Here's your black coffee and lemon drizzle cake.' The waitress appears by my shoulder. I thank her and tuck in, although I'm still full from breakfast with Brenda. I don't even want the cake. It's force of habit. Since my marriage broke down I seem to crave sugar. Some people lose weight when they're unhappy but I'm the opposite.

I sip my coffee, my gaze going to the window as I mull over Brenda's interview. A man outside catches my attention, mainly because he's acting oddly. He's looking up and down the street, and talking into his phone, as though he's waiting – or, more accurately, searching – for someone. Then he glances up at the window and I instinctively shrink back in my chair so he can't see me, though I'm not sure why. When I look again he's gone.

I return to my notebook and start scribbling what I've learnt about Ralph Middleton when the man from outside sweeps into the room. He's panting slightly from the exertion of the narrow staircase. He's about my age with dark brown hair that falls over his high forehead and he has to stoop to get through the doorframe. He has one of his hands in the pocket of a black North Face padded jacket over a shirt and tie.

'Wesley.' One of the waitresses, an attractive brunette, perhaps late twenties, trots over to him. *Wesley?* Olivia's boyfriend? I give him the side eye while pretending to read my notes. He's good-looking and knows it.

And then it strikes me. Was it me he was looking for outside? Olivia must have mentioned I spoke to her earlier.

'Izzy,' he says, wrapping an arm around the waitress's slim waist. The older couple at the next table are watching him too, the woman with barely concealed contempt. Now this is interesting, I think, sitting up straighter and sipping my coffee.

Wesley banters with Izzy and the young waitress who showed me to my table – I deduce she's called Chloë. His arm hasn't left Izzy's tiny waist. Oh, so that's who you are, I think, as I survey him. A bit of A One, as my mum would say. I know he's noticed me because of the way he's pretending not to. It's as though this room is his stage and he's the lead actor. He's playing to me.

Izzy leads Wesley to a table diagonally opposite mine. He avoids looking in my direction as he sits down and orders from the menu. Izzy disappears to fetch his food and I pretend to read my phone while surreptitiously watching him. He's fidgeting now, his fingers drumming on the red-checked oilcloth, his eyes darting about the room. And then, finally, they land on me. I look up just in time to meet his eyes. They are very blue, penetrating, challenging. He narrows them but doesn't say anything. I lower mine and carry on scrolling through my phone, even though the signal is sketchy and I can't load anything, aware that his gaze is still on me.

I decide I don't like him. He's too cocksure, his arrogance undignified, brash. I look up from my phone and catch his expression. He's glaring at me, dislike written all over his face. It takes me aback for a moment and I can't help but return the look.

'You're that journalist, aren't you?' he says loudly, across the room, his eyes flashing. The woman at the other table looks up from her mug to stare at me.

'That's right.' I try to keep my voice calm although my heart is beating furiously, I'm not sure whether from anger or embarrassment or both.

'I suppose you think this is all some big joke, don't you? Coming here and ruining other people's lives.'

I frown. 'I'm not trying to ruin other people's lives.'

'Dredging it all up again.'

'I'm just here to make a podcast.'

He laughs nastily and turns to Izzy, who's walking in with his full English. He raises his eyebrows at the older couple in the corner. 'She thinks she's going to come here and solve it all,' he mocks, addressing the room like a politician. 'The police haven't been able to solve what happened to your sister and her friends, Iz, not in twenty years, but Nancy Drew here thinks she's got it all sorted.'

Izzy's related to one of the girls? I'm intrigued.

'I don't think that. I'm here to gather information. That's all.' I wonder if Izzy is related to Sally. They have the same dark hair and clear skin. I need to interview her.

Izzy places his food in front of him. 'Now, come on, Wes. I don't want you here upsetting the customers. Eat your food in peace.'

I'm surprised. I wouldn't have thought Izzy would speak to him that way given how she was purring around him earlier.

She flashes me a warm smile and, thankfully, Wesley shuts up.

I snap my notebook closed and push away my unfinished coffee and cake. I've suddenly lost my appetite. I pay, and then I walk out, aware that Wesley's eyes are burning into me.

It starts to drizzle as I exit the tearoom. Next door is a tiny shop selling trinkets and jewellery. It smells of incense and, on the spur of the moment, I dart in there. I have a feeling Wesley might follow me, and I'm right because two minutes later he's on the pavement, looking left and then right. What is his problem? I'm aware I'm acting cagey. I hope the girl behind the counter doesn't think I'm a shoplifter, although she's taking no notice of me, too busy flicking through a magazine and twirling her pink hair around her fingers. 'Last Christmas' is playing on the radio and the shop assistant is singing along to it half-heartedly. I pretend to browse. I'm intrigued by Wesley. Why does my being here unsettle him so much?

I hide behind a stand of glittery scarves and watch as Wesley fishes his mobile from the pocket of his padded jacket. 'I've lost her,' I hear him say. I steal a glance at the young assistant but she still seems oblivious to me and to the situation. 'I'm going back in to finish my food. Yeah, babe, I said that, didn't I . . .' The rest of his words die as he heads back inside. I take the opportunity to hurry to my car before he sees me from the window.

Did Olivia send him? And if she did, then why?

10

THE HEAVENS OPEN AS I SIT COCOONED IN THE CAR SCRIB
bling notes, my breath steaming the windows, the rain blurring
the hills and the sky outside. *Izzy Thorne?* I write. I need to speak
to her urgently. I have no idea where she lives so I'll have to go back
into the tearoom and ask her, although I want to avoid doing it in
front of Wesley. I check my watch. It's been half an hour since I left
and I hope he's finished with his brunch.

I pull my hat firmly down on my head, shove the notebook
and phone back into my bag and get out of the car. I'll lurk in one
of the shops and wait for Wesley to leave, then try to speak to Izzy.

Just as I'm walking across the car park my phone vibrates. A
number I don't recognize flashes on the screen. I shelter under
the canopy of a block of public toilets to answer it, pleased when
the male voice introduces himself as DS Crawford.

'Thanks for calling,' I say. 'I know you must be busy.' I angle my body away from a sudden gust of wind. I can hardly hear what he's saying. The rain beats down on my back.

'. . . as a favour to Brenda but I don't know how much I can tell you.'

'Okay.' I cup the phone to my ear so I can hear him better. 'I'm trying to gather as much information as I can at this stage. If you're free for a coffee at any point it would be great to pick your brains.'

'I'm having a frantic day but could meet you for a quick drink after work.'

I tell him I'm grateful for any time he can spare and his voice is warmer when he says he'll meet me at The Raven at 7 p.m.

My spirits are lighter as I put the phone down and head back to Bea's but then I see Wesley coming towards me. Shit, I was hoping to avoid him.

He stops in front of me, blocking my path. I push my shoulders back. I won't let him intimidate me. I've met enough of his type before.

'Still hanging around then, like a bad smell,' he says.

'It looks that way.' I fold my arms across my chest.

He sighs but his expression softens. 'Look, I don't want Liv upset, okay? She's been through enough.'

I hesitate, thrown by the change in Wesley. I had pinned him down for a bit of a thug. But, with him standing in front of me, I wonder if he's just a man who's worried about his girlfriend. 'I don't want to upset her either,' I say, trying to assure him, 'but this podcast will shine a light on what happened here twenty years ago. It might even help jog someone's memory. Wouldn't you and Olivia and everyone else want to know what happened to Sally, Katie and Tamzin?'

He knits his dark brows together. We're both getting soaked and a raindrop hangs from his fringe. 'There's lots you don't understand about this town. Strange things happen here.' He lowers his voice. 'The forest is haunted and so is the Devil's Corridor. The standing stones are said to be full of mystic energy. Do you know about ley lines?'

'No, not really.' I try not to look sceptical. 'What are you trying to say? That their disappearance was something . . . What? Supernatural? Paranormal?'

He runs his hand through his rain-soaked hair. 'Who knows? Look, I don't care what you do. If you want to waste your time on this that's your choice, but leave Liv out of it, okay? She's been vilified enough by the people around here.' He doesn't wait for me to answer and I watch as he strides away, his hands in his pockets and his head bent against the rain.

I continue to the tearoom, thinking over my conversation with Wesley. Vilified? I wonder how. It can't have been easy for her and I do understand why Wesley is so protective.

I can hear the cacophony of the lunchtime rush as soon as I climb the stairs and the smell of warm coffee and bacon engulfs me. Nearly every table is full and the waitresses are dashing around like magpies in their black-and-white uniforms. My heart sinks. I hesitate in the doorway trying to spot Izzy, and then there she is, crossing the room, her glossy dark brown ponytail swinging as she carries a tray full of empty plates. I wave to get her attention and she comes over.

'Hello again,' she says pleasantly. 'Back so soon? There's a table over in the corner but I'd grab it quick.'

'Actually, I was here to speak to you but you look really busy.'

She frowns. 'Oh, I see. About your podcast? So you know I'm

Sally's sister?' I nod and she chews her lip, her eyes darting about the room before landing back on me. 'Give me a card and I'll ring you.'

I grab one of my business cards from my wallet and leave it on the tray she's carrying. 'Thanks so much. I really appreciate it. I'm here until Friday but would love to speak to you as soon as possible.'

She smiles at me again, but more uncertainly this time, then moves away towards the kitchen. I just hope she calls.

I have no choice but to go back to the cabin for now so I head down the high street towards the car park. The rain has seeped through my wool coat and my trousers are wet and heavy from the knee down. I long to change into something more comfortable – I feel cold to the bone. It was a mistake wearing work clothes instead of jeans, wellies and a raincoat. I'd wanted to look professional, to be taken more seriously. Ha, like that happened. I realize I've laughed out loud as a woman walking towards me shoots me a strange look. She's pushing one of those tartan shopping bags on wheels and I recognize her from the tearoom earlier. I smile at her now and as she passes she stops and grabs my arm. Her grip is surprisingly strong. 'Ain't you that journalist?'

'That's right. My name's Jenna Halliday.'

She lets go of my arm and blinks at me. Her hair is tobacco-stained yellow and her face is hard, her mouth thin. She doesn't offer me her name. 'I lived here when it happened,' she says. 'Next door to that Tamzin Cole and her parents. Weird lot. Loud. Common, you know?'

I keep my face impassive.

'That Tamzin had a string of boyfriends. Wouldn't surprise me if she'd run off with one of them.'

'What about Sally and Katie?'

She draws her lips together like she's taking a drag of an imaginary cigarette. 'Didn't know much about those two. But think the lot of them were up to no good. Fancy running away like that and not telling your parents. It ain't right.'

'Maybe they didn't run away.'

She laughs mirthlessly. 'And what happened to them, then? They were abducted by aliens, like some folk around 'ere like to think? What a load of tosh. That Olivia Rutherford knows exactly what happened, mark my words. She was in on it too. She'd be with them now, I reckon, if it hadn't been for that accident. She plays the whole butter-wouldn't-melt routine down to a T, that one. Just like her mother. Stuck up. Haven't got time for the pair of them.'

It doesn't sound like this woman has time for anyone. She's obviously a gossip with no concrete information. Still, she might be good for the podcast. I ask her if she'd like to be interviewed but she looks horrified. 'No, thank you. You're wasting your time here anyway, if you want my opinion.'

'Why do you think they ran away?' I ask, to keep her talking.

'Well, I can't speak for the other two, but Tamzin Cole's parents rowed like cats and dogs. Think the husband ran off with another woman before Tamzin went missing. Oh, but the shouting I used to hear coming through the walls. It turned the air blue, all their cursing. It wasn't a particularly happy home. Maybe Tamzin wanted a new start, away from the lot of them.'

'Do the Coles still live in Stafferbury?'

She shakes her head. 'They moved away in the end. Don't know where. Good riddance, I say. Anyway, got to get on. Can't stand around here all day gossiping. My Stan's waiting in the car and I still need to buy bread. Oh, my name's Rita.' She grimaces at me showing large front teeth, then seizes the handle of her trolley and wanders off towards the other end of the high street where there is a small Co-op on the corner.

Thunder rolls overhead and the rain falls even heavier as people dart into shops or quicken their step. I almost run to the car park, grateful when I get into my warm, dry Audi. I wonder if Rita's opinion on the missing girls is widely shared in the community and make a mental note to ask around, conscious of Wesley's comment about Olivia being 'vilified'. I exit the car park, having to slam my brakes on as three teenage girls dart across my path, giggling and leaning on each other. One is wearing a Santa hat, the other has pink tinsel wrapped around her hair. They look college age. The same age as Tamzin, Sally and Katie were when they went missing. I watch them as they trip along the high street, arms interlinked, my heart heavy. And then I continue driving, my windscreen wipers swishing back and forth trying to keep up with the downpour. I can barely see as I drive along the Devil's Corridor and have to slow right down so that I don't miss my turn. When I pull up outside my cabin I turn off the ignition and sit for a while. The trees bend and stretch in the wind, their leaves rustling as though whispering secrets, the rain plopping into muddy puddles.

Reluctantly I get out of the car and scurry towards the front door, stopping briefly to extract my heel from the matting on the drive. As I reach the door I nearly slip on something. I look down at the step, slick and wet, recoiling when I see blood and flesh. It looks like a rat or some kind of rodent, or part of one. I kick it to the side and open the front door, my pulse quickening. Nausea washes over me. I close the door on the dead animal, hoping that a fox or cat has left it and it isn't some kind of warning.

11

Olivia

IT'S NEARLY 3 P.M. WHEN WESLEY'S MIDNIGHT BLUE BMW pulls up outside the stables just as Olivia's exiting the office shed. Apart from a quick chat earlier when she told him about Jenna's visit and he went haring off after her, she hasn't had the chance to ask him about where he disappeared to last night. He's talking to her mum in the car park, their heads bent in conversation. It's started raining again, the sky a deep charcoal behind them. They look up in unison when they hear her and she holds the gate open for them.

'Well?' she asks, letting it slam closed behind them. 'Did you catch up with the journalist? You've been gone ages.'

'I had to go back to work. I've got a job, you know. I managed to leave early, saying I had a stomach upset. Which,' he says, holding on to his stomach and grimacing, 'isn't a lie. It hasn't been right all day.'

'I'll leave you to it,' her mother says, winking at Olivia as she strides past her into the office, and Olivia realizes that Wesley must have been filling her in already or she would have stayed to listen. Her mother always has an ear to the ground: she likes to know everything that's going on in Stafferbury. After the accident Olivia asked if they should sell up and move away. Not far. Maybe to the next town so she could keep seeing Wesley. But her mum had been horrified. 'I can't possibly leave the stables. It's a family business. Your grandparents would turn in their graves.' So they had stayed, and Olivia had had to put up with the stares, the accusations and gossip, and then, by the time she felt well enough, strong enough even to consider moving away, her life was so interwoven with the fabric of the town that to leave seemed unthinkable.

'So?' she asks now. 'Where did you run off to last night?'

'Last night?' Wesley shuffles his feet. He's wearing a new pair of ugly platform trainers that wouldn't look out of place on a guy half his age.

'I woke up and you'd gone.'

'Oh, that . . . yeah, I couldn't sleep. I needed my own bed and you looked so peaceful I didn't want to wake you.'

She frowns. 'So you just snuck out in the middle of the night?'

'It was actually the early hours of this morning.'

Was it? She can't remember what time it was. All she knew was that it had been dark. But considering it doesn't start getting light until after 7.30 a.m. he could be right. Either way it was before 6 a.m. as that was when her alarm went off.

'Did you see Izzy in the café?' she asks, hating herself for it. She knows she sounds needy and insecure. But she looks so much like Sally. Wesley must notice too. Sometimes, especially in the early days, Olivia would stop in her tracks when she saw Izzy, and for a wild moment, a millisecond really, it was as though Sally had never gone missing, as though she'd been in the town all along and was walking carefree down the high street, her dark glossy ponytail swinging. And it would be so painful it winded Olivia, sending her into a spiral of nostalgia and grief for the only best friend she's ever had. Olivia tried, about ten years ago, to befriend Izzy despite their eight-year age gap and had asked her if she wanted to go for a drink. Izzy had agreed – her parents might not have wanted anything to do with Olivia but Izzy was delighted to swap memories and humorous stories about her sister. They'd spent a few nights out reminiscing about Sally, but being with Izzy just reminded Olivia that although Izzy looked like her best friend she was an imposter, and it made her miss Sally all the more. Olivia realized then that friendship couldn't be forced, no matter how much you both might want it.

Now Wesley tries to look nonchalant. 'Yeah, we had a quick chat. Anyway, when are you finishing up here? Thought we could go to the pub tonight.'

'About five,' she replies.

He laughs. 'God, Liv, at least fake some enthusiasm.' He reaches over and tenderly touches her face. For a moment she sees rare vulnerability in his eyes. 'I know it's a hard time of year. But I do love you, you know, and I'd do anything for you.'

'I know you would.' She nudges the concrete with the toe of her boot.

'I just want to take care of you.'

She doesn't need taking care of. She's a grown woman and

everyone treats her like a child. But she would never have survived through it all without him. And now she wonders if she does love him or whether she feels like she owes him.

'I know neither of us wants kids . . .' he says, and she looks up at him in surprise.

'Whoa! Isn't this a bit of a heavy conversation to be having on a Tuesday afternoon?'

He laughs. He has a wide mouth that is too big for his face. It can make him look happy one minute and sulky the next. 'I just think maybe we should move things forward. It's about time. Live together. I can look after you. You need me, Liv. And I need you. We'd be a proper couple.'

'We are a proper couple.'

'You know what I mean. You could move into my flat with me. Get away from . . .' He inclines his head towards the office where her mother is.

Does she want to get away from her mother? They've always been close and Wes gets on well with her. And it's a big house to live in all by herself. She'd feel guilty leaving her all alone. Not to mention that she hates Wesley's poky flat. 'What about Mum?'

'She'll be fine. She's a strong woman. And you'd still work here, wouldn't you, so you'd see her every day.'

'Can I think about it?'

He sighs. 'This can't be a surprise. We've been together for twenty years.'

But it is a surprise and she can't help wondering why he's mentioned this now.

12

The Charmer

DERRECK SMILED BROADLY AS THEY ALL TROOPED PAST HIM *into the villa. Stace could hardly believe her eyes at the sheer opulence of the place. It was like a palace, with a marble floor and a sweeping staircase that led to five double rooms. There were two bathrooms with tubs as big as swimming-pools and a kitchen with modern appliances. The views from the front overlooked the river, and at the back the garden was private, hidden from the other two properties at either side by exotic trees and bushes. Although, according to Derreck, the other properties were vacant. There was also an oval swimming-pool sunk into the lawn and a terrace with an awning and a barbecue.*

'How can Derreck afford this?' Stace whispered, after they'd all been shown to their rooms.

'Everything is much cheaper in Thailand,' said John-Paul, by

way of explanation, as he placed his clothes in the polished wooden chest of drawers. 'And he has a good job now. Investment banking. He's settled down at last.'

'Girlfriend?'

He looked up from the suitcase and raised his eyebrows. 'Why? You interested?' He laughed. John-Paul wasn't the jealous type and he was sure of her. Too sure, sometimes, she felt. It would have been nice for him to show a little bit of jealousy on occasion. Anyway, he need not be jealous. They might not have been getting on that well lately but this holiday had come at the right time.

'Now you come to mention it, this does have a corporate air about it,' she said, unpacking her new skimpy bikini.

John-Paul laughed. 'A corporate air! Like you'd know what that is.'

She punched his arm playfully. 'By what I've seen in films.'

But she couldn't shake the feeling that the villa didn't feel like a home. It felt like somewhere Derreck had maybe hired for a few weeks to impress. There were no homely touches, no vases with flowers or personal effects. No photos on the walls or art work or anything that showed any individuality. She imagined that both villas either side of this one looked exactly the same inside.

Still, now she was here, now she had survived the hideous twelve-hour plane journey through the night, and the trek from the airport, she was determined to relax and have fun. They were in beautiful surroundings with – thank goodness – air-conditioning and all mod-cons. Hannah, Leonie and Maggie were right. This was a holiday of a lifetime. When would she get to stay anywhere so magnificent ever again?

Maggie and Martin burst into the room, giggling, their arms wrapped around each other. 'Wow, this is all just . . . wow,' exclaimed Maggie, her brown eyes flashing with excitement. 'Have you seen the bathroom? It's bigger than my whole flat!'

'Mate, I could kiss you for sorting this out,' said Martin, wrapping an arm around John-Paul's neck and making lip-smacking noises against his cheek.

It made Stace's heart soar to see the easy way the lads had accepted him into their group. She knew John-Paul still felt he needed to prove himself, even though it was unnecessary.

'We'd never have been able to afford a holiday like this if it wasn't for you.'

'Gerroff,' laughed John-Paul, pushing Martin away. 'It's what mates are for. And, anyway, it's Derreck you have to thank, not me.' His cheeks reddened. 'It was his idea.'

'Yes, it was,' agreed a voice from the doorway. They looked up to see Derreck leaning against the door jamb, his shirt unbuttoned to reveal golden skin. He was no longer wearing his hat and he flicked his blond fringe away from startling blue eyes. He was disarmingly handsome and Stace was annoyed with herself when her stomach flipped. She bet he had the pick of most women. 'My maid is downstairs preparing the barbecue.'

'You have a maid?' spluttered Maggie. 'Blimey.'

'She comes with the place,' he said nonchalantly.

The wealth was a stark contrast to the way they all lived their lives back home, in their small flats with not much money. Stace wondered if John-Paul felt envious. She couldn't help feeling a twinge of jealousy.

'JP,' Derreck strolled further into the room, 'would you mind coming with me? I'd like to catch up properly with my old mate. That's all right, isn't it?' he said, his gaze washing over her. Stace felt it wasn't really a question.

John-Paul glanced at Stace and she raised her eyebrows. 'Sure, would love to,' he replied, following Derreck out of the room and winking at Stace over his shoulder, but she noticed the tension in his body, which hadn't been there before Derreck walked in.

'We'll meet you outside in ten,' called Derreck. 'Tell the others.'

'Well,' said Maggie, when they had gone, 'Derreck's done all right for himself, hasn't he?'

'Yeah,' agreed Martin, pushing the suitcase to one side so he could join his girlfriend on the bed. 'Do you know much about him?'

Stace continued to hang the rest of her clothes in the large wardrobe. 'Not much. John-Paul said Derreck was brought up in Australia but his mum is British. They met when John-Paul was travelling in Vietnam. He's twenty-seven and . . .' She shrugged. 'That's all I know, really.'

'Hmm,' said Maggie, chewing her lip thoughtfully. 'Well, he seems nice enough and obviously hot.' Martin swiped at her playfully and Stace felt herself blush. 'Anyway.' Maggie jumped off the bed. 'We'll leave you to unpack. Come on, Mart.' She took his hand and led him from the room.

After Stace had finished unpacking she headed to the garden. As she descended the marble staircase she could smell the barbecue and her stomach rumbled. She hadn't eaten since the plane. But as she passed the front-room door she heard raised voices. She stopped, her hand on the door knob.

'If I'd known I'd never have fucking agreed to come.'

'Aw, come on, mate. There's nothing like a freebie in this world, you know that.' It was Derreck.

Stace's heart pounded and she was filled with a sense of dread so powerful she felt sick.

'I thought we could put the past behind us.'

'We have!' Derreck sounded jovial compared to John-Paul's surly tone. *'But you do owe me.'*

'For Goa, I suppose.'

Stace felt a flash of heat to her face. What did Derreck mean? Why did John-Paul owe him?

'It's just this one thing,' said Derreck, his voice cajoling. *'Please, mate.'*

'I don't know. What'll I tell the others?'

'That we're meeting an old friend, don't . . .'

The rest of the sentence was drowned out by the sound of Griff and Leonie, followed by Hannah and Trevor coming down the stairs and Stace moved away from the door.

'Hey,' said Griff, clapping her on the back and making her cough. *'Are we going to get a drink, then? Smells like the barbie's on.'*

The door opened and John-Paul stood there, his face pale. She noticed that he couldn't quite meet her eye as he took her hand wordlessly and led her down the hallway. The titters of Leonie and Hannah from behind her made her hackles rise. She didn't even have to turn around to know they were flirting with Derreck.

The air was still hot and sticky as they walked through the huge kitchen and out onto the patio. The sky had turned a beautiful shade of pink and gold but, despite the humidity, Stace shivered. What had Derreck and John-Paul been talking about? And what happened in Goa? She suddenly realized John-Paul and Derreck had a whole past that she knew nothing about.

13

Jenna

I FIRE UP MY LAPTOP AND TYPE 'DS DALE CRAWFORD' INTO
Google. Thankfully, there is Wi-Fi in the cabin even if it is a little sketchy at times. As soon as I enter his name a photo comes
up of an attractive guy in his thirties with hooded hazel eyes
and messy light brown hair. It's from a piece in the *Guardian*
about how he helped crack a decades-old cold case involving an
elderly couple who had been found suffocated at their cottage in
Devizes. Another article describes him as a 'rising star at Wiltshire CID', then goes on to detail all the recent investigations
he's worked on, mainly from years ago and involving murdered
or missing people. I'm impressed. I check the time. It's almost
3.30 p.m. I'd better get a move on if I want to visit Ralph Middleton. I should do it now before it gets dark.

I'm wearing more practical clothing this time: my bright yellow wellies and a raincoat over jeans and a warm jumper. Brenda

had said Ralph's caravan wasn't far from this cabin. Let's just hope I don't get lost trying to find it.

When I open the front door I'm half expecting to see the dead animal remains back on my porch, but fortunately there's nothing. The rain has stopped but a mist is suspended between the trees and there is dampness in the air. I inhale the smell of soil and scented pine as I hover on the porch, not sure which way to head. There is a path that snakes through the forest, past the cabin diagonally in front of mine – the same path the person with the German Shepherd took yesterday. I decide to go that way, pull my bag strap across my body and hunch my shoulders against the wind. I have my mace in my pocket, just in case. Mud squelches under my rubber soles as I make my way past the other cabin. Now I'm closer to it I can see it is named Foxglove. There are no signs of life from inside. I follow the footsteps that are already formed in the mud as the pathway curves to the right. Over to the left I see two more cabins poking out of the trees.

As I head deeper into the forest my heart starts to beat that little bit faster. I keep to the path but the terrain is rougher in here, the treetops like a green canopy above my head so that, when the rain begins again, I barely feel it. I can just hear the tap of it as it hits the trees. It's as though I'm walking into another world and I can smell smoke, like a dying bonfire. I trudge on. I hope I don't get lost and that this main path leads me to Ralph Middleton's caravan.

I walk for another ten minutes, feeling less and less sure of myself until eventually I stumble into a clearing and find the source of the smoke I could smell. A bonfire is smouldering half-heartedly, and next to it stands a small beaten-up caravan that can't be bigger than a four-berth. It has rust around the window and a pair of ugly orange curtains hanging limply. This must be it. I hear the tinkle of a windchime I can see swinging from a nearby tree. The sound is eerie. The rain is heavier here without the protection of the canopy of leaves. I walk around the fire. There are no flames, which isn't surprising, given the rain, just wood, black and charred. In front of it is an old camping chair, the fabric coming away from its metal frame.

I stop, holding my breath. I can hear raised voices inside the caravan. I hesitate, wondering whether to knock, but before I've had the chance, the door is flung open and I have to jump back to avoid being hit in the face.

Olivia steps down onto the grass, a black beanie pulled over dark blonde hair. She turns to me, her face white and pinched, her eyes puffy. I take a step towards her but she cowers away from me. She turns without speaking and strides past me in the direction I've just come. I notice she's limping slightly.

Ralph appears in the doorway, confusion written on his face. His hair is thin on top and gathered at the base of his neck in a ponytail. He looks like an ageing rocker. He's wearing a baggy black jumper and khaki cargo trousers with heavy biker boots. He looks from me to Olivia's retreating back. By his side is his three-legged dog, which fixes me with huge dark eyes.

'Hi,' I begin. 'I don't know if you remember me from yesterday?'

He frowns and strokes his greying beard but he doesn't take his eyes off Olivia's yellow coat, which flickers through the trees until she's out of sight.

When she's gone he turns to me. 'She's upset,' he says matter-of-factly.

'Why?'

He touches the top of his head where the hair is thinning, looking agitated. 'She's upset,' he repeats. 'I've upset her.'

'What did you do?'

He shakes his head. 'I can't say. I'm not allowed to say.'

'Did . . . did you hurt her, Ralph?'

His dark eyes are sad. 'Of course I didn't hurt her. I'd never hurt her.' His shoulders droop and he pats the dog's head.

'Can I . . .' I clear my throat, not sure how to ask '. . . I was wondering if I might come in and have a chat?'

He looks at me suspiciously. 'Why?'

'My name is Jenna Halliday.' I smile encouragingly at him and, hating myself for it, I pull my long hair over my shoulder. The red hair that Gavin used to say was like the colour of russet autumn leaves. 'I'm making a podcast about Olivia's accident and her friends' disappearance and was wondering if I could interview you.'

'Why? I don't know anything.'

'Just because you found her that night. You saved her life, Ralph.'

He assesses me as though he's not sure whether to believe me. But then, to my relief, he stands aside to let me in. 'I . . . It ain't much, mind.'

I tell him I don't care about that as I step up into the caravan. Straight away I'm hit by the smell of wet dog mixed with beef soup, but his caravan is tidy yet sparse. I can see it has a small bedroom off the main area and, next to it, a toilet. He indicates the table at the opposite end and I inch past the kitchenette to get to it. The brown sofa is ripped in places, foam oozing from the cracks, and a tabby cat is curled up in the corner.

'Would you like a cup of tea?' he asks. 'I ain't got no milk, mind. Olivia used the last of it.'

I spot two green plastic camping mugs on the melamine worktop. 'I'd love a coffee if you have any. I have it black anyway.'

He nods and opens a little cupboard above his head and takes out two clean plastic mugs. I notice how his hands shake as he switches the little kettle on and my eye goes to a bin in the corner piled high with empty lager cans.

'How long have you lived here?' I ask, as he scoops some Nescafé into my mug.

'Years and years,' he says. His accent is thick West Country. 'My stepdad threw me out when I was seventeen. I've been here ever since. The caravan was my ma's, like. She took pity on me, I think. Not pity enough to kick out that scumbag of a husband, mind.'

I watch as he pours the hot water into the mugs, then ambles towards me. He seems too big for this small space. He sits opposite me, sliding my mug across the table. The tabby cat stretches and resumes its sleeping position. I stroke its soft head. Out of the corner of my eye I see something scurry out from under the table and towards the bedroom. I squeal with surprise.

'That's just Timmy Willy,' he says, grinning at me.

'It's . . . a mouse?'

'Yep. A field mouse. Olivia named him. From Beatrix Potter. He likes to come in and I give him summit to eat.'

I shudder at the thought that rodents just wander through the caravan and surreptitiously scan the floor to make sure no other furry friends are about to make an appearance.

He laughs. 'He won't hurt you.'

There is something so childlike about Ralph and I feel a lump form in my throat. Since I've had Finn I've become soft. I see the little boy that Ralph once was and wonder how he could have ended up like this. Was he loved growing up? Did his mother do enough to protect him? Who cares for him now? I wonder if Olivia does. Is that why she visits? The rain thrashes against the window and the wind whistles through the gaps in the caravan. Yet I don't feel afraid here with him, even though I probably should. This could be exactly what Ralph is banking on. Luring his victims here by pretending to be a simple soul with animals for companions. As I reach for my phone to record him I place the mace inside my handbag but within easy reach.

'You're happy for me to record you?' I ask, setting my phone up on its stand between us.

He nods. 'Sure.'

'So why did Olivia come and see you?' I sip my coffee while I wait for him to answer.

He shrugs. 'She comes often. She's my friend. She's always been kind to me. I know what people say about me, but Olivia's always treated me like a person, not a joke.'

'Did you know her before the accident?'

He shakes his head, his giant hands clutching his mug. 'Only after her friends went missing.' He's silent for a few moments, looking into his coffee. And then he says, 'They were nice girls. Pretty.'

I try to fight the preconceived idea that he's some kind of pervert just because he lives alone in the forest and is a little bit odd.

But then I remember Olivia's pinched white face, her puffy eyes. Had he tried it on with her?

'Did you like the girls, Ralph?' I say carefully. 'Do you like Olivia?'

He looks up at me. 'I didn't know them. And, like I said, Olivia is just a friend.'

'Did you see anything that night? Anything suspicious?'

He bites his lip, as though he's trying to stop himself saying something he shouldn't.

'Olivia claims to have seen a figure in the road. And that's why she'd swerved. Did you see anything?'

He shrugs again, avoiding eye contact. 'No. I didn't see a person in the road.'

'You said something about a bright light? And then you retracted it?' I press.

He sighs. 'It was a long time ago. I can't remember.'

'Did you see a bright light?'

'Olivia told me not to say.'

'Olivia told you not to say what? About the light?'

'People would laugh. That's what she said. People would laugh at me.'

'Why?'

'Because I believe in aliens.'

Oh, yes, his alien theory. 'Did Olivia see the bright light too?'

He nods, just a fraction. 'This place ain't right,' he blurts out suddenly, with feeling. 'I've been saying that for years. It's haunted.'

'What did you think the bright light was, Ralph?'

'A UFO, of course. It blinded me. And then . . . and then it just sort of disappeared.'

He eyes me stubbornly. Does he really believe what he's saying? I decide on another tactic. 'Why did Olivia leave here crying earlier, Ralph?'

He presses his lips together stubbornly. And then he stands up, his leg knocking against the table and nearly unbalancing my phone stand. 'I think you need to go now.'

I experience a thud of disappointment. 'Ralph, are you protecting Olivia?'

'I don't want to talk about Olivia any more. She told me not to say anything. I'm fed up with everyone asking questions . . . everyone blaming me!' His cheeks have turned red and spittle forms on his lips.

'Told you not to say anything about what?'

'Please leave now.' He strides across the caravan and flings open the door. I reluctantly gather up my phone and its stand, dropping them into my bag, and hurry out. 'Ralph . . .' I begin, as I step down onto the wet grass, but he has shut the door in my face.

14

THE SKY HAS DARKENED CONSIDERABLY IN THE TIME I'VE been in the caravan. As I head back through the forest I'm thinking about Ralph and our strange conversation when I hear a twig snap behind me. I pause, my body rigid, a creeping sensation at the back of my neck. I turn but nobody's there. I'm not far from my cabin so I break into a jog, wondering if Ralph has followed me, if I got him wrong and he isn't some harmless loner after all but a psychopath. I feel a surge of relief when I notice a light is on in Foxglove, the cabin opposite mine, and a shadow passes across the window.

I'm cold and damp by the time I let myself into my own cabin and turn on the lights. I go around closing the curtains, wanting to shut out those trees, which feel like they're encompassing me, threatening to swallow me. They remind me of a *Doctor Who* episode I once watched with Finn where trees started sprouting out of the ground and growing out of control, threatening to engulf the town in a blanket of nature. I peel off my wet things and make myself comfortable in the armchair by the fireplace. Then I Face-Time Finn.

My son is in the living room when he answers. Behind him I can see the ink blue feature wall I'd painted last year. He flashes me his cheeky smile but he looks tired. I hope Gavin isn't letting him stay up too late.

I tell him about the forest and remind him of the *Doctor Who* episode.

He laughs. 'Really, Mum! That sounds pretty rad.'

'Sometimes it feels like they're going to come in through the windows, their branches like gnarled fingers, trying to grab me. I'm literally in a box in the middle of a forest.'

He giggles and asks to see so I take my phone to the window and pull aside the curtains to show him the forest beyond. A flash of a waxed jacket catches my eye. Is it Ralph coming to find me? Or the person I saw in the cabin opposite? I peer out but everything is smudged due to the rain splatter on the glass and I can't tell if it was my imagination. I close the curtains and concentrate on what Finn is saying.

'Wow, I wish I was there,' he says, as I turn away from the window. 'We could explore.' My heart lurches. I wish he was here too. Or that I was there. Right now I'd give anything to be at home with him, curled up on the sofa watching *Doctor Who*.

'It's not exactly Center Parcs,' I say, and a shiver runs through me at the thought of my excursion to Ralph's caravan earlier. I'm just glad I managed to get a recording of our conversation.

We talk about school and I spot my mum in the background, zooming in and out of shot as she hands Finn some biscuits and milk. 'Can I talk to Nanny after?' I want to ask him about the woman I heard earlier but I don't want to put him in an awkward position. He just thinks Gavin and I are having a break from each other. And that, soon, we'll all be back under one roof. It must be confusing and unsettling for him.

He talks more about school and his teacher, Mr Carter, whom he adores, while munching his biscuit. He has ink at the tips of his fingers and his nails are bitten down.

'Do you want to talk to Nanny now?' he says.

I nod and say goodbye, blowing him kisses and wishing I was there to give him a hug. The screen blurs as he hands over the iPad to my mum. The top half of her face appears on screen so all I can see is her strawberry-blonde fringe and green eyes.

'All right, love?'

'Mum, I can't see your mouth!'

'Oh   right. Hold on.' She moves the screen down. 'Is that better?'

'Yeah, much.'

'How are you getting on? What's it like there?' she asks, and I fill her in on everything that's happened so far. My mum should have been a journalist herself; she's even nosier than I am. She asks for a tour of the cabin so I turn my phone around to show her the kitchen and the living area, then the bedroom. 'It's smart,' she says approvingly.

'I miss you all, though. I miss Finn,' I say, returning to my armchair. I've been away with work before, usually just a night, and Finn hasn't really worried about it. But this is the first time I've been away since the split and never for so long.

Mum has now moved into the kitchen and is standing in front of my pale grey Shaker-style pantry. I know she's left Finn on his own so we can talk freely. 'You'll be home Friday. Make the most of it. Everything is under control here.'

'Have you spoken to Gav much?' I ask.

'Only about Finn. I get the sense he doesn't want me poking my nose in.' I suppress a wry smile. I know she'd like nothing more.

'I'm trying to give him space, Mum. But I'm running out of patience. I don't know what to do. And this morning . . .' I hesitate and lower my voice. 'I thought I heard a woman.'

Mum grimaces. 'What do you mean, heard a woman? Heard a woman doing what?'

'Laughing. Quite early, before school.'

Her eyes narrow. 'Look, Gavin isn't stupid enough to have a woman spend the night, if that's what you're thinking. Not with Finn here. Stop being paranoid. It was probably the TV or radio.' She is smiling as she says it but her voice is stern.

'You're right,' I say. Mum has made me feel better, like she's been doing since I first had my heart broken when I was twelve and the boy I fancied called me Rat Face. Maybe it had been the radio. In any case, I have to forget about it for now.

I pull up in the pub car park at just gone 7 p.m. It's stopped raining and I'm still wearing my big chunky green jumper and my jeans from earlier but with my smarter wool coat now it's dried. I pull my bag over my shoulder and walk purposefully into The Raven. I scan the wooden tables and the comfy checked sofas but I can't see DS Crawford, just an older couple in the corner and two women chatting on one of the sofas. I go to the bar and order a glass of white wine and lemonade from an old guy with a nose ring. I'm just handing over my debit card when the door opens letting in a gust of fresh air and DS Crawford comes in. He's a bit older than he appears in his photo, tall and rangy and his hair looks like he's just walked through a wind tunnel. He pats it down self-consciously. He has an air of dishevelment about him, like he's been rushing around all day.

His hazel eyes light up when he sees me. 'Jenna?'

'Hi, yes, you must be DS Crawford.'

He thrusts out a hand to shake mine. He smells of rain and woodsmoke. 'Please, call me Dale. Great to meet you. If you find a table I'll grab a drink and join you.'

I choose the table in the corner next to the leaded window and shuffle onto the padded bench seat with my back to the wall so I have a view of the door. I take two large sips of wine. Dale crosses the room, pint in hand, and takes a seat opposite. He sets his glass on the table and shrugs off his black wool coat revealing a shirt and a tie that's askew.

'So, Jenna. I hear from Brenda you're making a podcast.'

'That's right.' I explain a little about it while he listens. 'It's for BBC Sounds and it's the first I've done, although I've been a reporter for over fifteen years.'

'So Brenda told you I've recently been assigned to the case?'

'She did. I just wondered, why now? Have there been any developments?'

He arches one of his expressive eyebrows. 'Not really. This happens every now and again. It's never been closed but now with more funding . . .' He waves a hand. 'I won't bore you with the red tape.' He picks up his pint and takes a long gulp.

'So they decided to bring in the cold-case expert,' I say, smiling.

He chuckles. 'Ha. No. It's been twenty years. A fresh pair of eyes and all that.'

He's being modest. I've read all about the cases he's helped solve and some were high-profile.

'And you come from Stafferbury?' I'd read that too.

He lowers his glass. 'Yep. My dad still lives here, in one of the retirement flats, although I moved away a while ago now with my wife – ex-wife.' He flushes slightly. 'But not that far. Devizes. Do you know it?' I shake my head. 'I used to drink in here as a teenager.' He looks around wistfully. 'It's changed quite a bit. It was a dive back then.'

He must surely have known the girls. I try to guess his age, but it's hard because there is no grey in his thick hair and only a few lines around his eyes. He could be a few years younger than me. I decide to ask him.

'Yes. I did know them a bit.' He coughs. 'I was in the same year at school as Katie and Tamzin.' I calculate that he must be a year older than me. I'm surprised.

'And did you know Olivia or Sally?'

He swallows. 'Um. Not really, no. They were in the year below.' He picks up a menu from a stand in the middle of the table. 'I'm starving, and I've hardly had time to eat today. Do you mind if I order some food? Do you want anything?'

Now I think about it I could do with something to eat.

We decide on pizzas and Dale goes to the bar to order, insisting it's on him. As he walks back I notice he's wearing pale blue socks with little white penguins on them underneath his smart suit trousers that are just a tad too short. For some reason the sight of them puts me at ease.

He slides back into his seat and grins. 'Shouldn't be long.'

'So,' I say, leaning back against the wall, regretting taking the uncomfortable bench seat, 'you were saying you were at school with Katie and Tamzin.'

'Uh. Yeah. That's right. But then I went to university in Edinburgh and it was while I was there they went missing.'

I play with the stem of my wine glass. 'There was something Brenda mentioned that I wanted to ask you more about.'

'Oh, yes?'

'She said Olivia reported that she was being followed in the days leading up to the accident.'

He pulls a thread from the cuff of his powder blue shirt. 'Yes. She said to the police she saw a man driving a white van. So the police interviewed all the men in the area who drove a white van and none fitted the description. There was building work going on at the time, so it might not have been a local. But there was hardly any CCTV around in Stafferbury in 1998 and Olivia didn't know the registration plate. So it all came to a dead end.' He hesitates as though wondering whether to continue. 'And then it was thought, perhaps, that she was lying to maybe hide her own guilt.'

'Did the police think Olivia was guilty then?'

'I think, to this day, many of the locals believe she's hiding something.'

'And do you?'

'I'm not at liberty to say. I haven't even had the chance to interview Olivia myself yet since reopening the case.'

'Were there . . .' I pause as a woman with dyed black hair and heavily drawn-on eyebrows arrives at our table with the pizzas.

Ham and pineapple for me and pepperoni for Dale. I wait for her to leave before continuing. 'Were there ever any sightings of the girls?'

Dale takes a bite out of his pizza and chews, then swallows. 'Yes. Especially in the early days. Mainly in the UK and about ten years ago there was a sighting in Germany.'

'Of all three?'

He nods. 'Apparently they were spotted in Munich. But it was never verified. An anonymous source claims he saw them wandering around the grounds of Nymphenburg Palace. I dunno . . .' he shrugs '. . . it doesn't sound very feasible. Another time a woman with blonde hair matching Tamzin's description was seen in Thailand. But, again, nothing came of it.' He finishes his pizza slice in a few mouthfuls. 'Sorry.' He grins. 'I didn't have time for lunch.'

I smile and take a bite of my pizza to show solidarity. 'I bumped into a woman in town today.' I explain about Rita. 'She said she used to live next door to Tamzin but her parents split up and moved away.'

Dale has a swig of his pint. 'Yes, that's right. They were always arguing.' He bows his head. 'So I heard anyway.'

'And Sally and Katie's parents?'

'Sally's parents are still together and live in Stafferbury. Katie's dad died a few years ago but her mum is still around.'

'Do you think they would talk to me?'

He wipes his mouth with a paper napkin. 'It doesn't hurt to try. They've been very private over the years, though. No press interviews, apart from a televised appeal not long after they disappeared. But they've always been helpful to the police.'

I tell him about my visit to Ralph Middleton earlier and witnessing Olivia storming out of the caravan crying. 'Ralph said Olivia had asked him to keep something secret.'

His expression grows serious and he puts the napkin down. 'And he didn't give any clue as to what that was?'

I shake my head. 'He basically kicked me out of the caravan when I asked and . . . Oh.' I stop mid-flow. Wesley has just burst into the pub, bringing with him a blast of cold air and a buzz of high-octane energy. He's talking nineteen to the dozen and I spot Olivia behind him, a more subdued presence. He turns to help her down the stone step and gently leads her to a table. She's limping quite a lot, more than earlier. They haven't seen us. She looks downcast but he seems excitable, regaling some story of a recent night out. The odd words like 'Such a laugh . . .' and 'Stan couldn't stand up for hours' drift over to us.

'What is it?' Dale cranes his neck to look at them, then turns back to me, his eyes wide. 'I heard they were still together. God knows what she sees in him. He was a bit of a knob in school.' He coughs. 'Sorry, not very professional of me. But let's just say we weren't in the same crowd. In fact, he was a bit of a bully at school. Pushed me up against the lockers once.' Dale is a good three inches taller, although slighter, than Wesley. 'I was a late developer.' He laughs as though reading my mind.

It's not until Olivia sits down that she sees us.

And when she does I observe the flash of fear in her expression.

15

WESLEY SEEMS NOT TO HAVE NOTICED US. OLIVIA LOOKS
pretty in a deep rose blouse that brings out the colour in her
cheeks. She scrubs up well. I don't know how she can work with
horses all day – they terrify me with their flaring nostrils and
large teeth. Wesley's voice carries over to us, loud and brash.

'Stop staring,' whispers Dale, a laugh in his voice.

Olivia is sitting diagonally across from me and is doing her
best to pretend I'm not here but there's something in her expression I can't read. Panic, maybe. I pull my gaze away from her and
back to Dale. 'Am I that obvious? I'm so nosy.'

'I can tell. Subterfuge wouldn't be your thing, would it?' He
chuckles. 'Now do you want another drink?'

'Let me get it this time. You paid for the pizza.'

'It's not going to break the bank.' He grins. 'What do you
want?' He stands up and I ask for another wine and lemonade.

While he's at the bar I finish my pizza. Wesley is chatting away, loving the sound of his own voice, unaware of our presence. And then I see his eyes go to Dale at the bar. He leans forwards and whispers something to Olivia. Then they turn in my direction. I smile but they look away.

'I see they've clocked us,' says Dale, returning with our drinks. 'We'd better be careful what we say now.'

Damn it. 'I've still got so much I want to know . . .'

'Well, hold off on those questions. There will be other opportunities. I'm staying with my dad in Stafferbury for the next few days so I won't be far.'

'And you're happy for me to interview you for the podcast?'

'Sure. Why not? You might want to wait a few days, though, until I have more information.'

It's there again, the nagging feeling that there is a reason for reopening the case. Something he's not yet ready to share.

'This works two ways, though,' he adds, in a low voice. 'If you find out anything while conducting your interviews I'd appreciate being kept in the loop.'

'Of course.'

Since we can no longer discuss the case, he starts telling me about his family, how his mum died a few years ago of cancer and how he tries to stay with his dad regularly to keep him from getting too lonely. He has a sister who lives in Spain – he sees her twice a year. 'And you're from Manchester? I can tell by the accent.'

'Yes. I've lived there all my life.'

'Have you ever thought of moving away?'

I shake my head. 'Not really. My son is happy at school and I wouldn't want to uproot us all.'

He glances at my wedding ring. 'And what does your husband do?'

'He's in finance. He's . . .' The wine burns in the back of my throat. 'We're actually separated at the moment.' I instantly regret saying this. Gavin says I often overshare.

Dale looks a little uncomfortable. 'I'm sorry to hear that.' Then he adds softly, 'I've been there.'

'I'm sorry.'

Now he tries to look nonchalant, even though I'm not fooled. A broken marriage – I'm coming to realize – hurts like hell.

'It is what it is.'

'How long ago?' I ask.

'Two years now.'

'Kids?'

'No, thank goodness. It was messy enough without bringing a child into it all.' Then he's mortified. 'God, I'm sorry. That was thoughtless of me.'

I wave away his apology. 'That's okay.' But there is a lump in my throat.

'How old is your son?' he asks.

'Finn is only ten. And I love Gav. Gavin, my husband. I've been with him since I was nineteen. Half my life. I really want to make it work.'

'So it was his idea?'

I nod, my eyes smarting. I shouldn't be drinking. I've already shared too much with someone I barely know.

'Jody, that's my ex, well, it was her idea too. It sucks, doesn't it?'

I laugh despite the pain behind my eyes. 'It does.'

'I'm sure it'll be okay. Hopefully you guys can sort it out.'

'I hope so too.'

Dale's mobile buzzes on the table next to him. He glances at it. 'Shit. Sorry, it's work. I'd better get this.'

I nod and take a sip of my drink. From across the room I see Wesley get up to go to the bar.

'I see,' says Dale, into his mobile, his expression stern as he fiddles with the edge of his paper napkin. 'Right. Okay. Yes, yes, I'm in the area. I'll go now.'

'Is everything okay?' I ask, when he ends the call.

He has a distracted look about him now and his face is grave. 'I'm so sorry, Jenna, but I've got to go. Something's happened.' He gathers up his coat and I follow suit.

As we're leaving I hear a peal of Wesley's fake laughter. It sends prickles of irritation shooting up my spine. The cold air hits us as we step outside and I wrap my coat further around my body. 'I bet they're relieved to see us go. They can enjoy their night now,' I say.

Dale gives a snort of laughter. 'I expect so.' He strides off towards our cars, which are parked near each other, and I fall in beside him.

'Are you okay to drive?' I say, when we reach his car, a blue Volvo with a dent in the bumper.

'I'm fine. I had a very weak shandy and there was hardly time to get started on my second pint. But thanks for your concern.' His lips twitch. 'Maybe you should have been a police officer.' I wonder if I've offended him but his tone is light.

I hesitate as he points his keys at his car and the lights flash on. 'Are you able to say why you've been called away urgently?'

He opens the car door and my heart sinks with disappointment. He's not going to answer me. But he seems to change his mind. 'A man's been found dead.'

'In Stafferbury?'

He nods curtly, then gets behind the wheel.

My journalistic brain is crying out to know more. 'Who?'

'I can't say yet. But I'll be in touch when I can, and we can set up an interview. Bye, Jenna.' He closes the door and I have no choice but to get into my own car.

I turn the ignition on and watch as Dale pulls away.

And then I slowly follow him.

16

Olivia

OLIVIA IS RELIEVED WHEN SHE SEES DALE CRAWFORD LEAVE with Jenna. The whole time they were in the same air space she felt like the oxygen was being sucked from the room. She'd heard he'd become a cop and was now working on her friends' disappearance and it irritates her that Jenna is already trying, no doubt, to charm information out of him.

The mood has now changed between her and Wes. While Jenna and Dale were here he acted his usual chirpy self, even a little hyperactive. Now he seems subdued, as though they'd taken his spirit with them when they left, leaving behind just a shell.

'Well, that was weird,' he says, getting up from the table. He looks troubled as he pulls on his puffy coat. Their food remains half eaten. Olivia had lost her appetite as soon as she walked through the door and saw Dale and Jenna together. 'What do you think they were talking about?'

'Me, I expect,' she says, shouldering on her jacket. She tries to keep her voice even to hide how rattled she feels. 'Jenna will try to speak to everyone connected with the case.'

'Hmm, well, as long as she doesn't bother you again.' They are both equally shaken by seeing Dale and Jenna conspiring, and their unvoiced concerns float between them, creating a barrier. As if to counter that Wesley takes her hand and leads her out of the pub. 'My flat tonight, yeah?'

She'd rather go home, sit in the cosy living room with her mum and watch reruns of *Only Fools and Horses* or *Friends*. Something comforting. Something to make her forget everything else. All her fears and dark, tortured thoughts. The stables have always been her place to hide from the world.

'You don't want to come back to mine?'

'I'm always at yours, Liv, and we have more privacy at mine.'

'Your place is small, though.'

'That's why we need to find somewhere of our own. I really like your mum and everything but I'd rather it just be the two of us.'

It's begun to drizzle, beads of rain landing softly on Wesley's dark head. He holds his arm out and she takes it obediently and they wander towards the high street. He is trying his best to be chipper, chatting away about a comedy he watched the other night, but she can sense an underlying anxiety to his tone. Just as they reach Madame Tovey's they spot Izzy and her boyfriend, Joe, ambling towards them. Izzy is gazing up at Joe adoringly and he's laughing at something she's said. Seeing Izzy will always take Olivia's breath away and make her think of Sally, even after all these years.

Izzy smiles as she passes. But she doesn't say anything, her head bent into Joe's burly shoulder. She was only nine or ten the night of the car crash. So much younger than Sally – a happy accident, Mrs Thorne always said. Izzy has stayed on the polite side of friendly with Olivia since their reminiscing days. She's never crossed the road to avoid her, like her parents do, or openly glared at her when she's out and about, like Katie's mum does. She's relieved that at least Tamzin's parents have moved away and she doesn't have to face their judgement and hostility.

The flat is dark when they get back. Wesley has rented it from Madame Tovey downstairs since his mother turfed him out in his late twenties. Initially they were supposed to live in it together but back then Olivia still had difficulty with stairs. She forgets sometimes how much her health has improved over the years with the advances in procedures to her leg. It will never work like it did before the accident but at one point she couldn't imagine ever walking again. The crooked staircase wasn't enough to put Wesley off renting the place, though. And she'd often wondered if it was because, deep down, he wasn't ready to live with her either.

The flat is tiny – mostly one large room with a beamed ceiling, a small kitchen in the corner and a bathroom off it. Wesley's double bed is unmade, a pile of clothes strewn over the ugly leather armchair in the corner. Facing it, and the massive TV, there is an equally ugly three-seater black leather sofa. The flat is sparsely furnished and it has a funny smell. It will never feel like home to her.

Wesley switches on the kettle, then settles on the sofa, patting the seat next to him.

'So?' he says, when she's beside him. 'What do you think about buying a flat together? I've been saving for years. I know a bank teller doesn't earn that much but I've been saving for a deposit. We'll own it jointly. Both our names on the mortgage.'

She surveys his new trainers, his expensive North Face coat, the new 49-inch TV on the wall, with a cupboard full of gaming equipment underneath, and presses her lips together. Not to mention the two-year-old BMW he bought last spring. She can't think about all this now. It's too much.

'I think we could even get one of those nice two-bed apartments that are being built the other side of the stones,' he continues. 'We could afford to furnish it nicely. I know you don't like this sofa.'

'They won't be ready any time soon. If they get built at all. You know the locals are opposed to them.' She wishes he'd stop talking, let her drink a bottle of wine and drown her sorrows in peace.

'I'm sure Jay Knapton will get around that. He managed to build those cabins, didn't he? Even though everyone moaned about it! You know what people can be like around here. They don't like change.' He sighs. 'I've been renting for years but I want to invest in something.' He turns to her with a disarming smile. 'In us.'

Her heart sinks. She doesn't want to live in a soulless new build. She doesn't want to live anywhere but the ramshackle house she grew up in, with the sound of horses whinnying at night and the tranquillity of the surrounding countryside. Not overlooking a bunch of centuries-old stones that give her the creeps. And she can't think about all this now. Her head is filled with Jenna and Dale. *What were they talking about?* What did they say about her? 'I haven't really got much money, to be honest, Wes. Not enough for a deposit on a flat anyway. You know Mum can't afford to pay me more than a pittance for my work at the stables. The place is only just ticking over, especially in the last few years.'

He rolls his eyes. 'I don't know why your mum just doesn't sell it.'

'Of course she's not going to sell it. It's been in the family for generations. And who would buy it? Stafferbury isn't exactly a prosperous town.'

He shrugs. 'It does all right. And that's fine. Like I said, I've been saving and have enough money to put down.'

'How could you have saved up enough, though, Wes? You've been spending loads.'

She knows instantly it was the wrong thing to say. His face darkens. 'Why do you always have to go and ruin everything, Liv? I've got a handle on it all, okay? I'm trying to do a nice thing for us and you throw it back in my face. And now look at you. Sitting there like a frigid little mouse with your coat still on. I know it was a shock seeing Jenna and Dale together but you were in a foul mood before we even got to the pub. What's going on?'

Fear pierces her heart. She hates it when Wesley gets mad. Not that he's ever hurt her. He'd never do that. He doesn't even shout at her, not really. It's more the resigned disappointment followed by the silent treatment that he stretches out like an elastic band, getting tauter and tauter until she can bear it no more.

'I don't know,' she lies. 'It's this time of year. The anniversary and everything. It's just a shit time.'

His face softens. 'I know.' He inches nearer to her on the sofa. 'Why don't we go to bed? Have an early night?' He leans over to kiss her but they are interrupted by his phone chirruping on the coffee-table. Some rap song that Olivia's never liked. 'Sorry, babe,' he says, reaching for it. 'Hello,' he barks into it, glancing at her and rolling his eyes. He gets up and goes to the window. 'Right.'

His voice is serious now and he stands with his back to her. 'I can be there in ten.'

Be where? She wraps her coat further around herself. It's freezing in the flat. She just wants to go home. He slips his mobile into the back pocket of his jeans. 'Sorry, babe. Something's come up.'

She frowns. 'What do you mean?'

'I need to pop out. A – a friend has asked me for a favour. You can stay and wait for me here or I can drop you back home . . .'

She gets up from the sofa and he comes towards her and tucks a lock of her hair behind her ear. 'Which friend?'

'Stan,' he says, too quickly. Wesley has lots of friends she doesn't know, all with monikers like 'PJ' and 'Sickboy' and 'Pod'. Even Stan isn't his real name – she has no idea what it is. She doesn't think any of his mates go by the names they were actually born with. She doesn't care that she has never got to know them even though she remembers some from school. They were immature then and they're immature now. On the odd occasion she's bumped into Wesley with these mates they're usually talking about football or the latest PS4 game. She suspects that when Wesley isn't staying at hers he spends way too long on his gaming station talking to his mates through headphones. He's like a seventeen-year-old in the body of a thirty-nine-year-old man.

'That's fine.' She doesn't ask what's come up at nine o'clock at night. She finds that she doesn't care right now if it means she can fall asleep in her own bed.

He can't get her into his car fast enough. He has a parking space around the back of the high street where all the delivery entrances and garages are. She gets into his BMW, shivering and tired, desperate for bed and oblivion from her racing thoughts.

He pulls up outside her house, brushes her cheek with his lips and has driven away before she's even got to the front door. The TV is blaring as she walks into the hallway. Her mum is watching a sitcom with canned laughter. She suspects it's a rerun of *Seinfeld*.

'Hi, love,' she calls, when she hears Olivia come in. She turns as Olivia stands in the doorway. The room is dark and the television casts a bluish hue over everything. 'Not staying at Wesley's after all?'

Olivia slumps onto the sofa next to her. 'No. He had to go out to see a friend.'

'Right,' she replies, looking back towards the TV.

'Do you think Wesley's cheating on me?' she asks. Is that why he raced off tonight? An image of Izzy pops into her head. Beautiful, young. Like Sally had been. But, no, she shakes the thought away. Of course he isn't. Why would he ask her to move in with him otherwise? Wesley might irritate her sometimes but she'd be lost without him, wouldn't she? She tries to imagine her life without him in it and finds she can't. It's as unfathomable as living without oxygen. He's always telling her she needs him. And she does.

'Of course he isn't. Wesley adores you.' Her mother doesn't take her eyes off the TV. But she reaches out, clasps her daughter's hand and gives it an uncharacteristically affectionate squeeze.

17

Jenna

I MAKE SURE TO STAY A GOOD DISTANCE BEHIND DALE'S Volvo but not too far so that I lose him, which is harder than it looks on TV. It's started to rain again and Dale's brake-lights blur against the dark night. He's continuing on to the Devil's Corridor and I follow. He doesn't take the left turning to the cabins but keeps on the main A-road and I follow suit. Where is he going? He said the man was found dead in Stafferbury so he shouldn't be going that far. Up ahead his indicator winks and he takes the next left. My heart quickens. That's interesting: there must be another way into the forest. I take the left too, careful to slow right down so that my headlights aren't visible in his rear-view mirror. The track is windier and longer than the one that leads to my cabin and I worry that I've lost Dale. I drive slowly over the bumpy terrain. I switch to my side-lights so as not to draw attention to myself but I can hardly see.

After a few more minutes I notice that Dale has pulled into a kind of lay-by on the right, next to a police car. I stop and turn off my engine as I wait, hidden by the thicket of trees. I'm too far away to see Dale but I hear the slam of a car door. I leave it a while before I turn the ignition back on and then I drive very slowly into the lay-by and pull up next to Dale's car. I plan to be quick, just to see where Dale has gone, and I'll be back to my car before he notices it. I don't want to risk him seeing me and annoying him because then he might not be so willing to help me. The ground is spongy as I step out but at least it's stopped raining for now. From deep within the bowels of the forest I hear the hoot of an owl and I'm momentarily paralysed by fear. This is mad. What am I doing? I should just go back to the cabin and wait until I hear from Dale. But patience isn't my strong point. I have to be doing something proactive. And what kind of a journalist would I be if I just stayed behind?

I continue walking, my mobile's torch lighting the way. The track is narrow, more like a trench, and mud splashes up the back of my jeans and seeps into the soles of my flimsy fashionable boots. I don't know if this is the way Dale went but I'm assuming so as it's the main path. I concentrate on the way ahead, trying not to feel freaked out by the sounds of the countryside and the dark pressing in on me from all sides, except for the arc of light where I'm pointing my phone. Eventually I see the clearing up ahead. The same clearing I was in earlier today. Bile rises at the back of my throat when I notice a hub of activity near Ralph's caravan: a white tent, two policemen erecting tape around it. There are flashes of torchlight and I can just about see someone I assume to be Dale heading into the tent with a woman in a forensic suit who is carrying a metal suitcase.

I hide behind a tree trying to catch my breath. The snap of a twig makes me freeze. The back of my neck prickles, as if someone has blown on it. I turn slowly, expecting to see someone behind me. Dale perhaps, furious, even though I'm sure I saw him go into the tent. But I can't see anyone. I'd better get back to the car. I need to keep Dale onside if I want him to confide in me about what's happened here tonight.

I make my way down the track, almost stumbling in my desperation to reach the safety of my car. Crime tape. Police. Forensics.

Ralph was murdered.

And the person responsible could still be here, in the forest.

Watching me.

As if on cue another twig snaps underfoot and I gasp in fright. There's no denying it now. Someone is behind me. I can feel their presence. I don't turn around. Instead I break into a run, slipping and sliding down the mud track. A brush to my shoulder. A hand trying to grab me. I scream, my legs buckling beneath me. A flash of pain to my head and then everything goes black.

18

I CAN HEAR A YOUNG CHILD CRYING. IT'S GRATING AND IN-
sistent. Is it Finn? *Finn . . .*

Where am I? There is a shooting pain in my head, and when
my eyes flicker open I see trees, so many trees, soaring upwards,
their dark branches bobbing in the wind, the pine needles pressed
together and eclipsing the sky. And then I remember. I'm in the
forest. I'm lying on my back in the mud. I was being followed.
The back of my head is throbbing. Someone attacked me. They
could still be here. I have to get up. I need to get out of here and
back to my car.

My hands sink beneath the mud as I try to winch myself up,
and my whole body feels weak. Panic sets in at the thought my
attacker is still here, waiting. My legs flail as I try to get a foothold
on the ground but I manage to pull myself up and scramble to

my knees. I need help. I look behind me, half expecting to see the perpetrator standing over me, but nobody's there.

'Hello?' I hear a familiar voice from between the trees, then see a flicker of torchlight, bleaching the ground in front of me. It's Dale, thank God. As he comes closer I see the disapproval on his face. 'Jenna? What are you doing here?' I'm still on my hands and knees and he bends down to help me to my feet. 'What happened? Are you okay?' I'm covered with mud – I can feel it in my hair and soaking into the back of my jeans. He's still holding on to my elbow. 'Did you fall?'

I feel like such an idiot. 'I . . . I'm sorry. I wanted to see what was going on but then, on the way back to the car, someone was following me. They . . . they hit me . . .' I must look a right idiot standing here in my mud-stained city clothes. What was I thinking?

He drops my elbow. Even in the dark I can tell he's angry. 'You shouldn't be here, Jenna.'

I've messed everything up. He's not going to trust me now and he won't help me with my podcast. I wince as pain shoots up my neck and into the back of my head.

'Are you hurt?' His voice softens.

'My head,' I say, reaching up and touching it. I can feel something sticky. It's either mud . . . or blood. Dale must take pity on me because he snakes an arm around my waist and helps me back down the track to my car. It's started to rain again, heavier this time. I feel utterly miserable and in pain. 'Did you hear that child crying?' I ask desperately. I can see the dark shadows of our cars parked up ahead.

'I think you should get checked over. You might be concussed.'

'There was a child . . .'

He leads me to his car. When I try to protest, he says, 'Jenna, you're in no state to drive back yourself. I'm going to take you to A and E.'

Everything spins as I sink into his passenger seat gratefully, conscious I must be getting mud on it. How long had I been lying there unconscious? It must have been a while if Dale had finished and was heading back to the car. I touch the back of my head gingerly, and when my hand comes away I see blood all over my fingers.

'Shit,' says Dale, his face full of concern. 'You're bleeding quite a lot, Jenna. Here, take this.' He hands me an old cloth that he must use for wiping the windscreen and I press it to the back of my head. 'You think someone did this to you?'

I nod, and wince as the movement causes lights to erupt in front of my eyes. 'Yes. Someone was following me. I felt a hand on my shoulder and then I – I can't remember. I . . .' I feel close to tears and swallow a few times, trying to compose myself.

As Dale reverses out of the lay-by I squint, trying to spot anyone lurking among the trees. But there's nothing other than dark shadows flickering between the branches.

'It was reckless of you,' admonishes Dale, as he pulls onto the Devil's Corridor.

'Is it Ralph? Who was found dead?'

'Yes,' he says quietly.

'What happened?'

'It's unexplained at the moment. We'll know more after the pathologist's report.'

'Do you think he was murdered?'

'Jenna.' A warning in his tone.

I press my lips together and we don't speak for a while. Despite the pain in my head guilt weaves its way around my insides until I blurt out tearfully, 'I'm so sorry. This is the last thing you need after a busy day.'

'It's fine, Jenna. Really. I just want to make sure you're okay.'

We lapse into silence and I stare miserably out of the window, the rag still pressed to the back of my head. I feel slightly sick.

'Jenna . . .'

I turn to him. I notice he has a smear of mud on his cheek. His face in the dim light is hollowed out in shadows but he looks tired. I feel another tug of guilt that he's having to drive me to the hospital. 'I'll need to take a formal statement from you about your conversation with Ralph earlier today, the time you visited him and what he told you about Olivia.'

'Okay,' I say, nausea rising. I'm not sure if it's because of the intense pain in my head or because it's hit home that I was one of the last people to see Ralph Middleton alive.

19

Night Visitor

JOHN-PAUL HAD BEEN DISTANT AFTER THE BARBECUE AND HIS chat with his old mate. Stace had asked him about it as soon as they were alone, but he'd brushed it off and told her he was too jet-lagged and drunk to talk: he just wanted to crash. Stace had fidgeted next to him, wishing she could fall asleep as easily. The light from the moon fell onto John-Paul's sleeping form, illuminating his bronzed back, his strong shoulders, and she reached out and ran her finger down the length of his torso. He didn't stir. What was he hiding from her? She'd thought she knew him so well, but their romance, which had burnt brightly for the first few months, had been slowly getting dimmer as soon as they'd moved in together last year. Something she hadn't wanted to admit to herself because she hoped that things would return to how they had been at the beginning. He'd rarely spoken of his past or Derreck and she'd never thought to ask. They'd been so wrapped up in the here and now, their little cocoon, which *she'd always felt was untouchable. But now . . . now she realized she was naïve. How well did she really know John-Paul?*

It was no use. She was worrying too much to sleep. She stepped carefully out of bed so as not to wake him and pulled on the sundress she'd been wearing earlier. She'd go to the kitchen and fetch herself a glass of water.

When she reached the bottom of the winding staircase, the marble tiles refreshingly cold beneath her feet, she saw a light coming from the patio beyond the kitchen. And there, in the amber glow of the garden lights, sat Derreck, his back to her. She could see he had a cigarette in his hand, the smoke curling away from him and disappearing into the warm night air. She hesitated. She didn't fancy sitting alone with Derreck, a man she hardly knew. Something about him unsettled her. Unless . . . she thought back to his heated conversation with John-Paul. Could she dare ask him about it?

'Are you going to stand there all night?' His voice was low and growly, with a hint of an Australian accent.

She padded through the kitchen. It was immaculate, unlike how they'd left it earlier, and she felt a pang of guilt that Derreck's maid, Anya, had had to clean up after them. She stepped onto the patio. The air smelt smoky, sweet and not entirely unpleasant. His shirt was open and a lock of his blond hair fell over his tanned face. Despite herself her tummy did a weird little flip and then she felt guilty, as though just being here with this man, finding him attractive, had somehow meant she'd betrayed her boyfriend. He indicated the lounger next to him, the tip of his cigarette like a firefly against the velvet sky. She slid into it. They were facing the swimming-pool and didn't speak for a few minutes, just watched as the water rippled under the moonlight. It was peaceful, and beautiful with the sound of the crickets and the water of the pool lapping gently against the sides.

'Couldn't sleep, huh?' he said eventually, flicking the butt of his cigarette into the undergrowth.

'Too hot. And air-con too loud.'

She stole a glance at him but he wasn't looking at her, his head resting against the back of the lounger. He was wearing chino shorts and his feet were bare. Wrapped around his left wrist was a jumble of leather braids. His skin was golden-brown, even and unmarked, like the topping on a cake.

'So,' she said, swinging her legs around so that she was facing him. She tried not to feel a touch of pride when she noticed his gaze sweeping over her bare calves. 'It's kind of you to invite us here. John-Paul speaks highly of you.' She felt her cheeks grow hot at the lie.

Derreck laughed. 'I bet JP's barely mentioned me. Coke?'

'Pardon?' Was he trying to give her drugs? She suddenly felt out of her depth, provincial. Something about Derreck scared her. He was so worldly. Then she saw he had reached over to a bucket full of ice between their sun-loungers and was proffering a can of cola.

'Thanks,' she said, taking it from him and pressing the cool metal against her chest. 'To be fair, John-Paul doesn't talk that much about his travelling days. So why don't you tell me about them?'

He narrowed his eyes. 'What is it exactly you want to know?'

'I got the impression that John-Paul thinks he . . . well, owes you for something that happened in Goa.'

She could feel her heart beating hard in her chest. Could he tell she was bluffing? She noticed a flicker of surprise in his eyes.

'He told you about Goa?'

'Well, no. Not exactly.' She opened her can and took a sip, trying to hide her discomfort.

He laughed. 'I thought as much. JP certainly wouldn't want to look bad in your eyes.'

Her heart sank. 'What did he do?'

'You need to ask him that.' He sat back against the sun-lounger so that he was facing the pool again. 'But it doesn't sound like he's been very open with you about his past.'

'Did he do something illegal?'

A muscle in his jaw twitched but he didn't answer. She felt sick.

'Do you fancy a swim? It might cool you down, make you able to sleep. I know this heat can take a bit of getting used to,' he said, suddenly breaking the silence. Without waiting for an answer he stood up, took off his shirt and stepped out of his shorts. She averted her eyes. But when she looked up again she could see the flash of his naked bottom as he jumped into the pool. She felt herself blushing. What was he playing at?

She had to leave. She'd ask John-Paul about Goa in the morning. She'd get nothing from Derreck tonight. She stood up.

'Don't fancy coming in?' he called, from the middle of the pool. He had pushed his wet hair back from his face. She noticed what a lovely straight nose he had. All she could think about was that he was naked beneath the water. It was too much.

'I . . . no, I need to get back. Thanks, though,' she said scurrying from the sun-lounger, clasping her can of Coke to her chest without looking behind her.

Day Three

20

Jenna

IT'S THE TWENTIETH ANNIVERSARY OF THE NIGHT THE THREE girls went missing. It's 3 a.m. and I'm finally back from the hospital. Thankfully just one small stitch and no concussion. I still can't believe that Ralph is dead and that someone attacked me. I'm sure I heard a child crying. Was it real, or just another incidence of the strange occurrences that Stafferbury is famous for? I need to sleep now . . .

When I wake up I still have a slight headache. I can hear someone clattering around in my kitchen and panic flares until I remember. Dale offered to sleep in the spare room last night after the nurse said I shouldn't be alone, with the possibility of concussion. He had sat with me for the three-hour wait in A and E, bringing me lukewarm coffee from the machine and trying to make me laugh with stories of growing up in Stafferbury. And he'd stayed with me while I was getting stitched up.

There is a soft rap on my door and I hear Dale's voice asking if I'm decent.

'Yep, come in,' I say, sitting up in bed and tucking the duvet around me. I remember dressing in my fleecy pyjamas last night and pulling on my thick bed-socks, although I'm still wearing yesterday's makeup.

'How are you feeling?' He hands me a black coffee and I'm touched that he remembers how I like it. He's fully dressed in last night's clothes and I feel a fresh wave of gratitude for all his help.

'I'm fine, thanks,' I say, sipping the coffee. 'I really appreciate you coming with me and staying over.'

He smiles in response, his hazel eyes warm, and checks his watch. 'I'd better get going. I need to go to my dad's and change before my shift starts. What are your plans for today? You should probably take it easy.'

There's no chance of that. I've got too much to do. I take another sip of coffee, not caring it's too hot. My mouth feels like the bottom of a birdcage. 'I'm going to try Katie's mum. And I still haven't given up on Olivia. I just need to find a way to convince her to talk to me.'

He shuffles his feet. 'That's great, but . . .' He suddenly looks uncomfortable. 'You don't really think that we'll solve this case while you're here, do you? Because I'd hate to disappoint you but I sincerely doubt you'll get any answers. It's been twenty years.'

I laugh. 'When did I say I wanted to solve the case? That's your job.'

His lips twitch. 'Yeah, I know. But there might never be a resolution for your podcast, that's all I'm saying.'

I shake my head and wince at the movement. 'I know. I'm not here for that. I'd just like more local interviews for the podcast. It's an intriguing mystery. Obviously it would be great if you could solve it while I'm here . . .' I grin to show I'm joking.

'Hmm.' There's a twinkle in his eye. 'I'll give you a call later. Let me know if you need a lift to fetch your car.'

'I'm a grown woman. I'll be fine in the broad daylight.'

'Also,' he looks a little uncomfortable again, 'could you pop into the station at some point and give a formal statement about your visit to Ralph?'

'Sure.' I pull back the duvet.

'No, don't get up,' he says. 'I'll let myself out.'

When he's left I reach for my phone. Time to call Finn before he leaves for school.

I don't mention my head injury or Ralph's murder to Finn or my mum so as not to worry them. I'm surprised to see her at my house so early and ask where Gavin is. Mum tells me he had to go into the office for a breakfast meeting. I wonder how he would feel if he knew another man stayed with me last night – even if he was in the spare room. Would he even care? I think of the woman's laugh I was sure I heard yesterday. I can't believe Gavin would have anyone staying over. Finn would surely have mentioned it. Can I be so sure about what Gavin is up to in his rented flat? I thought I knew everything about him but after he told me he wanted space from our marriage I feel like he's a stranger. I had trusted him but now I can't help the nagging voice in my head taunting me that he wants space from our marriage because he's met someone else.

After I've finished chatting to Finn I fall back against the pillows and close my eyes, trying to dispel the slight headache.

Olivia and Wesley pop into my head and how unnatural they had seemed last night. Olivia had more or less squirmed with us there. And Wesley had acted oddly too.

I must have fallen back to sleep because I'm woken by a thud against my bedroom window, as if something has been thrown against the glass. I sit bolt upright, my heart scudding. What the fuck was that? I look at my phone. It's nine thirty. I hurry out of bed and throw open the curtains, terrified of what I might find. There's a streak of blood trailing down the glass. I dart out of the room, fling open the front door and am hit by a cold gust of air. There's nobody there. My breath fogs in front of me as I step onto the freezing slabs, my socks sticking to the thin layer of ice. I go back into the hallway to thrust my feet into my wellies and pull on my coat over my pyjamas before I hurry back outside to where my bedroom window is – the blood looks worse out here, smeared across the glass, and I take a sharp breath. A dead bird is at my feet, its neck bent. I look at its sad, unseeing eye and feel a twinge of melancholy.

'Happens a lot, I'm afraid,' says a voice from behind me, and I jump in fright. 'Stupid wood pigeons flying into windows.' I turn to see a man standing at the end of the driveway, half expecting it to be the person I saw the other night who's staying in the cabin opposite. But this man isn't wearing a big overcoat that hides his face and is instead smartly dressed and business-like. He looks to be in his late sixties with closely cropped grey hair and neatly trimmed beard, an expensive-looking beige mackintosh over a well-made navy blue suit. 'Sorry to startle you. You must be Jenna Halliday?' He thrusts a large hand in my direction.

I nod as I walk up to him and shake his hand. 'And you are?'

'I'm Jay Knapton, the owner. We spoke on the phone.'

'Oh, yes.' Relief floods through me. 'Nice to meet you properly.'

He smiles in response. 'Likewise. I just came to do a checkup of all the empty cabins. Yours is the only one occupied at the moment. It's not a very busy time but I'm hoping that changes by the summer.'

'What about that cabin there?' I point to the one opposite. Foxglove.

He shakes his head. 'No. Just you.'

'But . . .' That can't be right. 'Has the person left?'

He looks puzzled. 'What person?'

'Someone was there when I arrived. I assumed it was a man by their height and build but it was hard to tell. I saw him yesterday too. He had a German Shepherd dog with him. Whoever it was, he was wearing a long hooded coat.'

Jay's face darkens. 'Nobody else is booked into these cabins and there hasn't been anyone for weeks. It's just you here. Could you have been mistaken? Lots of dog-walkers use the forest.'

'Definitely not mistaken. There were lights on in the cabin. I saw the person go in there myself.' Now I'm freaked out.

Jay's face is serious. 'You're sure about this?'

'Yes. Yes, I'm sure. Could it be squatters?'

He straightens. 'I doubt it. These cabins are checked on regularly by myself mostly, and if not me, then my team. Stay there. I'm going to look.'

He marches off across the uneven dirt track to the cabin opposite and I quickly pull my front door to, making sure the key is in my pocket, then jog after him.

Jay takes what must be a master key from a chain in his pocket and opens the door. I flinch, expecting a dog to charge out, but there is silence.

'Hello,' calls Jay almost theatrically, walking further into the cabin which is a mirror image of mine. I shadow him. He pushes open the main bedroom door but it's empty. He does the same with the next bedroom and then the living room. They, too, are empty. The whole cabin looks unlived in.

Jay stands in the white gloss kitchen, looking into the living room that is so similar to mine, except the sofa is lime green and there is no animal head on the wall. Instead there is a cow-hide rug on the wooden floor. 'It looks perfectly empty.'

I put a hand to my head. My brain feels frazzled. 'I don't understand it. Someone was here yesterday.'

'Well,' he says, a note of irritation in his voice, 'there's nobody here now.'

I can't believe this. Surely whoever was here would have left some sign. I return to the main bedroom. The duvet on the bed is unwrinkled. The wardrobe is empty. There's nothing under the bed. I sniff the air. Not even the smell of dog. I go into the en-suite, open the cupboard under the sink and check the shower for signs of use. Nothing. I do the same in the twin room.

'Well?' says Jay, standing at the doorway, his brow creased.

I shake my head. 'It's weird. Someone was here. But now there's no sign of them.'

'The lock hasn't been tampered with. There's no sign of a forced entry.' He sighs. 'This is sadly the kind of thing that goes on here.'

I turn to him. 'What do you mean?'

'Oh, just strange happenings. Talk of the supernatural, the paranormal.' He shrugs as if he doesn't believe any of it.

I remember Ralph's talk of alien abduction. 'Ah, yes, I've read a few things,' I say. 'For research.'

'You said on the phone when you booked that you're making a podcast on the Olivia Rutherford case.'

I nod.

'Well, if you'd like an interview I'm more than willing. I wasn't living here when Olivia's friends went missing, I moved here the year after, but I know the town very well. And the people in it. All the crackpot theories and the charlatans.'

'The charlatans?' I'm intrigued.

'Oh, there's a medium who vows she knows something. She's got a lot of people fooled around here. Not me, mind. I don't believe for one moment that she's got the second sight or whatever it is she claims she has.'

I think back to the sign on the high street I noticed when I first arrived. 'Do you mean Madame Tovey?'

'Yep.' He clasps his clipboard to his chest. 'She might be worth talking to, but take everything she says with a pinch of salt.' He sniggers. 'She'll definitely add a . . . How shall I put it nicely? Some local flavour to your podcast.'

'Great,' I say, pleased that someone actually wants to be interviewed. 'Can I meet you later? I need to get my car. I've left it in the forest.'

'Oh?' He raises his eyebrows questioningly.

'Long story,' I reply. I wonder if he knows about Ralph Middleton. I'm assuming he must, considering he was found dead on his land. I decide to wait until later to ask him about that.

'I've got a few things to do this morning but why don't you come by the offices around two p.m.?' He opens his briefcase and extracts a card. 'Here, the address is on there. But if you turn down Halfpenny Lane and make a right, opposite Stafferbury Stables, and keep going until you get to the end of the road, my offices are on the industrial estate there.'

I take the card and return to my own cabin, suffused with unease and paranoia. I change quickly, without showering, suddenly desperate to escape the cabin, the forest and the unshaken sense of being watched.

21

Olivia

WHEN OLIVIA OPENS HER EYES SHE IS INSTANTLY HIT WITH a sense of impending doom, fear and regret. And then she remembers why. It's the twentieth anniversary today. She wishes she could go back, close her eyes and wake up on this day in 1998. She would do so many things differently.

The doorbell rings as she's getting out of bed. Her mum will be in the yard feeding the horses. She hastily pulls on yesterday's jodhpurs and jumper and makes her way down the stairs, holding on to the banister for support.

Her stomach plummets when she opens the front door and sees Dale with a younger man at his side. Dale's hair is standing up in peaks and the end of his nose is red from the cold. 'Sorry to bother you so early,' he says, blowing on his hands. The air feels icy and swirls around her bare ankles. 'This is DC Liam Stirling. Can we come in? We'd just like to ask you some questions.'

Her mouth goes dry and she wishes desperately that she'd stayed the night at Wesley's after all. She doesn't think she can do this alone. But she has no choice other than to step aside and let them in. They follow her down the narrow hallway and to the kitchen. They look wrong sitting at the little pine table, Dale and his weird socks and this DC Liam Stirling with his bright blond hair and boyish dimples. He looks like he should be at college, not on the police force.

She offers them both a coffee, which they accept. As she's pouring boiling water into their mugs, Dale says, 'I'm afraid we've got some bad news.'

Her hand shakes as she lowers the kettle. She doesn't trust herself to bring their mugs to the table without dropping them or spilling the coffee.

'I think you should sit down,' suggests Dale. He gets up and helps her carry the coffees.

When he's sitting, facing her, he says gravely, 'Ralph Middleton was found dead last night.' He gives her a moment to digest this information.

She can't speak. She remembers their last conversation. The hurt in his eyes. Her tears. *Oh, Ralph.*

She buries her head in her hands as blood rushes to her ears. She can hear Dale's soothing voice telling her how sorry he is, and asking if there is anyone who can come and sit with her. She lifts her head. 'No. I'm fine.'

'I understand you went to visit him yesterday. Around four?'

She nods, her palms sweating. She can't tell him what they talked about.

'You were seen leaving his caravan in tears.'

She glances across at DC Stirling. He hasn't said one word, but has a notebook open on the table and is looking at her intently with his clear blue eyes.

'Yes.' She blinks back tears. 'We had a silly disagreement. It was nothing, really. I was . . . I was trying to tell him to cut down on the drinking. To eat more healthily. To look after himself. I felt a sense of duty, I suppose. He saved my life all those years ago.'

Can they tell she's lying? She's never been very good at deception, at keeping secrets. DC Stirling scribbles something down.

'How?' she asks, gulping. 'How did Ralph die?'

'We think it was a head injury although we won't know for sure until the post-mortem,' Dale says.

'Could he have fallen and banged his head?'

Dale shakes his head. 'It's looking suspicious at the moment. I'm so sorry, Olivia. I know it's a horrible thought that someone would want to hurt Ralph deliberately.'

Her chest tightens as it hits her that Ralph is actually dead. His animals. Oh, God, she hadn't thought about them. Where are Bertie and Tiddles and Timmy Willy and all the others? She'll need to find them. She'll adopt them, bring them here. It's the least she can do.

'Olivia?' Dale's voice penetrates her thoughts. 'I think I should get your mum, or Wesley. I don't think you should be alone.'

'I'll be okay,' she says curtly, getting up to fetch some kitchen towel to blow her nose. Her voice sounds heavy, strange, like her emotions are trapped in her throat. She swallows. She can't break down. Not in front of them.

'Can your mum bring you to the station later to make a formal statement?' asks Dale, as she hovers at the sink.

'W-why do I need to do that?'

'It's just procedure.' His voice is gentle. 'Because you were one of the last people to see him alive.'

'Can't I just do it now?'

'Of course, if you feel up to it.'

The thought of going to the police station makes her feel sick. So she sits down. Dale gets out a notebook and asks her a series of questions about her visit to Ralph. She answers, while clenching the kitchen towel so tightly in her palm that it turns damp.

'And that was all you argued about? That he wasn't looking after himself?' queries Dale. A shadow passes behind his eyes. Suspicion maybe. Or disbelief?

'Yes, I already said.' She bristles with irritation. She just wants them to go away and leave her alone.

'Is there anything else you can think of?' probes Dale. 'About who might want to hurt Ralph? Was he in any trouble? Did he owe money?'

He smoked weed and popped the occasional pill, she knew that much, but she feels it would be disloyal to divulge that information to Dale. 'I honestly don't know.'

He stands up and College Boy follows suit. Thank goodness they're finally going.

'Okay. Thank you for your time.' She follows them to the door. As Dale steps outside he turns to her and says, 'Please call me if you think of anything. No matter how small.'

It's not until she closes the door on them that she breaks down in tears.

As she walks across the yard she feels like someone has carved her insides out, her mind full of Ralph and Sally, Tamzin and Katie.

From one of the stables she can hear Radio 2 and she freezes. Pixies' 'Where Is My Mind?' is playing, and grief washes over her. It had been one of Sally's favourite songs. She used to play it over and over again. Olivia stands, hidden by the wall of the stables, and listens to it, a lump in her throat. How strange that it should play today on the twentieth anniversary. She hasn't heard it in years. And straight away she's back there, in Sally's bedroom at fourteen, watching her best friend put the album on the turntable, the hiss of the record as she lowered the needle, the haunting guitar intro. Sally would replay that song over and over. She closes her eyes as a thousand memories flood through her: the smell of the mini meringues Sally's mum used to buy from Tesco and they used to eat straight from the plastic tub, the sweet taste of Dr Pepper on their lips, the blue nail varnish, the black-and-white Kurt Cobain poster pinned to the woodchip wallpaper. She can almost see Sally standing in front of her in her faded black jeans, her favourite checked shirt and leather bracelets entwined halfway up her arms. Her first best friend and her last.

Sally hadn't wanted her to start dating Wesley. It had put a bit of distance between them for the first time ever.

'But he's a creep,' she'd said, when Olivia first told her about it. They had been in Sally's bedroom – Olivia had raced straight over there to tell her as soon as Wesley had asked her out on a date.

'He's not,' Olivia said. 'He's funny and popular and charming.'

'He might have been in school, but he's turned weird,' Sally replied dismissively, and Olivia had felt instantly irritated. It was all right for Sally, she'd thought, with her swishy hair and perfect skin and pick of the boys. But this was the first time someone like Wesley had asked her out and there was no way she was going to say no.

'Don't you remember how he hounded me?'

Of course Olivia remembered. She'd been jealous as hell when Sally had told her that Wesley had pursued her the year before. He'd bombarded her with love notes and roses through the post and mix tapes. Olivia had thought it charming but Sally hadn't been so enamoured. In fact she'd got cross with him after he sent one Forever Friends teddy too many and told him if he didn't stop she'd go to the police. Olivia had thought that a little harsh. Wesley had a crush on her. That was all. If only, she'd thought wistfully, someone felt so strongly about her.

Wesley did eventually stop and then, one night at the Raven, she'd got talking to him and when he'd asked for her number she'd thought she'd combust with happiness. She'd mentioned the Sally thing to him, of course, and he'd laughed it off, his cheeks pink with embarrassment, and said he'd been an idiot but that he'd thought she'd liked him and wanted to be 'wooed'. 'I didn't read the signs properly,' he'd said, lowering his bright blue eyes, and all she could think of was how she wanted to snog him so badly that she had to contain herself from throwing her arms around him there and then.

But it continued being awkward between him and Sally, so Olivia had met up with her friends away from him, making Saturday nights their night. And then, just months later, the accident happened and all their lives had changed for ever.

'Where have you been? Roxie and Sabrina still need mucking out.'

Olivia jumps, her eyes snapping open at the sound of her mother's voice. She's aware she's been standing with her hand on the stable door, her eyes closed, swaying. Her mum will start to think she's on something. She straightens. 'Sorry. It's been . . .' She swallows. 'Mum, something awful's happened.'

The annoyance freezes on her mother's face, replaced by fear. 'What?'

'Ralph Middleton was found dead last night.'

For a few seconds her mother doesn't move – she doesn't even blink. Olivia wonders if she's even heard her. 'Mum?'

'I . . . How?' she asks, seeming to come to. In the background they can hear the murmur of the Radio 2 DJ talking. Her mother puts a hand to the corduroy collar of her waxed jacket as if it's too tight and threatening to strangle her. Olivia knows the feeling.

'A head injury. They think . . .' her lip wobbles '. . . they suspect he was murdered.'

'Oh, my God. When?'

'Last night. They didn't say what time.'

A gust of wind blows through the yard and sends a hay-net skimming across the concrete. Her mother makes a dash for it, then strides back to Olivia, the hay-net over her shoulder, her face grave. She pulls her daughter into her arms for a rare hug. 'It's really sad about Ralph,' she murmurs, into Olivia's hair. 'I know you liked him. I didn't know him very well but I always felt for him, living in the caravan all alone like that. There was something sad about him.'

This makes Olivia cry even more.

'It's a difficult day even without that,' her mother says 'What with it being the anniversary. All sorts of emotions must be flooding to the surface right now.'

Olivia sighs and pulls away. When she looks up at her mother's face she sees something she can't quite place. Grief, perhaps, or guilt.

22

Jenna

THE FOREST LOOKS LESS FRIGHTENING IN THE LIGHT OF day with the weak winter sun slanting through the trees and refracting in the frost-coated leaves. The mud has dried underfoot so that it crunches with each step I take.

After Jay left I looked up the address on the electoral roll for Katie Burke's family. Her mother still lives in Stafferbury and, once I've got my car, I plan to drive over to her house after I've given my statement to the police in Devizes. Whether she'll agree to speak to me remains to be seen. As I trudge along the track I try calling Dale to tell him about the man who has been staying without consent in the cabin opposite but the reception is sketchy this deep in the forest so I pocket my phone and pick up my pace. The parent in me wants to run away, back to the safety of Manchester and my beautiful son, but the journalist in me knows I need to stay and brave it out until Friday. It's doubtful that Ralph's death is linked to what happened to Olivia's friends back in 1998 but, even so, it will add to the intrigue about the town for the podcast.

The thick branches eclipse the sunshine and a few times I stumble over potholes. Then I get to the place where I was attacked last night. There is a kind of dip in the track, still boggy in places from yesterday's rain. I touch the back of my head gingerly. It's still bruised and tender and I can feel where they put in the stitch. I stand still and listen. I can hear the faint faraway sounds of voices coming from the clearing, which must be the police still at the scene, and the solitary bark of a dog. I shudder when I remember the hand on my shoulder last night, the feeling of being followed before I was struck with something. Did whoever it was mean to kill me too, like Ralph? Or was it just to frighten me? To stop me snooping?

How lucky it was that Dale was the one to find me when he did. I wonder if he scared off my attacker. I'm not sure how long I was lying on the ground.

I walk on, faster now, suddenly desperate to get back to my car. I almost run the last few steps but then I stop. Something has been shoved under my left windscreen wiper. My first thought is it's a flyer, until I register I'm in the middle of a forest. On closer inspection I can see a message has been scribbled on lined paper that looks like it's been ripped from one of my notebooks. I slide it out from under the windscreen wiper and my blood runs cold as the words swim in front of me. They are written in neat block capitals slanted to the left.

LEAVE TOWN OR YOU'LL BE NEXT.

23

I DRIVE ERRATICALLY OUT OF THE FOREST, MY HEAD ALMOST bumping against the ceiling as my car bounces over the potholes on the track as though I'm being chased. I don't even know if I should be driving after my head injury last night. *Calm down*, I tell myself. It's not like me to be so spooked. But a lot has happened over the past twenty-four hours. I only start to breathe easier when I'm back on the Devil's Corridor and heading towards the next town. It's a relief to be driving away from Stafferbury for a bit. Devizes is bigger and more bustling than Stafferbury and I park outside the police station. When I arrive, a young detective with a baby face called DC Stirling says he's expecting me. It doesn't take long to give him my statement, and once I've signed it I'm on the road again. I didn't mention the note because they might take it and file it somewhere, and I want to keep it to myself for now. At the back of my mind there is the possibility of using it as some kind of bargaining tool – in exchange for more information from Dale.

It isn't long before I'm back on the Devil's Corridor and I try to imagine what it must have been like for Olivia that night, with the wind and the rain. The WELCOME TO STAFFER-BURY sign is up ahead with its warning to drive slowly through the town.

I head along the high street, which looks prettier in the winter sunshine. A large Christmas tree has been erected near the war memorial since yesterday. I can't even think about Christmas and how it will be this year. Will we spend the day together for Finn's sake? As I drive towards Blackberry Avenue, where Katie's mum lives, I have to pass the stables. I can see Olivia chatting to a woman I don't recognize across the saddle of a chestnut pony. *What do you know?* I wonder. Is it conceivable she knows nothing about her three best friends' disappearance?

Blackberry Avenue is a small road that joins with another at the end and is set with a row of detached houses from all eras. Number five is a mock Tudor with symmetrical windows, a drive-way and a garage on the side. It's small but tidy, almost sensible-looking, and I wonder if this is where Katie grew up. According to the electoral roll, Sally's family live a few streets away.

I pull up outside and knock at the door. The street is quiet and there are no sounds coming from within the house. The driveway is empty and a green bin has rolled over and lies on its side. I knock again but no answer. As I turn away to pick up the bin I hear a voice. 'What are you doing?' I look up to see a woman striding out of the side gate in a quilted vest, holding a pair of gardening gloves, a small black-and-white dog at her side that starts yapping at me.

'I . . . um . . . Sorry. Your bin had fallen over.'

'Ssh, Walter,' she says, to the dog. She's tall with a long, weath-ered face and light brown hair threaded with grey pulled back in a clip. I can tell straight away that she's Katie's mother: the same pointed chin and hazel eyes. Her face is criss-crossed with lines, etched with years of grief. She frowns. 'You came to pick up my bin?'

I start to introduce myself but she holds up a hand. 'I'm not interested. I've heard about you and I have nothing to say,' she snaps.

'But this podcast will shine a light on this case. Someone might come forward who knows something . . . anything about that night, something overlooked, a clue . . .'

'It's been twenty years,' she interjects wearily, moving her dirty gloves from one hand to the other. 'Don't you think some-one would have come forward by now.' It's not a question and I open my mouth but she charges on. 'I've given up thinking that my daughter is going to walk through that door. My husband . . .' she inhales and touches her chest as though it's painful '. . . he died not knowing. And I'll die not knowing. I have my son to think about now, and a granddaughter. I have to . . . I can't . . .' Her eyes smart and she shakes her head. 'You need to go.'

'But . . .'

She heads back through the gate, her dog trotting behind her. I swallow. I can't begin to imagine her pain and my eyes fill when I think of Finn. Fuck. Having a child has made me soft. The old me would have followed her, kept on trying to persuade her. I would probably have made a nuisance of myself. But I can't do that to her. She looks like she's got the weight of the world on her skinny shoulders.

It'll be different with Izzy, I hope, as I head back to my car.

Not that Izzy won't be in pain too – but a mother's grief . . . I swallow the lump in my throat. I can't think of it. I just want to go home, hug Finn tightly and never let him out of my sight again. I sit behind the wheel in the quiet street. The back of my head is still throbbing and I reach into my handbag for two more painkillers, swallowing them with a swig from a warm bottle of water that's been in my car since Monday. Then I check my mobile, disappointment flooding through me when I see that neither Izzy nor Dale has called. I know Dale must be run off his feet, especially now with Ralph Middleton's death, and it might not have shown up on his phone that I'd tried to call him due to the sketchy reception in the forest. But Izzy . . . I really need to speak to her. If she's willing to be interviewed for the podcast she might be able to convince her parents to cooperate. I couldn't find either of Tamzin's parents on the electoral roll.

It's not yet noon and I decide to try Izzy at the café and hope she isn't too busy. I park by the standing stones and head into Bea's again. The young girl, Chloë, greets me at the top of the stairs – her hair has been newly bleached so that it's almost silver. It would be ageing on anyone over thirty but it gives her an almost angelic look. It's piled high on her head. 'Sorry,' she says brightly, when I ask if I can have a quick word with Izzy. 'She's not in today. She's doing a course at the college. Beauty, I think.' She frowns. 'Or hair. Can't remember.'

'Oh, right. Do you know what time she finishes?'

She shakes her head, her topknot wobbling. 'Nah, sorry. Although,' she glances at the clock, 'she did say yesterday she was going to the stones today at lunchtime.'

'The stones?'

'Yeah.' She lowers her voice. 'Her sister was one of the girls who disappeared back in 1998 and Izzy's parents set up a memorial bench there.'

I wonder why Sally's parents would do that when their daughter could still be alive. You hear stories of young girls being abducted by a psycho and kept in a cellar for years sometimes. It's rare, but it happens.

'Anyway,' Chloë is looking past me now to a couple with two young kids who have come in behind me, 'got to get on.'

'Thanks,' I say, moving past the family and heading back down the stairs.

I can't help thinking that as Izzy hasn't rung me yet she has no intention of doing so. I'll walk past the stones and see if she's there. I don't want to interrupt her memorial to her sister, but I might be able to catch her as she's leaving.

There are a few people out and about on the high street. Two old ladies dawdling arm in arm in front of me. A group of smartly dressed young office workers walking as one entity towards the pub. I shuffle behind the pensioners, who are gossiping about a friend's new widower boyfriend.

By now I've reached the stile. I climb over it and nearly rip the lining from my coat in the process. The field is expansive. And deserted. The stones spring out of the ground like something from *Indiana Jones*. Up close, they are huge and imposing. Brenda said they've been here for more than five thousand years. I walk between them, the ground crisp beneath my boots. I wonder when they were put here and for what purpose. There is a plaque attached to a post near the first stone and I stop to read it. It's mostly folklore, about how it's believed the stones were placed there to align with the sun and the moon. I move away, trudging further into the field, wandering in and out of the stones. The field is empty, and from where I'm standing I can no longer see the high street. From my peripheral vision there is a flicker of movement. I turn, hoping it's Izzy, but I can't see anybody. The sky darkens a shade and the cloud seems lower. I feel like I could reach out and touch it and the sensation is oppressive. I walk faster, unable to shake the disconcerting feeling that someone else is in the field with me. Someone who keeps darting between the stones so that every time I look round I can't see them. A macabre game of hide and seek.

I try to concentrate on my surroundings and look for the memorial bench Chloë mentioned. And then, towards the back of the field, I notice a large oak tree in the corner and, just to the side of it, half shaded by branches, a wooden bench. On closer inspection I see all three girls' names etched onto a brass plaque with the words, 'Always in our hearts'. And then I see that someone has left a bunch of pink roses on the arm. Izzy must already have been. I sit down on the bench and sigh. And that's when I see the note scribbled on lined paper almost hidden beneath the leaves. The writing is in block capitals and slanted to the left. There's something familiar about it. I pick it up and read.

KATIE, TAMZIN & SALLY

And then, underneath, just two words.

I'M SORRY.

It's the same handwriting as on the threatening note left on my windscreen.

24

Olivia

OLIVIA CAN'T STOP THINKING ABOUT RALPH. SHE KNOWS people think it's odd that she and Ralph are friends. *Were* friends. Were, were, were. Her heart contracts. Ralph was a good person, a kind person. He liked the simple life but he was surprisingly astute, yet all his life people had taken advantage of him. Even her, in the end. There's so much she wishes she could change. Ralph had told her once that the truth would set her free. That was a typical Ralph statement. He liked to talk in slogans. But he was wrong about that. The truth wouldn't set her free. Far from it.

The truth was a Pandora's box and she had to keep the lid firmly closed.

Not for the first time she wishes she had someone to confide in. With a pang of sadness she realizes that Ralph was her only friend, the one person she thought she could trust. And now he's gone. She feels more alone than ever.

She checks her watch. It's five past twelve. Wesley said he'd meet her here by the stones: they could visit her friends' bench, lay down some flowers, then grab a bite to eat before he has to go back to work. The bouquet feels heavy in her hands. Where is he? And then she catches him walking towards her with his familiar loping gait and his big puffy jacket that makes his top half look out of proportion to the rest of him, like one of those characters in the Guess Who? game. He'd texted her this morning to tell her to meet him here and she had assumed it was him being sweet and thoughtful, wanting to commemorate the fact it's been twenty years since her friends' disappearance. But from the look on his face as he approaches she sees she assumed wrongly. He looks furious.

'Ralph Middleton is dead,' he says curtly, when he gets up close. He grabs her arm and almost forces her over the stile and into the field. 'And you were *seen* coming out of his caravan in tears yesterday. What the fuck, Liv?'

She feels like she's been punched in the gut. Why is he so angry?

'Has that fucker Dale been to see you? Because he came to my flat earlier.'

'Why did he want to see you? You hardly knew Ralph. And weren't you at work this morning?'

He runs a hand across his chin. 'It was before I left for work,' he says, too quickly. 'It was just routine apparently.'

His eyes have gone flinty, like they always do when he's lying. Instead he deflects the questioning back to her as deftly as a tennis stroke. 'What were you doing at Ralph's caravan yesterday?'

How did he know? Did Dale tell him? Her heart races beneath her waxed jacket and the arm holding the bouquet feels dead. 'I'm devastated about Ralph,' she says quietly. 'And I'll always feel guilty that our last conversation ended with heated words.'

'Heated words about what?'

She toes the muddy grass. She's still in her riding gear. 'It was a stupid misunderstanding.'

'He was *murdered*, Liv. Did Dale tell you that?'

She looks up and for the first time today she notices real fear in his eyes. 'More or less.'

'That fucker . . .' He sighs, and she wonders if he's talking about Dale or Ralph. She knows Wesley and Dale were in the same class at school and never liked each other. But Ralph . . . Wesley didn't know him that well. It was she who kept in touch with him, who would visit him to make sure he was okay, that he wasn't too lonely living in that caravan all by himself. It was she who had cared.

Wesley balls his fists at his sides and his expression darkens as he stares at her. 'What are you keeping from me?'

'I'm not keeping anything from you, Wes, I promise,' she lies. 'But you have to trust me. I don't question you about where you went last night.'

'I told you, Stan needed –'

'And I don't care,' she says, in the same calm tone. She's learnt that to raise her voice to Wesley just makes him rear more, like Sky, the hot-tempered grey at the stables.

'I'm just trying to look out for you, to protect you,' he says. 'But you seem to thwart me at every turn. You're vulnerable, emotional. It's the twentieth anniversary today and you're not thinking straight. But if there was something going on between you and Ralph I need to know.'

She wants to laugh in his face. Something going on? Surely he can't think there was anything romantic between them. But she knows better than to laugh at Wesley.

'I felt sorry for him and I felt I owed him. That was all. I was upset because I knew he wasn't going to change. That he was killing himself with the amount of drinking he did . . . the drugs.'

Wesley doesn't say anything, just presses his lips together and assesses her. She concentrates on keeping her face impassive to give nothing away. She knows Wesley can be jealous, irrational, watching for signs of betrayal that aren't there in a raise of an eyebrow or the quiver of a lip. She's learnt how to deal with it over the years. Ralph – a lonely man in late middle-age who drank too much – was her only friend, yet Wesley even begrudged her that. She has often wondered over the years if they would have stayed together if she'd never had the accident, if her friends hadn't gone missing. She wouldn't have been so dependent on him. Sally would probably have made her see sense. And then she feels a rush of guilt and compassion. Wesley isn't a bad man. And he does love her, she knows that.

'Wes . . .' she begins, but he turns away from her.

'I need to go back to work. You'll have to visit the bench without me.'

'But I thought we were going to grab lunch.'

He swivels around to face her, his eyes flashing spitefully. 'I've lost my appetite. I'd rather spend my precious lunch hour with someone who actually gives a shit about me.'

She's confused. 'What are you talking about?'

'You. Running to Ralph. Confiding in him. You were talking

about me, weren't you? I know you don't want us to buy a place together. It's so obvious.'

A man has died and all Wesley can think about is himself. 'Not everything is about you,' she finds herself saying.

His eyes widen in surprise, his face reddening. 'Fuck you, Liv.' And then he storms off.

'Fuck you too,' she mutters. She stomps across the field, her heart racing with fury. How dare he speak to her like that? He knows this is a hard day for her and he's just abandoned her here to lay these flowers by herself. Where is his support when she needs it? And her leg is really aching after walking here from the stables. She'd hoped Wesley would give her a lift back on his way to work but he's just fucked off and left her. Angry tears form in her eyes and snake down her cold cheeks. And then she slows when she sees that she's not alone in the field, like she first thought, but that someone is sitting on the memorial bench under the oak. At first she's worried it might be Sally's parents, Katie's mum or, even worse, Tamzin's, but as she gets closer she recognizes the mane of red hair, the familiar green bobble hat. Shit. She can't face Jenna Halliday right now. She's tempted to turn and head back across the field, but her leg really hurts and she's exhausted.

Jenna stands up when she sees her approach. Olivia notices that she has a bouquet of pink roses in her hand. She's brought flowers with her?

'Hi,' says Jenna, smiling sheepishly. She lays the flowers on the bench. 'These were already here when I arrived. I'm sorry to impose . . .' She must notice the pain etched on Olivia's face, her tear-stained cheeks. 'Are you okay?'

'I . . . need to . . . sit . . .' she manages, before collapsing onto the bench.

Jenna gently takes the flowers from her and places them next to the roses. 'You look really pale,' says Jenna. She reaches into her bag. 'I have a bottle of Coke. It might help.'

Olivia reaches for it and takes a swig. It's flat and warm but she's grateful for the rush of sugar. Jenna perches next to her – the flowers between them.

'Thanks,' says Olivia, handing it back. 'My leg . . . It's a long walk.'

'Can I give you a lift home?'

Olivia would rather sit here all night than get into a car with Jenna Halliday. 'No, I'm fine, thanks.' She's aware her voice is curt.

'I'm sorry to hear about Ralph,' Jenna says, much to Olivia's surprise. Although she shouldn't be surprised. Of course Jenna will know. The whole town will by now. Jenna touches the back of her bobble hat. 'I think the same person attacked me last night too.'

'What?' Olivia stares at her in disbelief. 'You were attacked last night?'

Jenna then launches into a story of walking through the forest on a mission to follow Dale and find out the scoop on the murder when someone hit her over the head. 'Dale was really kind and took me to A and E. I had to have a stitch,' she finishes.

'What time did this happen?'

Jenna deliberates. 'I think around ten-ish. I can't remember exactly.'

Olivia wonders who would do such a thing and why. She was at home by ten. Thank goodness she hadn't walked home from Wesley's – although she rarely did after dark.

'I'm sorry that happened to you. It must have been scary,' says

Olivia, as the silence stretches between them. She wants to get up and walk away from this woman, despite how nice she's being right now. But she doesn't think her leg will carry her. She's a captive audience. Jenna must be thrilled.

'Olivia . . .' Jenna hesitates. 'When this podcast is broadcast by the BBC it might trigger a memory, a clue to someone listening.'

'Like what?'

'Oh, I don't know. A tiny little detail that maybe they hadn't thought at the time was important. Maybe seeing someone on that day . . . someone who, in hindsight, might have been acting suspiciously. Or if your friends were abducted maybe someone will confess. Will a relative remember that their son, husband, father was acting strangely that day? Or on the days after?'

Olivia has never thought of it in that way before. She glances at Jenna. Maybe she's right. She sighs. 'Wesley would go mental if I spoke to you – or any journalist. He's dead against it.'

Jenna frowns. 'Really? But why?'

'He doesn't trust authority. The police. The press. The government.'

'Hmm,' says Jenna, crossing her legs.

'He's just trying to protect me.'

'I understand that but, Olivia, it's a podcast. I'm not writing a piece for the tabloid press. And it would only be a quick interview with you. About what happened that night. In your own words. You and Ralph were the only two there when you came to. And now . . .'

Olivia lowers her head, Jenna's words hanging between them in the air. It's only her now. Her words. Her story. Nobody can twist things, say things that aren't true when the words are coming out of her mouth and recorded. Maybe she should agree to the interview. She'd have a voice at last, a way to control the narrative, to stop people speculating. People would be forced to listen to what she's got to say. Yes, it would be her word on what happened that night. *The final word.*

'Okay, then,' Olivia finds herself saying. 'I'll do it. I'll do the interview.'

Jenna leans forward, her face shining with delight. 'You will? Oh, that's amazing, thank you, Olivia.'

'But please don't mention it to Wesley. Or to anyone for now. Is that okay?'

'Of course. Do you want to come over to my cabin this evening? Around five-ish? It will be quiet there and private. I can pick you up.'

'Um . . . I don't really want anyone to see us.'

'Okay. What about if I wait for you in the road opposite the farm? I'll park down the lane a bit so I'm not seen.' Jenna looks so keen that Olivia doesn't want to disappoint her. Her obvious approval gives Olivia a rare, warm glow, like she's given the right answer in class. And then she feels a flash of uncertainty. Can she really do this? Wesley will be furious with her. *But he already is*, a little voice inside her head says. *So what difference does it make?*

And doesn't she owe it to her friends? And to Ralph? The hero who saved her life that night? Everyone should know what he did. Her heart lurches when she thinks of him. Oh, Ralph. He was the spectre of the forest. He knew things, saw things, kept secrets.

After all, he'd kept hers for all these years.

25

Jenna

'ARE YOU SURE YOU WOULDN'T LIKE A LIFT HOME?' I ASK OL-
ivia, as I stand up. She'd looked so pale when she first arrived, and
even though the colour is back in her cheeks, I can see from how
she winces every few minutes that her leg is giving her pain.

Olivia shakes her head. 'It's fine. Thank you, though. I'll
give my mum a call in a bit and she'll pick me up. I'd like to stay
awhile . . .' She touches the petals of one of the pink roses, concen-
tration on her face. 'Did these flowers come with a card?'

'Um . . . actually, I saw this note.' I reach over and pluck it
from the roses to show her. I've already taken a photo of it. 'I was
just being nosy and wondered who they were from.' I don't want
her to think I'm being underhand. That she's agreed to be interviewed for the podcast is a massive coup but I can see she's a bit
wobbly about it, and I imagine it wouldn't take much for her to
change her mind. I notice how her hand trembles when she reads

the note. Does she recognize the handwriting? 'Do you know who it's from? The same person wrote a note on my car.'

Her eyes widen. 'What kind of note?'

'It said, "Leave town or you'll be next." Charming.' I roll my eyes.

She shakes her head and composes herself. 'It could be from anyone. I imagine everyone is sorry, and most around here don't like journalists poking their noses in. It doesn't imply guilt.'

I'm intrigued by her defensive tone. I watch her carefully: her composed expression and the fingers that still tremble as she folds the note and slips it back into the bouquet. But I don't want to say anything that might upset her. I can ask her more about it after she's done the interview.

When I'm halfway across the field I turn back to see Olivia has her head in her hands. I waver. Should I go back and insist that I drive her home? No. She's a grown woman, for goodness' sake. Just because she has vulnerability about her I shouldn't treat her as a child. And time is getting on. I need to head to Jay Knapton's place now.

But I do feel a surge of excitement as I get back into the car. The podcast will be so much better now that Olivia has agreed to an interview. I hope Wesley isn't too hard on her when he finds out.

It's about a seven-minute drive to Jay's offices on the edge of town, behind the shops and back-streets of Stafferbury. It's not as salubrious out here on the side of the town that the tourists don't see: a winding maze of 1960s office blocks and industrial estates.

Jay's office is in a typically unappealing industrial unit that shares a car park with a few other equally soulless buildings. It looks as though five different companies share this building with him. I press the buzzer for Knapton Developments and I'm buzzed through straight away.

It's just gone 2 p.m. but the reception area is empty and surprisingly small, with just one desk crammed up against a tiny window and a dusty Swiss cheese plant in the corner next to a filing cabinet with a cheap plastic kettle on top. There is another door off the reception area, which is suddenly flung open. Jay rushes out, clasping an A4 leather-bound book to his chest.

'Oh, hi,' he says, staring at me as though he's forgotten who I am even though he only saw me this morning. He looks around the small space. 'Where's Lydia?'

I shrug in response. 'It was empty when I got here but someone buzzed me in.'

'I bet she's gone for a fag again. I keep telling her not to take so many breaks. Anyway, come in, come in,' he says, ushering me through the door into his office. It's even smaller than the 'reception area', with just enough room for a desk, two chairs, and a table in the corner on which sits a compact archaic coffee machine. He waves his notebook in its direction. 'Would you like one?'

'Yes, please, black. Decaf if possible,' I say, pulling out the chair in front of his desk and sitting on it. It's claustrophobic in here and smells of new carpets and old ashtrays.

He dumps the notebook on his desk and takes off his jacket. He's wearing a short-sleeved shirt that shows off his tanned arms. I can see the edge of what looks like a tattoo on his left bicep. 'Ah, yes, something stupid I did in my youth,' he says, when he sees me looking. He pulls up the hem of his sleeve to show me. It's some kind of symbol, in Chinese.

'What does it mean?' I ask.

'Courage. It was to remind me to take chances in life. To take risks. Silly, really.' And I try to imagine what type of man he was in his youth before he was a corporate businessman in an expensive suit. He goes to the coffee machine. We're silent as the machine gurgles away and then he hands me a white mug with KNAPTON DEVELOPMENTS written on the side. He pushes his glasses onto his nose and smiles broadly. He has very tanned skin, as if he uses a sunbed. There is nothing personal on his desk, no family photos or homely trinkets, and his hands are bare of any rings.

'Do you mind if I record you?' I ask, as I get out my phone. 'I might not necessarily use everything you say.' I'm wondering whether I'll need Jay's interview now that I'll have Olivia, Dale and Brenda. He wasn't even living in Stafferbury at the time so I don't know if he can tell me anything useful. I'm hoping he can just give me some local colour – rumours that have never faded about the case maybe. Or other eerie happenings.

'Um . . . well, sure. Sure, that's fine,' he says, as though he's trying to convince himself.

I ask him a few warm-up questions to relax him, like how long he's been living in the town – nearly nineteen years – and if he has any family nearby ('No, never been married. No children.').

'Can you tell me a bit about the town? I know you weren't here when Olivia Rutherford's friends disappeared but there have been so many reports about strange goings-on. The haunted forest. A child crying . . .' I remember hearing that myself on the night I was attacked. I shudder and he notices.

'You've heard it, haven't you? The child's cries?' When I nod he charges on, more animated than I've seen him so far. 'The contractors who built the cabins heard it too. They told me. And others over the years. Ralph Middleton was convinced that the forest was haunted. And he should know. He lived in it. Other things too. Bright lights by the standing stones. A figure haunting the Devil's Corridor. There have been many accidents on that road over the years, you know.' He sounds almost proud of this fact. 'The local pub, the Raven, is haunted by a woman in grey.' I want to laugh in disbelief. It's always a woman in grey. 'Stafferbury is known as one of the most haunted towns in the UK.'

'And do you believe it all?' I ask him.

'Of course.' He crosses his arms and juts out his chin. 'It's hard not to when you've seen or heard things yourself. Once, many years ago, when I was staying in the high street I woke up in the early hours of the morning and saw a pony and trap overturn in the street. When I looked it up afterwards I found out that a horse and carriage accident had taken place here in the early 1800s.'

'And what do you think happened on the night the girls disappeared?'

'I wouldn't want to rule anything out,' he replies noncommittally. 'But I do know that Ralph believed it was an alien abduction.' I expect him to laugh or scoff but he remains serious. Then he adds gravely, 'As you're probably aware, Ralph was found dead last night.' I nod, willing him to continue. 'His caravan was stationed on my land – I own a large portion of the forest. And he worked for me – a bit of cash in hand – to keep an eye on the place. He told me over the years that he'd seen a lot of strange things. And it does make me wonder, you know. About his death.'

'Wonder what?'

'If it was perhaps . . .' he pauses for dramatic effect '. . . supernatural.'

I stare at him in shock. Does he really believe that? My mum used to say, when I was little and scared that a ghost was under my bed, it was the living who could hurt you, not the dead.

'You know,' he continues, 'that a long time ago human sacrifices were made at the stones.'

I remember Brenda telling me.

'There are rumours of a pagan group living in Stafferbury. Not a cult exactly but . . . I'm not saying they sacrificed the girls or anything but . . . they're a weird lot.'

'Who do you think might be in this "group"?'

'Well, I've only heard rumours, of course, but maybe Madame Tovey. And a few others. They're mostly elderly now. Apparently they like to do some kind of ceremony at the stones in the summer.' He waves his hand dismissively. 'I don't get involved. I'm not into that kind of thing although I have to admit there is a strange energy around those stones.'

I remember how I'd felt in the field earlier, that I was being watched, that a shadowy force was lurking, but I don't answer. Instead I sip my coffee and ask him if he knows the families of the missing girls.

He hesitates. 'Not really. They all keep themselves to themselves. Especially the Rutherfords.'

'What about Ralph? You said he did a bit of work for you, looking after the forest and keeping it clean and litter-free. What do you think happened to him? Did he have any enemies you knew about?'

He pushes his chair back to fiddle with the blinds behind his desk. 'Do you mind if I pull this up? It's dark in here.' He adjusts the vertical blinds without waiting for an answer. He spends a bit of time at the window, hassling with the cord, and I wonder if it's some kind of delay tactic. The light in the room was perfectly fine.

It seems unnecessary, but then I dismiss it. I'm becoming paranoid about everyone in this town.

'Ralph?' I remind him, when he's returned to his seat.

'Oh, he was a simple soul. I can't believe anyone would want to hurt him. He was harmless.'

'But someone obviously did.'

A shadow passes across his face but he doesn't say anything and I mentally kick myself for being insensitive.

'Anyway,' I say, wrapping up, 'thank you for talking to me.'

He flashes a relieved smile as I stop recording and fold up my stand.

As soon as I get back to my car my phone rings and Dale's name flashes up on screen.

'Jenna,' he says, as soon as I've answered, 'we've found something in Ralph's caravan that I think you need to see.'

26

I'VE AGREED TO MEET DALE IN BEA'S TEAROOM FOR A LATE lunch. I've been so busy today I haven't had the chance to eat since this morning. Thankfully, it's quiet now it's nearing 3 p.m. and we find a table in the corner furthest away from the counter. After he's ordered coronation-chicken baps for us both, Dale reaches inside his briefcase and takes out a manila folder.

'This was found in Ralph's things,' he says, opening it and taking out a clear plastic wallet. He slides it across the table. It looks like it contains a series of Polaroid images, slightly grainy and out of focus, taken of a teenage girl in various outside locations. One looks like a petrol station, the other a park, the next the high street.

I peer closer at the photos. The girl is young. Maybe eighteen with a round face and a 1990s layered haircut, with caramel-coloured streaks. 'It's Olivia.'

Dale nods. 'Before the accident. Look.' He points to the photo of Olivia wrapped in a fake-fur coat at the petrol station filling up a white car. 'Her Peugeot 205. It was written off after the accident.'

'Do you think it was Ralph who was following her?'

'Why else would he have them?' Dale runs a hand through his already messy hair. He looks exhausted, and I feel a tug of guilt, remembering how late he'd stayed up with me in A and E.

'Did he ever drive a white van?'

'Ralph couldn't drive.'

I hold the photos up towards the light to get a better look. They've been run through a colour photocopier so that they all fit on one page of A4. 'So, Ralph was obsessed with Olivia and was following her before the accident? Is that what these photos mean?'

Chloë appears with our baps and drinks, and I turn over the page of photos so that she can't see them. Only when she's gone do I turn them back. Something doesn't add up about this. 'Wouldn't she have recognized Ralph? If he'd been following her?'

'Hmm. You can see she's quite far away in them, though.' Dale takes a bite of his bap. Creamy coronation chicken oozes out of the side and drops onto his plate. He swallows. 'I'm wondering now if Ralph was the figure Olivia saw in the road. Did he hang around waiting for her to regain consciousness, then pretend he'd just happened upon her crashed car?'

'I know I only met Ralph once – well, twice if you include our encounter on the Devil's Corridor when I first arrived – but he didn't strike me as a criminal mastermind. Could he have pulled off something like that? Causing a crash, yes, but the missing girls? Where would he have taken them and why? Hardly his two-berth caravan – and if he had killed them, then what? He buried three girls all by himself?' I pick up my bap and take a bite, waiting for Dale to answer. His expressive eyebrows rise so that they are nearly hidden in his mop of hair.

'I don't know what it all means,' he says eventually. 'Ralph might have known what happened and that's why he was killed. Ralph was obviously following her. He'd kept these photos for twenty years. He befriended her, saved her from the crash. Maybe he played the hero.'

'And for what?' I ask. 'And why would someone wait twenty years to kill Ralph if he did know something about the girls' disappearance all that time?'

He exhales in frustration.

I pick at the corner of my bread. 'Did you find anything else?'

Dale sits back in his chair. 'Well, yes. A huge stash of money. In a box.'

My eyes widen. 'How much?'

He lowers his voice and leans forwards. 'Nearly ten thousand pounds.'

I gasp. 'That's a lot of cash to be lying around. Where would he have got it from?'

He sighs. 'There are some things I'm not at liberty to tell you. Yet. Things that cross over with another case I'm not working on. We're not even sure if the two things are linked yet.'

I feel a thud of disappointment. Of course Dale can only tell me so much. He's a police officer. A detective. After everything that happened last night – our long spell waiting in A and E confiding and chatting, him making me laugh – I haven't exactly forgotten but perhaps I've allowed the boundaries of our roles as police officer and journalist to blur. It just feels so easy with him.

I finish off my bap in silence. Dale takes the photos and puts them back into his briefcase. He knocks back the remainder of his Coke. 'I'd better be off,' he says, replacing his glass on the table.

'Before you go, I tried to ring you earlier, but the reception was bad.'

'Okay.'

I quickly fill him in on Jay Knapton's visit to me earlier, then the notes I found with the same handwriting.

'Do you have the notes?'

'Only the one from my car, but I've left it in the cabin,' I lie. I'm not sure why. 'But I took a photo.'

'Can you send it to me?'

I reach for my phone and do so while he's still sitting there. 'And the cabin being empty is weird, isn't it?' I continue, after I've sent the image. 'Jay said there was no guest staying in Foxglove, the cabin opposite mine,' I clarify, 'but I definitely saw someone in there.'

'And you're sure you weren't mistaken?'

'Definitely not. The lights were on and someone walked out of the front door on the night I arrived with a big dog, like an Alsatian or a German Shepherd.'

Dale's lips twitch. 'Think that's the same thing.'

'Oh, yes.' I laugh at my mistake. 'I prefer cats. Less needy.'

'Then you haven't met my dad's.' He checks his watch. 'I've got a meeting in twenty minutes so I need to go. But I can pop over later. Around seven p.m., if you still want to interview me.' He looks around as a group of six teenagers walk in and noisily grab a table. 'It'll be quieter than here.'

'Okay. That's great. Thanks.' I watch as he lumbers away, almost bumping into one of the teenagers, who has got up to move seats. Dale has to duck his head to get out through the doorway.

I drain the rest of my drink, still reeling from my conversation with Dale. I'm confused about the photos, still not convinced it had been Ralph following Olivia. But the money. He must have been involved in something dodgy to have that much cash sitting around.

I'm still thinking of Olivia and our conversation on the bench earlier as I drive through the high street. She had looked so sad but something else too. Almost resigned to her unhappiness. Defeated.

Just as I'm nearing the end of the high street, with the Co-op on the corner before it merges onto the Devil's Corridor, I see a woman up ahead, on the grass verge. She's gesticulating at the man she's with. I slow down to get a better look. It's Olivia's mum. She's pointing angrily in the direction of the high street. The man is tall, straight backed and wearing a navy blue overcoat, with the collar turned up. He has close shaved grey hair, and even though I can't see his face, I'm certain it's Jay Knapton. It looks like they're having a heated discussion. Why would Olivia's mum be so cross with Jay? He told me earlier that he didn't really know the Rutherfords. She looks over Jay's shoulder, her eyes landing on my car. Has she seen me? I drive faster, and when I look in my rear-view mirror she's storming away, leaving Jay standing there with his arms wide.

27

Olivia

OLIVIA IS JUST COMING OUT OF THE STABLES AFTER REPLAC-
ing Sabrina's hay-net when she notices a dark shadow looming
over her. She turns, the hairs on the back of her neck standing up,
to see Wesley watching her.

'Wes,' she says, in surprise. She thought he'd gone back to
work. It's nearly 4 p.m. He doesn't clock off for another hour.
'What are you doing here?'

'You really upset me earlier,' he says, thrusting his hands into
his pockets. 'So I pulled a sickie.'

'Another? Oh, Wes. You don't want to get sacked.'

'They won't sack me. I've been there too long.' He toes the
hard ground. She knows he won't apologize for earlier. He never
does. Instead he'll moon around her, like he's the victim, until
she's forced to say sorry or make it up to him in some way even
though she's the wronged party.

'I thought we could spend tonight together.' Wesley's voice is plaintive. 'It's an important night. Twenty years. I don't think you should be on your own.'

She pushes the bolt across the stable door and walks towards the tack room. She can hear Wesley following her. Her stomach flips knowing she's about to lie to him. 'I can't tonight. I . . . I'm meeting . . . friends.' She takes down a bridle and runs it through her fingers. She has to keep moving so that Wesley can't see her face and the lies written all over it. She always comes here in times of anxiety. She finds it soothing among all the saddles, bridles and numnahs. She loves the smell of it: a mixture of leather cleaner and the warm whiff of horse hair.

'Friends? You've got no friends.'

She knows it's true but it still feels like a stab to the heart. She had friends, of course, lots of friends, before the accident but in the years that followed she'd allowed them to drift away. She'd stopped making an effort to see them. It just seemed easier to stay in with Wesley. To hide away. Her three best friends had disappeared and she'd wanted to do the same. So she had. She'd disappeared in plain sight.

'I've made a new friend recently,' she says, moving the bridle to a different peg, her back to him. 'Someone . . . a girl who helps out at the stables.' Considering most of the girls who help out at the stables are aged eleven to fifteen this is a huge lie. The only person around her age is the instructor, Mel, but she's married with two teenage sons and, on the odd occasion Olivia has suggested going for a drink after work, Mel would throw her a horrified look and say she had to get back for 'the boys'.

'Really? What's her name?'

'Charlotte.' She plucks a name out of thin air. She's always liked it. She thought if she had a daughter that's what she would call her.

'Where are you going?' He sounds so suspicious she almost wants to laugh. Does he think she's really going out with a guy? He has a boys' night out, as he calls it, every week and goodness knows where he was or who he was with last night, despite his assurances he was with Stan. He'd disappeared around the time that Jenna was attacked. She inhales deeply. She immediately dispels this thought. Wesley wouldn't hurt anyone. *Would he?* But she knows better than most what a person is capable of, if pushed.

For some inexplicable reason her eyes fill with tears. She stares ahead at the racks of saddles on the far wall. This is the life she deserves, she thinks.

This time twenty years ago she was going about her life, happy, innocent, unaware that it was about to change. She was getting ready for her weekly girls' night out, dressed up in her knee-high boots and checked mini skirt, her hair streaked a beautiful honey colour and heavily layered around her plump, youthful face. She was excited about the future, her new relationship with Wesley, her best friends. She was excited about trying out the new nightclub in the next town that has now long ago closed down. Her life had been filled with expectation, with colour, but now it's black-and-white, a pencil drawing that's fading slowly over time. She is greying at the temples, she's put on a stone and she can't remember the last time she'd felt truly excited about something. How she wishes she really did have a friend called Charlotte. A bubbly, fun friend, who would encourage her to wear something inappropriate and drag her out to nightclubs and encourage her to get pissed and flail about with abandon in the middle of a sticky dance floor.

What would her life have been like if Sally, Tamzin and Katie hadn't disappeared twenty years ago tonight? Would they all be married now? Mothers? Would they all have stayed friends or would they have moved away, moved on, grown up?

'Liv? Have you gone off into Dreamland again? I asked where you were going.'

'I don't know yet. Look, I have to get on now.' She turns and faces him at last. 'I've still got a bit of work to do before I finish for the day.'

'What am I supposed to do tonight?' he whines. 'They were my friends too, you know.' No, they fucking weren't, she wants to shout. Sally couldn't stand you! But she presses her lips together. She doesn't want to hurt his feelings. God knows why when he's always hurting hers. 'I thought we'd spend the night together.'

'Well, you thought wrong, then, didn't you? I didn't say we would. And after you flounced off at lunchtime I didn't think you'd want to see me today.'

There's a shocked pause. 'Is this about last night?' he says, in a strangled voice.

She sighs. 'No, of course not.'

'You've been funny with me ever since. I didn't like the way you spoke to me earlier either,' he says. 'You can't do this when we live together, you know.'

'Do what?'

He thrusts his hands deeper into his pockets. 'Just go out gallivanting. That's not what couples do.'

'Oh, really? So, no more boys' nights out for you, then? Is that what you mean?'

He hesitates. 'Well, no . . . that's different. We get together to watch football. It's not like we're clubbing or chatting up girls.'

She closes her eyes. She suddenly feels bone tired. She realizes in that moment that her injuries have helped Wesley keep her on a lead. He's stifling her and she wants to run, run, run.

'Wes,' she sighs, 'it's one night. We can't live in each other's pockets. I didn't question why you had to run off so quickly last night –'

'I told you. Stan needed help. Woman trouble.' Not one of his friends is in a couple as far as she's aware. 'It's never bothered you before.'

'Well, it bothers me now.'

He laughs nastily. 'Oh, I see, I get it. You've just used me for all these years, is that it? And now you're stronger, now your leg is getting better, you don't need me any more. Well, fuck you, Olivia. Fuck you.'

'Wes . . .'

He storms out. She doesn't follow him.

She is still in the tack room, slumped on the bench, when her mum walks in. The fading light casts shadows along the tiled floor.

'What are you doing sitting in here alone?' asks her mother, when she spots Olivia. She's holding a red grooming kit with a hoof pick sticking out of the top. She places it on a shelf along with the others. Olivia hadn't known her mother was back. She'd picked her up from the standing stones earlier and dropped her home, then said she'd had to go to the cash-and-carry to get supplies. Her mother has been gone for ages. 'Have you brought Sky back in from the field?'

'Yes, she's in the stables.' Olivia brushes down her jodhpurs. She must stink of horses. The soles of her riding boots are caked with mud. 'And the vet came earlier and sorted out Pickles.'

Her mother turns to her, her face softening. 'It's a hard day, I know.'

Olivia doesn't say anything. Instead she plucks the horse hair from her jodhpurs.

'I love you so much, you know that, don't you?'

Olivia's head shoots up in surprise. Her mum doesn't often profess endearments. 'Of course. And I love you too.'

Her mother comes and sits beside her, reaches over and pats her knee awkwardly. 'I like Wesley, you know I do, but I'm worried you're not happy.'

It's on the tip of her tongue to blurt it all out, to confide in her mother – her doubts about Wesley, her unhappiness. And to ask the questions she's always been afraid to. But once she says it all she'll never be able to unsay it. It will be out there, in the ether.

'Don't you ever worry that our lives are just so . . . small?' she asks instead.

Her mother fidgets next to her. 'Small?'

'It's always been the two of us. And then Wesley. You've never really had a relationship apart from my father, and you said you were only together for a short time.'

Her mum laughs suddenly. 'What? Of course I had other boyfriends before that, and since you were born. I just didn't advertise it. You were always my priority.'

'And friends. You never see them any more either. Since . . . well, since the accident.'

Her mother closes her eyes. 'How could I? Let's not rake all this up now, love.' She presses her thumb and forefinger to the bridge of her nose and sighs. Then she seems to rally herself. 'Come on.' She gets up and holds out a hand. 'Why don't we watch a film tonight, a feel-good movie? *While You Were Sleeping* is on at nine.'

'There's something I need to do first. But maybe later.'

Her mother nods and smiles but Olivia can see the worry behind her eyes. They walk back through the stables and towards the house together. She'd better hurry – Jenna will be waiting. Her mother goes into the house and Olivia keeps walking until she reaches the end of the car park. She wavers. Can she really do this? Yes. Yes, she can. She must. She's got a voice and for the first time in twenty years she's going to use it.

Olivia zips up her yellow raincoat over her thick jumper and black jodhpurs and pulls her bobble hat further down onto her hair, her breath fogging out into the gloaming. Then she heads out of the stables to the lane opposite, towards Jenna's waiting car.

28

Suspicion

WHEN STACE WOKE UP THE NEXT MORNING SHE FOUND SHE *was alone in the huge bed. The French windows were ajar, the white voile curtains fluttering in the slight breeze, and voices rose from below. She grabbed the dress she'd discarded on the chair last night and pulled it over her head before stepping onto the veranda. The impressive wrought-iron gates were open and John-Paul and Derreck were heading out of them, with Trevor, Griff and Martin following, nattering away like excitable kids off on a school trip. What was going on? She didn't even know what time it was. She must have overslept. And where were the girls? She felt disoriented and a little irritated that John-Paul hadn't woken her. Their first day in a strange country and he was already off gallivanting with this Derreck and the other lads. She was tempted to call after them but didn't want to look like some possessive girlfriend in front of*

Derreck. Instead she watched as they headed onto the busy street and hailed a couple of tuk-tuks.

After she'd changed into a pair of frayed denim shorts and a strappy vest, making sure to slather her skin in sunscreen, she headed downstairs, the marble tiles cool against the soles of her feet. The villa felt like a sanctuary, their own little oasis, but she knew that just outside stood a bustling, smelly, sweaty metropolis and John-Paul had just been swallowed into it. She didn't feel ready to face it.

'Hey, there she is,' called Hannah, as Stace wandered into the huge kitchen. The doors were flung open onto the garden and she could see Maggie perched at the edge of the pool in a bright cerise bikini, her legs immersed in the water, a glass of juice to her lips and large purple sunglasses pushed back onto her dark hair. She looked back at them over her shoulder and waved. Leonie was making herself at home in the kitchen in a garish floral one-piece, her deep cleavage already red. Hannah was standing in the doorway in a green bikini, her towel draped over the sun-lounger. She was tall and androgynous and her light brown curls were pulled back in a ponytail. She turned her freck-led face to Stace. 'Why haven't you got your suit on?'

Stace looked down at her shorts and top. 'I wasn't sure of the plan. Why are you all so chirpy? My body feels like it's made of lead.' They didn't seem affected by jetlag in the slightest but that was prob-ably because they'd gone to sleep at a sensible hour last night, un-like Stace, who was drooling over Derreck until three o'clock in the morning. It served her right. What would the others say if she told them he'd taken his clothes off and jumped into the swimming-pool naked? That he'd invited her to join him and that a part of her had wanted to?

'Iced coffee?' asked Leonie, proffering a tall glass. Stace grim-aced. She'd never tasted iced coffee in her life and she wasn't about to start now. She shook her head and Leonie took a sip of it. She smacked her lips. 'Surprisingly nice.'

'I saw the lads leaving. Where are they going?'

Hannah laughed. 'Worried John-Paul will make a run for it?' she teased, knowing Stace's insecurities. 'They've gone to the 7-Eleven on the corner.' They headed outside to join Maggie. Stace stood in the shade of the wooden arbour while Leonie and Hannah settled on the sun-loungers. Her heart fluttered when she remembered Derreck in the pool last night, the water rippling over his toned chest and the moonlight catching his gleaming strong shoulders. She took a deep breath, feeling disgusted with herself for the way her body betrayed her when she thought of it. It was because she was angry with John-Paul, she told herself.

'But they went off in tuk-tuks,' she said, perching on the edge of Leonie's sun-lounger, the wood hot against the back of her legs.

Leonie wiggled her stubby toes. Her nails were painted a frosted pink and she was wearing a silver ankle bracelet.

'Oh, relax, won't you? Enjoy the time with us girls instead of worrying about where your precious John-Paul is.' She closed her eyes. 'Anyway, I heard Derreck and John-Paul talking this morning. I sensed they wanted to get the other lads on their own to ask them something.'

'Ask them what?' Panic flared in Stace when she remembered Derreck and John-Paul's conversation behind closed doors last night.

'I dunno, but I reckoned he was taking them to meet a mate,' Leonie said, face turned up to the sun.

Why did Stace get the feeling that Derreck was trying to involve them in something ... What? Unscrupulous? She shrugged off the thought. She wasn't in a Robert De Niro film. She was being paranoid.

Stace got up and went back into the kitchen to get herself a drink. She was also starving. She hadn't eaten properly at the barbecue last night as everything had been a bit overwhelming. She desperately wanted a cup of tea. Not iced, just hot like she had it at home. Was there even a kettle in this place?

'Are you okay?' a voice at her shoulder asked. She turned to see Maggie standing behind her, her feet and ankles damp from the pool. There were wet footprints on the marble tiles.

Stace attempted a smile. 'Of course. We're in this amazing place. I mean, look at it! It's like a palace.'

'But?'

Stace's gaze flickered to where Leonie and Hannah were chatting quietly to each other, their eyes closed. It was nearly 104 degrees out there. They were going to burn if they weren't careful. 'It just makes you realize how bleak things are at home, doesn't it?'

Maggie's eyes widened. 'What do you mean?'

Stace ushered Maggie further into the kitchen so that the others were out of earshot. 'John-Paul has lost his job,' she said. 'I've not told anyone else yet.'

'Fired?'

'No, no, definitely not. John-Paul is a hard worker. The company aren't doing that well so . . .' She tried to quell the flurry of anxiety that assailed her every time she thought of it. 'Last in, first out. That kind of thing.' She lowered her voice. 'And, also, last night I heard John-Paul and Derreck talking. And it sounded like Derreck wanted John-Paul to do something for him. That John-Paul owed him.'

'For what?'

'I have no idea, and John-Paul brushed it off last night when I tried to ask him.'

'John-Paul's a good guy. He won't do anything stupid.' Maggie's voice was firm.

Stace opened the fridge and poured herself an orange juice. 'He seems different since we got here. Secretive. Morose with me. And Derreck is so . . . so . . .'

'Radiant. Magnificent. Sexy. Rich as fuck.'

Despite herself, Stace giggled. 'I was going to say persuasive,' she said, thinking of how close she had been to joining him in the swimming-pool last night. 'But, yes, your words too.'

Maggie linked her arm through hers. 'Come on, don't let your anxieties ruin your holiday. We'll probably never stay anywhere so plush again. Make the most of it.'

Two hours later the boys finally returned. 'We've bought supplies,' called Derreck, holding up a striped plastic bag as he led the others into the garden. Martin, Trev and Griff all looked in good spirits, particularly Griff, whose face was practically splitting with his huge grin. As soon as Stace saw Derreck she felt a ripple of excitment mixed with nerves. John-Paul was hanging at the back, a distracted air about him.

'It took you two hours to go to the 7-Eleven?' Leonie observed from where they were all sitting under a huge awning. It was too hot now to be in the sun. Leonie was looking particularly lobster-like.

John-Paul plonked himself down next to Stace and rubbed her bare knee. He flashed her a smile, which she supposed was meant to be reassuring but it didn't reach his eyes.

'Derreck took us on a bit of a journey,' sniggered Griff, slinging an arm around Leonie's shoulders. She shrugged him off, proclaiming it was too hot to be touched. He had large circles of sweat under the armpits of his Pink Floyd T-shirt.

'I'd say he did,' said Trevor, still wearing his ridiculous hat. He exchanged a look with Griff, who let out a dirty laugh. 'Who's getting in the pool?' He started stripping off his T-shirt and Trev followed suit. They jumped into the cool blue water, causing Leonie to shout in mock-horror when she got splashed.

'We need to talk,' whispered Stace to John-Paul.

'I can't . . .'

'Now,' she mouthed.

Without speaking he got to his feet and followed her wordlessly to the bottom of the garden.

'What's going on?' she demanded, as soon as they were far enough away not to be heard. Every now and again Leonie's cackle drifted over to them.

'What do you –'

She noticed John-Paul's top lip was sweating. 'Don't lie to me. I heard you and Derreck last night.' John-Paul paled. 'What does he mean by you owe him? Owe him for what?'

John-Paul's large brown eyes widened like a panicked animal's. 'It was . . . something stupid. I got into a spot of bother back in our travelling days. Derreck helped me out.'

'A spot of bother? Like what?'

'It doesn't matter.'

'I thought we knew everything about each other.' She grabbed his hand. 'But I'm seeing a different side to you. A secretive side. Why can't you tell me?'

He pulled his hand away and ran it through his dark hair instead. 'It doesn't matter. You have to trust me, Stace.'

'Okay, then. What does he want you to do? Why did he really invite us here?'

John-Paul cast his eyes over to their group of friends. Maggie and Martin were now in the pool too. Derreck stood on the edge, fully clothed, his body angled in their direction, a hand shielding his face.

John-Paul sighed heavily. 'It's nothing, really. Derreck has a mate who specializes in foreign artefacts back home. He wants me and the lads to smuggle some out of the country.'

'What? Why would you need to smuggle them out?'

'Because Thailand is very strict about not taking certain things out of the country. Like Buddhas, for example. And Derreck's friend back home wants to sell them in his shop.'

A sweat had broken out over her body yet she felt cold, despite the 104-degree heat. 'Are these Buddhas filled with . . . drugs?'

'What?' John-Paul laughed. 'Bloody hell, Stace. Of course not. It's just a load of antique ornaments.'

She frowned. 'Do you get paid to do this?'

'Well, yeah. Sure. But it's still technically illegal. The Thai government are very hot on it. I think you can take them out for religious purposes but you have to get paperwork and a licence and it's all a bit of a hassle, according to Derreck. And he wants us to export a couple each.'

'Us?'

'Well, yeah. Like two Buddhas per couple. That way if one of us is caught it will look like we're just stupid tourists who didn't know the rules.'

'And you've said you'll do this?'

He shrugged. 'At first I said no. But the pay . . . We could do with the money.'

'How much?'

'He hasn't said yet.' He glanced across at Derreck, then back at Stace. He rubbed the nape of his neck. 'Derreck took us to see the guy this morning. That's where we went. The lads are thinking about it, said they'll ask their other halves. This is just a sideline for Derreck.' He gave a hollow laugh. 'I think he has a lot of sidelines, judging by how much money he seems to have.'

'Could we go to prison if we're caught?'

John-Paul shook his head emphatically. 'God, no. No . . . we'd be fined, probably. But no . . . I don't think a prison sentence would be . . .'

Stace was appalled. 'You don't think? I'm not doing anything that could land us in a Thai prison, for fuck's sake. I don't care how broke we are.'

Just then Derreck strode across the grass to join them. He clapped John-Paul on the back and winked at Stace. 'What are you two doing over here being all anti-social?'

Stace held his gaze. 'John-Paul was just telling me about the Buddhas.'

'And what do you think?'

'I think it seems like a strange request.'

Something she couldn't read passed between the two men. And then Derreck laughed. 'Got yourself a suspicious one here, JP.' He winked again at her. 'Come on, let's grab some lunch.'

As they followed Derreck back to the others John-Paul tried to take her hand but she snatched it away. 'You'd better not be lying to me,' she hissed. 'And I want to see these Buddhas for myself before I agree to anything, all right? And I want assurances that if one of us is caught the most we'll get is a small fine.'

'Of course.' He reached for her hand again. This time she didn't pull away.

29

Jenna

IT'S ONLY JUST BEFORE 5 P.M. BUT DARKNESS FELL QUICKLY this evening, as sudden as if someone had turned off the lights. I park in front of the cabin and we get out of the car. The air is cold and smells of bonfires, pine needles and damp soil. Olivia has on a grey bobble hat that brings out the silver in her eyes, and she's still wearing her riding gear, which has a faint horse odour. She smiles uncertainly, showing white, even teeth. She has a healthy glow to her cheeks. For the first time I really notice her. She's attractive in a girl-next-door kind of way with a wide, toothy smile and a clear skin tone that tans even in winter. Mine is of the milky-white, burns-in-the-sun variety. There's something different about her today. She seems more determined somehow.

'Thanks for picking me up,' she says again. She stands and observes the cabin. 'This is lovely. Very remote, though. Don't you find it a bit scary, staying here by yourself?'

'It's fine. There are others.' I wave vaguely in Foxglove's direction although I don't admit they're empty.

'I'd better take my boots off,' she says, as she steps over the threshold. 'They're filthy.'

I laugh, 'Sure. I'll put the kettle on,' then remember the instant-boiling-water tap. As I go to close the door behind her I look out onto the dark night. There is no comforting glow from any of the other cabins and the mass of trees makes me feel even more claustrophobic, their dark bristly branches adding to the gloomy, unsettled feeling I've had since I was attacked last night, maybe even before that. The darkness seems to stretch into infinity but . . . Is it my imagination or is there a movement over there by the trees?

'Nobody knows you're here?' I clarify, as I close the door.

She takes off her bobble hat and shakes out her hair. 'No. I haven't told anyone.' She follows me through the living room into the kitchen. 'This is lovely,' she exclaims, looking around. 'Very plush.'

'They've been decorated beautifully.'

I offer her tea, which she accepts. 'White, no sugar.'

'How's your leg?' I ask, when I notice her limping across the kitchen to take a mug from me. She'd seemed in a lot of pain earlier when I saw her at the stones. I've read about Olivia's injuries after the crash. I know she still has metal pins in her left leg.

She grimaces in response. 'It's a lot better than it used to be. It helps to use it as much as I can. I find it stiffens up the more I sit around. But, you know, it could have been a lot worse. If Katie, Tamzin and Sally were abducted then my leg being trapped could have actually saved me.' She gives a self-deprecating laugh. 'So of course that means I've also got survivor's guilt on top of everything else.' Her tone is deliberately light but I can see the emotions she's unable to hide.

'I'm so sorry. I can't imagine,' I say sincerely.

She shrugs. 'It is what it is.'

We go into the living room. 'I've tried to light the fire,' I say, when I notice her shivering, 'but I'm useless at getting it to catch.'

'I can do it, if you like. We have one at home.'

She places her mug on the rustic oak coffee-table and bends down in front of the grate. Within minutes she has the fire roaring and stands back with a satisfied look on her face.

'You make it seem so easy. I don't know what I do wrong.'

'Make sure to light the paper,' she says. 'Not just the wood.' She moves to the sofa, picks up her mug and leans back, stretching out her legs. I've already got my mobile phone and stand set up on the coffee-table. She sips her tea and watches me over the rim of her mug as I click on the app and begin recording.

'So,' I say, taking a seat on the chair by the patio doors. 'Thanks for agreeing to this. I was a bit worried you might change your mind.' I tuck my feet underneath me. I want Olivia to feel relaxed, to forget she's being recorded. As though we're just two people having a chat.

'I still can't believe I'm here,' she says, gazing around. 'But . . . It's silly, really.'

'No, go on. What were you going to say?'

She warms her hands on her mug. Her fingernails are bitten down. 'Everyone always tells me what to do. My mother, Wesley. I know it's because they have my best interests at heart but it's almost like they think I stayed eighteen after the accident. I'm a grown woman. I have a voice!'

'Of course you do,' I say. I imagine this is her way of pushing back, against Wesley in particular. To rebel.

'What can you remember about the night of the accident?' I begin gently, wanting to ease our way into it.

She blows on her tea, then says wistfully, 'We were all so excited about going out. We got together every Saturday but there was a new club in the next town and we wanted to try it out.' She swallows. 'It had been a good night. Mostly. Tamzin got too drunk, but she often did. And she and Katie had a bit of a row. I was with Sally at the bar but when they came out of the toilets, both with faces like thunder, Sally said, "Oh, no, not again." They rowed a lot. They were best friends but they were also like sisters.'

'What did they row about?'

'No idea. Probably something trivial. Tamzin often acted like a bit of a dick when she was pissed. She'd probably made some comment to Katie about what she was wearing or her lack of a boyfriend.' Olivia sips her tea. 'And then driving back it started to rain really heavily.' Her eyes glaze over as though she's seeing the empty Devil's Corridor in front of her, like I imagine it would have been the night she drove home. 'One of the girls screamed that someone was in the road. I swerved and the car turned over. I blacked out and when I came to they were gone.'

I nod, not wanting to speak, to break the spell. I already know most of this, of course, but this is for the listeners.

'And then I lay there for a while, hurt, unable to move and that's when I saw someone hurrying towards the car, appearing out of the rain. I screamed thinking it was the person I'd seen in the road but it was Ralph. It was just Ralph. I knew him a bit. I'd seen him around the town and we'd always say hello to him when we passed him. He once helped Katie find her cat. I wasn't scared of him. And in that moment I knew I had to trust him because what choice did I have?' She laughs mirthlessly and crosses her ankles. One of her woolly socks has bagged away from the toe area so that it looks like she has one long foot.

'And what did Ralph do?'

'He rang for an ambulance, then got into the passenger seat with me while we waited for them to arrive. I was crying quite hysterically and he tried to calm me down by reassuring me that my friends had probably gone to get help but I knew – I knew that didn't seem right because Katie had a mobile, but I thought maybe her battery had died, or maybe it had broken in the crash. So I let myself be convinced. And, if I'm honest, I was more concerned with myself at that moment. My leg was trapped, crushed. I knew I'd have to be cut free. I worried I'd never walk again.'

'That's understandable. So you're sure Ralph wasn't the figure you saw in the road?'

'I'm not sure, no. But Ralph assured me that he wasn't. He'd been in the woods, tending some animal – I think a fox, Ralph was animal mad – when he heard the sound of, as he put it, exploding metal. It had taken him ten minutes or so to reach me.'

I hesitate. She catches my expression and frowns. 'What is it?'

I explain about the photos found in Ralph's caravan, describing them. 'I think they must have been taken in the days or weeks before your accident. You were filling up your Peugeot 205 and you were wearing winter clothes. You said you thought you were being followed? I think it might have been Ralph. If he was following you, it could have been him in the road. He could have been the one to cause the crash.'

'But . . .' She stares at me in confusion as though trying to reorder everything she'd thought she knew all these years. 'No, that's not right. I told the police at the time. The man who was following me drove a white van. And the man had a scar.'

'A scar?' Neither Dale nor Brenda had mentioned that detail.

'Yes. Here.' She touches her cheekbone. 'It was quite prominent and ran from the corner of his eye to the middle of his cheek.' She leans forwards and places her mug on the table.

'Did you tell the police?'

'Yes. Of course. I mean, I was drugged up. I'd just been through an operation but they came and interviewed me several times.'

I watch her carefully, not sure whether she's lying. If she'd mentioned the man with a scar to the police then there would be a record of it. Is this something she's just plucked out of the air now, for the purpose of this interview? To protect Ralph? Or have both Brenda and Dale decided not to tell me for some reason? I make a mental note to ask Dale when I see him later.

'So this man with a scar,' I continue, 'what else can you remember about him? How old was he roughly?'

She fidgets and wrings her hands in her lap. 'It was such a long time ago. But I'd say late forties. Very rugged. Unshaven. A few times I saw his van parked up and he was sitting behind the wheel, smoking.'

'And you never saw him get out?'

'Just once. I think he was trying to approach me. I was walking one of the ponies to the nearby field and I saw him on the other side of the road. He called over to me.'

'Did he call you by name?'

'No. No, just "Hey" . . . something like that. And I started running with the pony. I was freaked out. He was sinister-looking. Unkempt. He didn't run after me, thank God.'

'And that was the last time you saw him?'

'Yes. I think that was the day before the accident.'

I digest this information. 'And you've never seen him since?'

'No.' She blinks. 'I asked Sally about him. At the club that night. But she hadn't noticed anyone. And the police never found him or his van.'

'But that doesn't explain why those photos of you were found in Ralph's caravan,' I say, perplexed. 'You never saw the man with the scar with Ralph?'

She shakes her head. 'No. It doesn't make sense.'

'Ralph said something to me about a bright light at the scene of the crash,' I say, moving the interview on. 'Did you see the lights too?'

Olivia's brows knit together. 'I . . . No, I don't think so. I was in a lot of pain. I was dipping in and out of consciousness even after Ralph found me. It wasn't until the next day, when the police visited me in hospital and told me my friends hadn't come home, that I began to worry. But even then . . .' She stops and seems to consider her next words. 'In the days that followed I still thought they'd show up. That they'd have some funny madcap story as to where they'd been.' She uncrosses her ankles.

'What did Ralph tell you about the bright light he saw?' I feel she's evading my question.

She makes a *pah* sound. 'Aliens. Of course.' She gives a dismissive laugh. 'That was Ralph. Always believing in the paranormal and the supernatural.'

'Do you think he imagined it, then?'

'He must have done.' There's finality in her tone and, worried I'm losing her, I ask about the missing money.

She sits up straighter. 'Yeah. Petty cash went missing from

Tamzin's work. I think as soon as the police realized that they assumed Tamzin must have taken it and run away.'

'But it wasn't much by all accounts.'

'I know. And there was no proof to suggest Tamzin was the one who took it.'

'Wasn't she the one who dealt with the petty cash, though?'

'Well. Yes. But that doesn't mean she took it.'

'No,' I say. 'Of course not.'

Her cheeks are flushed. 'Tamzin wasn't a thief. She wouldn't have taken that money. I can't help but think someone else did that and blamed Tamzin. Someone, maybe, who knew she wasn't coming back.'

I stare at her in surprise. 'Like who?'

'That I don't know. Someone who worked with her, maybe.'

'And you don't think the three of them ran away?'

'There is no way that all three would just run away and never get in touch with anyone. Especially Sally. We were so close.' But she doesn't look very sure and her lips wobble as though she's trying to contain a deep betrayal. 'I don't understand why Ralph had those photos of me. It couldn't have been him who was following me. I mean, why? I don't get it.'

I pause, wanting to put my next question delicately. 'Did Ralph ever make you feel . . . like he was romantically interested in you? You . . . you were crying yesterday when you came out of the caravan.'

She looks appalled at the idea. 'Absolutely not! Ralph treated me like a little sister. He was never inappropriate. He never even flattered me, or commented on my appearance or anything. No. No way.' She looks down at her hands. They are calloused and dry. 'It was a stupid argument yesterday. I worried about him, that's all. He did too many drugs. Didn't look after himself. I thought he looked rough and I told him so. And he snapped at me and told me to mind my own business. It was – it was out of character for him to talk to me like that. He was usually so placid.' She clucks her tongue against her teeth. 'I don't understand why he'd have those photos. Why he took them and why – why he kept them. Did Dale show them to you?'

I nod. 'He's coming over later to be interviewed. He might still have them on him. I'm sure he'll want to talk to you about them anyway.'

'He's coming here?' She looks aghast at the thought of bumping into him. I remember her reaction at seeing us in the pub last night.

'Not for a while.'

'I'd heard he'd reopened the case.' She stares into the fire. The flames are dying down now.

'Yes. Apparently he's a bit of a hot-shot cold-case investigator.'

She presses her lips together. And then surprises me by saying, 'I wouldn't have thought that was very ethical.'

I'm confused. 'What do you mean?'

She angles her body towards me. 'He obviously hasn't told you, then. I wondered if he had.'

A cold sensation washes over me. 'Told me what?'

She flicks her hair away from her face, her eyes hard. 'That Tamzin was his girlfriend when she disappeared.'

30

'WHAT?' I SPLUTTER, ALMOST CHOKING ON MY TEA.

Olivia's face is serious as she folds her arm across her chest, although I can tell she's inwardly relishing this bombshell. 'Yes, they were totally loved up.'

'He told me that Tamzin and Katie were in his year at school, but he made it sound like he didn't know them that well. In fact, he said he was at university when your friends disappeared.'

'They managed to keep it going long distance while Dale was at Edinburgh uni.'

'Wow,' I say, feeling like I've been punched in the gut. I trusted Dale explicitly. I knew there were things about the case he wouldn't be allowed to tell me. But to keep this from me? Tamzin was his *girlfriend*. This is huge. He sat there in the pub last night and told me he hardly knew them. He lied to my face.

I get up to hide my shock. I think I've got everything I need for the podcast so I stop the recording. 'I need to open the wine. Do you fancy a glass?'

She looks how I feel. 'Actually, yes, I'd love one, thanks.'

I take our mugs and dump them in the sink, then crack open a bottle of Chablis that I'd brought from home. I pour two glasses, and knock mine back, then fill it again. The liquid is smooth and cold, and as it hits the back of my throat I feel instantly calmer. I carry our glasses to the living room and hand one to Olivia. She takes it gratefully. I notice how she knocks back a few large gulps too.

What else has Dale been evasive about? He was the one person I thought I could trust in this town. The betrayal feels out of proportion to how it should but I'm winded by it. Why would Dale not tell me about Tamzin? What is he trying to hide? 'Why do men always have to lie?' I blurt out.

'I gather we're not just talking about Dale here,' Olivia says astutely.

I hadn't realized I was thinking about Gavin. 'My husband moved out a few months ago. Says he wants space from our marriage but I don't think he's being truthful with me. Something's going on. I can just feel it, here.' I place my palm over my heart. I don't admit the other stuff, the things I've only recently admitted to myself. How I was so desperate to make our marriage work that I put aside my true feelings, my doubts about Gavin over the years. I saw my mum struggling to bring up me and my brother without my dad around. I saw how it affected Darren, how he went off the rails as a teenager, not having any male authority at home. I remember the years of uncertainty, and fear as my mum stayed up late worrying about what Darren was up to and which of his scummy mates he was dossing down with. Until I met Gavin and felt certain I'd found the security I'd always craved. I'd do things differently from my mum, I'd vowed when I got married. I'd provide a safe haven for Finn. A proper family with a mother and a father. How stupid of me. How naïve. Darren is married now with two brilliant kids of his own – I adore my niece and nephew. He could have gone off the rails even if my dad hadn't abandoned us as young kids but he sorted himself out when he grew up a bit and met Tracey.

Olivia is quiet for a while and then she says, almost under her breath, 'I feel the same. About Wes.'

'You think he's lying to you?'

She nods sadly, then tells me about the extra cash Wesley has been splashing. 'And he never seems to be at work. I'm surprised he hasn't been sacked for all the sickies he's taken lately.'

'What do you think he's up to?'

'I'm not sure. He's got a lot of undesirable mates. They could be up to anything.'

I inhale deeply. 'Do you think it could be something illegal?'

She picks at the corner of her jumper. 'I don't think so,' she says, into her lap, but she colours as she says it. What does she suspect?

'Dale told me that a large sum of money was found in Ralph's caravan.'

Olivia's head shoots up. 'Oh, my God.'

'Was Ralph involved in anything criminal, do you know? Drugs?'

Olivia takes another gulp of wine. 'I don't know. He does take drugs. *Did*.' She sighs. 'Mostly weed, although there were times when I'd turn up at his caravan and I could tell he was high on something. But . . .' she finishes off her wine and places the glass on the table '. . . I don't know much about drugs. I've had a very sheltered life.' She gives a sardonic little laugh but I can sense the sadness behind it. I offer her more wine. 'Just a bit,' she says. I get up to refill her glass, then sit down and do the same to mine.

'It must have been hard for you, being so badly injured at just eighteen,' I say, sipping my wine.

She nods. 'Wesley was great. He helped me a lot.'

There's something she's not saying. 'Are you . . . still happy with Wesley?' I wince when she looks shocked at my question. It was too personal, probably. Just because I like to overshare, it doesn't mean she will. 'Sorry, don't feel you have to answer that.'

'Can I ask you a personal question?' she says instead.

'Uh . . . sure . . .'

'Do you think you and your husband will get back together?' I play with my wine glass. 'I honestly don't know.'

She takes a sip of wine. 'Sometimes I'm not sure if I just stay with Wesley because I'm so used to him, that he's been around for so long, looking after me. Or whether I truly love him. You asked me if I was still happy with him? But it's relative, isn't it? Happiness. I don't know if I'm happy at all.'

She looks so heartbroken as she says it that I want to hug her. 'I'm so sorry,' I say again. 'But – and I know I'm not one to talk with my relationship in pieces – but don't feel you have to settle. Don't feel that this,' I throw my hands into the air, 'is all you deserve. Because you can change things, Olivia. If you want to.'

Her eyes widen in surprise. 'Thanks. I needed to hear that.' She flashes me a wide smile that shows off all her teeth. It's the first genuine smile I think she's given me. And I realize we're no longer interviewer and interviewee. We're just two people of the same age having a chat. And I realize I like her. There's something guileless about her. An honesty. We fall into a companionable silence, each sipping our wine, until she says, 'Wesley wants to move in with me. He wants us to buy a place together. And I . . .' she hesitates '. . . I don't want to. I can't explain why. It just doesn't feel right.'

We're interrupted by a knock on the door. It's nearly seven. It'll be Dale. Damn it. I'm tempted to cancel him, but I also want to ask him if he knew of Olivia's claim that the man following her had a facial scar. Not to mention why he kept the fact he was Tamzin's boyfriend from me.

I glance across at Olivia. She's trying to hide it by smiling but her whole body is tense. 'Is that Dale?'

'I think so. I'm sorry, I lost track of time. He'll have to wait while I run you home.' And then it hits me that I've had a few glasses of wine. What was I thinking? I'd been so swept up in our conversation that I forgot I was supposed to be driving Olivia home.

I get up to let Dale in. Olivia follows me and starts tugging on her boots. Dale has his scarf pulled up to his chin and his hands thrust into his pockets. I feel another thud of disappointment that he lied about Tamzin. Behind him the treetops are shaking in the wind.

'Hi,' he says, his hazel eyes softening. And then he notices Olivia behind me. 'Oh, hey, Olivia.'

'Dale.' She nods at him. 'I'm just going.' She takes her yellow raincoat from the peg and pulls it on.

It has started to rain, a faint drizzle that has settled on the shoulders of Dale's overcoat. I'm embarrassed to have to ask him to drive Olivia home. 'I'm so sorry,' I say to both of them. 'I didn't think when we started drinking.'

'Really, there's no need. I can get a taxi.'

'I'm happy to drive you,' insists Dale. He's still standing on the threshold and he takes his car keys out of his pocket. 'It's a horrible night out there and it'll take me ten minutes.'

'That's kind of you, Dale,' I admit grudgingly.

'No, please, it's fine,' Olivia says, looking mortified at the thought.

Dale holds up a hand. 'I wouldn't hear of you paying for a taxi.' He turns to me and grins. 'I'll be back soon. A strong coffee on my return would be appreciated.' He gives me a friendly wink.

And then he's ushering a clearly uncomfortable Olivia out of the door.

31

Olivia

IS IT HER IMAGINATION OR IS THERE A FLICKER OF SOME-thing, chemistry perhaps, between Dale and Jenna? She's sure he winked at her just now. She knows Jenna must be feeling vulnerable after her husband's rejection but she's only known him five minutes. Not that Olivia has much experience with men, only ever having been with Wesley.

Olivia decides it's none of her business as she thanks Jenna and follows Dale down the driveway. She stumbles on the uneven path and has to grab Dale's arm. 'Whoa,' he says. 'Are you okay?'

'No, it's badly lit out here,' she says, removing her hand from his arm, embarrassed.

'It's pretty bad,' he agrees. 'Mind your step here, there's a big stone.'

She treads carefully behind him, grateful when she gets to his car.

'So,' says Dale, as she closes the passenger door and reaches for her seatbelt. He starts the ignition but doesn't drive off. 'I'm surprised you agreed to talk to Jenna.'

'It was about time. I just hope something good comes out of it.'

He nods, just once, his eyes straight ahead. 'I'm glad. And I know I spoke to you already about Ralph but I'd like to have a more formal chat about the accident. Maybe tomorrow? I did leave a few messages with your mum.'

She's surprised to hear this. Her mum never said. 'I gave statements at the time. Do you really need to speak to me again?'

'I do, yes.' His tone is crisp now, official.

'Then, fine.'

Dale starts the car. Radio X blasts from the speakers and Dale turns it down. 'Sorry.' He grins. 'I have it much too loud when I'm driving on my own. My mum used to tell me I'd go deaf.'

Olivia is silent as Dale turns right out of the forest and onto the Devil's Corridor. She hates this road.

Eventually she says, 'Jenna told me about the photos you found in Ralph's caravan. Do you have them on you? I'd like to see them.'

His jaw tightens. 'I was going to talk to you about them when I saw you tomorrow.'

'I'd like to see them now, if possible.'

'Okay.' His mouth twists into a smile. 'I'll show them to you in a minute when I've stopped. So . . . what else did you and Jenna talk about?'

He's trying to sound nonchalant but she's not fooled. 'I told her you went out with Tamzin, if that's what you mean.' As soon as the words are out of her mouth she instantly regrets them. The mood in the car changes, and when he answers his voice sounds strange, as though his throat is constricted.

'Right.' There's that tone again. Officious. Tight.

She sneaks a glance at his profile. His mouth is set hard. She's always thought that Dale was good-looking in a grungy kind of way. Not conventionally handsome but he has sparkly hazel eyes and good hair, even if it's always unkempt. When he was going out with Tamzin he wore Adidas Samba trainers and retro T-shirts. It seems strange to see him so smartly dressed now. She almost expects him to have trainers on beneath his suit trousers.

There are no other vehicles on the road and she can't help but be reminded of that night twenty years ago. She grips the edges of the seat. She's never driven again, despite the doctors' assurances that using an automatic wouldn't put too much pressure on her left leg. It's had enough being a passenger. She'd rather walk or ride a horse, even though she knows it's completely irrational, considering how dangerous horse riding can be.

The atmosphere between them has turned and now she just wants to get out of the car. She shouldn't have told him. Had she done it to rile him? She suspects so. If she's honest with herself she's never really liked him. She knows Wesley is brash, and a lot of people find him arrogant, but he is what he is. What you see is what you get with Wesley – most of the time. Dale Crawford has always taken time, even back then, to hone and project a certain image to the world. One she felt was fake to his true self. She's aware that she might have formed this opinion because of Tamzin and the way he'd treated her, which wasn't great when he went off to university, or because after the accident she no longer trusted the police force. She might be being unfair to Dale. Either way she wants to get out of the car.

'You can just let me out here,' she says, as they drive into the high street.

To her relief he pulls over. 'Are you sure? I'm happy to drop you back at the stables.' And then he nods. 'Ah, you're staying with Wes tonight, then.'

Wesley's flat is only a few buildings along. Even though she's not planning on going there she grunts in what she hopes is a noncommittal way. She knows Dale and Wes dislike each other – they're as different as cat and mouse. She's just not sure which one is which.

He leans into her footwell and pulls his briefcase onto his lap to open it. 'Here,' he says, handing her an A4 sheet in a plastic wallet. 'They've been photocopied.'

She takes them from him, frowning at the photos, still shocked that they were found in Ralph's caravan. She looks so young, so carefree in them. So blissfully unaware of how suddenly her life would change. She remembers pulling into that petrol station. It was the day before the accident and she was filling up for the weekend. Had she felt watched while she was there? She can't recall. Although . . . another is also familiar. 'This,' she says, pointing to one in which she's walking a young mare, a strawberry roan that they'd only looked after for a short time, on a halter down a country lane towards a field. 'This is one of the places I remember seeing the man with the scar. He was sitting in a lay-by in his van, smoking a cigarette and just watching me. And then he got out and called to me.' It was the time she was telling Jenna about. 'He must have taken this photo.'

'You didn't see anyone with him? Nobody in the passenger seat?'

She thinks back. It was so long ago but, no, she's sure it was just one man in the van. 'He was alone. I'm sure of it.' Had Ralph been there too, in the vicinity? Was it just a coincidence? 'I wish I could remember more,' she says now, handing them back to him.

'If you do, please let me know. I'll see you tomorrow.'

'Thanks for the lift,' she says, getting out of the car. She watches as he pulls away from the kerb, and then she's alone. The high street is quiet, even though it's only seven fifteen in the evening. The Christmas lights strewn between telegraph poles flicker red and silver against the inky sky. She begins to walk, thrusting her hands into the pockets of her yellow raincoat. As she passes the pizzeria she notices a few tables are occupied in the window – one by a young couple she doesn't recognize and the other by Sally's mum and dad. Light spills onto the pavement and she presses her chin to her chest and hurries past before they spot her. She's near Wesley's flat and she rushes on, desperate to get home. She should have let Dale drive her all the way but being in that car with him made her feel claustrophobic. She turns left, down the side road and past The Raven – even that's quiet tonight. This is where the shops and houses fall away to countryside. Is it her imagination or can she hear footsteps behind her? She'd under-estimated how afraid she'd feel walking in the dark on her own, even though it's not late. It's not seven thirty yet. In her mind the journey on foot from the high street to the stables isn't far, but she's unused to walking it at night. She hadn't considered how intimidated she'd feel with the countryside pressing in on her from both sides, how the lack of streetlights would unnerve her, how her footsteps would echo so that it felt like someone was behind her.

But, no. It's not her imagination. Above the pounding of her heartbeat she can hear a heavy tread behind her, getting closer.

If something happened to her tonight – on the twentieth anniversary of the accident – there would be something almost poetic about it. Inevitable. And she realizes she's been waiting all her life for this moment.

Yet still she tenses as a hand clamps her shoulder.

Still she yells out.

But her voice is swallowed by the darkness.

32

Jenna

WHILE I'M WAITING FOR DALE TO RETURN I TIDY UP THE
wine glasses. I haven't eaten since the sandwich with Dale at
lunchtime, and the alcohol swims in my empty stomach. It's a
good job Dale offered to drive Olivia home. I inspect the cupboards, even though I know they're empty, wishing I'd picked up
some groceries at the Co-op in the high street. It doesn't escape
my notice that I'd prioritized booze and sweet things instead of
healthy food. I need to look after myself. I can't let my health fall
apart as well as my marriage. I've still got Finn to think about.
And this job. I need the money. I haven't even let myself consider
what I'd do if Gavin and I split up. Could I afford to keep the
house? I doubt it on my wages alone.

I sink back into the armchair, my head swimming. Dale's taking ages. The fire is still flickering in the hearth and it's making me

sleepy. I can barely keep my eyes open. I've been rushing around all day and have barely had time to stop, and those glasses of wine haven't helped. I need to be clear-headed to interview Dale. I'll just rest my head against the cushion while I wait.

I must have drifted off, because suddenly there is a loud knocking at the door. Shit. I glance at my watch. It's nearly eight fifteen. He said he'd be ten minutes taking Olivia home but he's been almost an hour.

He's standing in the doorway with a plastic carrier bag and the smell of vinegar and chips emanating from it makes my mouth water. 'Sorry. I stopped at the chippie. There was a queue. Thought you might need something to soak up that alcohol. It smells like a brewery in here.' He grins. 'I haven't eaten yet either.'

'Hey, I didn't drink that much.' I'm thrown. I want to stay annoyed at him for lying to me but I'm so grateful for the food that I can't help but soften towards him. 'Thanks, Dale. I'm starving.'

He takes out two foam boxes. 'Can you get some plates?' I do as he asks. 'Great, cheers,' he says, as he unloads battered cod and thick-cut chips from the cartons. 'I hope this is okay.'

'This is perfect.' I pick up a chip and stuff it into my mouth.

We carry our plates to the rustic oak dining-table and I get the cutlery from the drawer. Dale has taken his coat off already and he looks at home as he sits opposite me at the table, chomping his food. We eat in silence for a while, with just the sound of the rain hammering against the windows.

'So,' I begin. I have to say it now because even though I'm grateful for the food I'm still wondering why he lied about Tamzin. 'Tamzin. She was your girlfriend?'

He blushes. 'Olivia said she'd told you. I'm sorry I didn't mention it last night at the pub. I didn't want it to . . . uh . . . cloud things,' he says, through a mouthful of fish.

'Cloud things? I don't understand.'

'It's, well, it feels so personal.' He blushes. 'I wanted you to see me professionally. I didn't want you to think my judgement was impaired in any way.'

'I wouldn't have thought that.' But would I? Would I have looked at him differently? Would I have suspected him of being too emotionally involved?

'But you were open with me about Gavin,' he continues. 'I should have . . . well, I should have been more honest. Tamzin was my first serious girlfriend. We thought we were in love, but by the time I went to uni it had run its course. Tamzin and I hadn't seen each other for months before the accident. I'd been up in Edinburgh since September.' He shrugs. 'Anyway. We were kids.'

I watch him intently as myriad emotions pass across his face: guilt, embarrassment, grief. 'Does your boss know?'

He swallows a mouthful of fish. 'Yes. Full disclosure. Don't worry. I was never a suspect. I was in Edinburgh the night of the accident. I had an alibi and everything.'

'I'm sorry. It must have been an awful time. I can't even imagine . . .' I'm trying to put myself in his shoes.

The bravado falls away from Dale, like a cloak, and he transforms before my eyes into someone much more vulnerable. More real. 'It's – it's what made me want to become a detective,' he says quietly. He lowers his fork. 'It seemed so unfathomable to me that someone could just vanish like that.'

I reach out and touch his arm. Our eyes meet and something passes between us. It's so fleeting that I wonder if I've imagined it.

I look away first, get up and clear our plates. 'Right. We should get on with the interview,' I say briskly. 'Coffee?'

'Please.' His voice is lighter again now he's back in the role of detective.

We take our coffees and move to the living room. I set up my phone again. I can feel Dale's eyes on me as I busy myself with my equipment. Maybe the wine has gone to my head but I feel as though something has shifted between us and I don't know how or when it happened.

'I'll just start recording. I'll piece it all together with introductions during the editing stages, okay?'

Dale leans back against the sofa, cupping his coffee, and laughs. 'I have no idea how to make a podcast so, whatever you're doing, I'm impressed.'

I prop the cushion behind me on the armchair. 'Can I ask you about Ralph Middleton? Do you think his death is linked to what happened to Olivia's friends back in 1998?'

'We're keeping an open mind at the moment.'

'Ralph was killed after talking to me yesterday, you said around five thirty. That's just an hour after I left him. Do you think someone was worried he'd talk to me? Tell me something?'

'It's possible,' says Dale, frowning. 'And some of the evidence found at the scene does link Ralph to Olivia's accident back in 1998.'

I let Dale fill in the listeners on the photographs. When he's finished I ask him to recap the cause of death, which he does. 'The pathologist report said his death was caused by a blunt instrument to the back of his head. Drugs were also found in his body.'

'Weed?'

'No. Harder than that. Crack cocaine.'

I'm surprised by this and wonder if that's where he got all the money from. 'Do you think he was a dealer?'

'I really don't know,' says Dale, his eyes flickering to my phone. But I sense there's something he's not telling me.

'Olivia said that the man who had been following her in the white van had a scar on his face. That doesn't fit Ralph's description.'

'Ah, yes. The man with the scar.' He sounds disparaging.

I raise an eyebrow. 'You knew about it?'

'Yes. It was in one of Olivia's original statements.'

'She said she kept seeing him, though. On more than one occasion.'

'Yet the photos were found in Ralph's caravan.' He folds his arms across his chest. 'And the man with the scar in the white van was never found. Or ever seen again.'

'Do you think she imagined him or made him up?'

He sits up. 'Look, I don't know about that. She obviously believes that's what she saw.'

'But you don't?' I press.

A flicker of irritation passes across Dale's face. 'I didn't say that. We had to run with what we had. And we had no evidence of this white van or a man with a scar. No other witnesses.' He holds his hands up. 'What more can I say?' His expression softens. 'Memories can be muddled, especially after a serious accident like Olivia experienced. And now, with these photos found in Ralph's caravan . . . well . . .' he sighs '. . . it shines a new light on things.'

Maybe he's right. It's strange that no one else ever saw him.

We talk a bit longer and I ask him more questions, but Olivia has already covered a lot of it. I stop recording and Dale finishes his coffee.

'Sorry to go on about the man with the scar,' I say. 'Olivia was adamant about it when I spoke to her.'

'She mentioned it to me in the car too, when I showed her the photos,' he concedes. 'But it makes no sense.' He gets up and takes his mug to the sink, then stands with his back to the counter, his ankles crossed. He has another pair of funky animal socks on, black with pink flamingos. He sees me looking. 'An old girlfriend bought them for me.' He laughs. 'They're very comfy.'

'They look it.'

He holds my gaze for a fraction too long, then says, 'I'm sorry it wasn't the best interview. There's still a lot I can't say. Things that cross over with –'

'Another case. Yes, you've said. You're just a big tease!' My cheeks grow hot when I realize what I've said.

He lets out a throaty laugh. 'I'm sorry, I know it's frustrating. When I can say more I will.'

I'm tempted to push him but I need to keep Dale onside. We spend another ten minutes just talking about Stafferbury, his memories of the town before he left for university, and Tamzin.

'Did you know Olivia that well?' I ask, as we walk to the front door and he starts pulling on his coat. 'No bullshit now. Not like last night.'

'Hey, it wasn't all bullshit. I really didn't know Tamzin's mates that well. Sometimes I'd go to the pub and Tamzin would be there – usually with Katie, Sally and Olivia. Occasionally we'd all sit together and play drinking games. Olivia was probably the quietest but Tamzin could be quite loud.' He wraps his scarf around his neck and tugs at the ends. He pauses, his hand on the door knob. 'I never thought I'd be here twenty years later still with no clue as to what happened to them.'

I smile in sympathy. I wonder if it's shaped him, Tamzin's disappearance. I can't imagine my first love going missing. Although my first love was Gavin. And in some ways it feels like he is missing because he's definitely not the person I fell in love with. I don't know who he is any more.

'It haunts me sometimes,' he says, so quietly I can hardly hear him. 'Wondering if she was in some kind of trouble. That maybe if I hadn't gone to university she'd still be here.'

'You can't blame yourself, Dale. You were young too.'

'Guilt. Regret. Ugh.' He shakes his head. 'Why do we beat ourselves up?'

'I know that feeling. Gavin leaves me and I'm the one wondering what I did wrong.' Our eyes meet and there is a definite charge in the air between us. It makes me catch my breath. He opens his mouth to say something but seems to think better of it. 'I . . .' He clears his throat. 'Well, I should go. Make sure my dad isn't being led astray by Doris next door. She's definitely got the hots for him.'

I laugh and our hands brush as I reach for the door handle and open it. A gust of wind blows in just as Dale is about to walk onto the step. And that's when I see it.

'Stop!' I cry, grabbing his arm and pulling him back.

'What? I don't –' And then he notices it too.

Laid out on the concrete step are three dead crows, their necks bent at odd angles as though someone had deliberately laid them there.

And I know there's no mistaking it this time. It's a warning.

33

Ornaments

SPREAD OUT ON THE STARCHY WHITE SHEETS OF DERRECK'S four-poster bed Stace saw a cluster of seven or eight Buddha heads, made of smooth mahogany. Not the chubby-cheeked Buddhas she was used to seeing, but sharp-chinned and prominent-nosed. Regal. She could sense John-Paul's presence behind her, his hot breath on the back of her neck. To her left stood Griff, Trevor and Martin. Identical stance: arms folded, feet shoulder-width apart.

They had been there four days now and in all that time she felt John-Paul was doing everything to avoid being alone with her. When Derreck took them out to show them the sights he would fall into step beside her, informing her about the giant Golden Buddha or the Royal Palace, while John-Paul hung back with Griff and Trev. Despite her doubts about Derreck she couldn't deny she found him interesting and knowledgeable as well as handsome.

Now Derreck stood over the Buddhas, a serious note in his voice as he relayed again what he wanted them all to do.

'Nah. I'm out. Mags doesn't approve,' said Martin, stepping back. 'She's too law-abiding.'

Stace noticed Griff and Trevor exchange glances. 'Too much of a risk, mate,' added Griff. Which surprised Stace. She knew he'd bought stolen goods in the pub even though she acknowledged that was less dangerous.

'Yeah,' agreed Trevor. 'I don't fancy ending up in a Thai jail. Brutal apparently.'

Derreck laughed in that cocksure way of his. 'You won't end up in any jail. It's just a few ornaments. The most you'll get if you're caught is a fine.' He turned his eyes to her and John-Paul. 'My mate can't risk applying for a special licence because he knows he's likely to get turned down. They're even more strict if the Buddhas aren't in their true, whole form and . . .' he indicated where they lay, macabre without their bodies '. . . well, look at them.'

The other lads shuffled from the room muttering apologies and excuses, and Stace was tempted to do the same. But something held her back. Was it the money? Or was it the hold she felt Derreck had over John-Paul? He had been so excited when he first told her about their trip but now he walked around as though he had a death sentence hanging over him. For the past two nights, unable to sleep, she'd found herself walking down to the terrace and sitting beside Derreck on the sun-loungers, drinking Coke and talking about everything: books they loved – Derreck was surprisingly well read, like her, whereas John-Paul was not – and films. The only subject that appeared to be off limits was John-Paul. Maybe if they did this for the money things might be good between her and John-Paul again. If he didn't find a job soon he'd have no choice but to leave town.

But she knew it was more than that. She wanted to do this for Derreck, to make him happy, to make his startling blue eyes shine.

Stace walked over to the bed and picked up one of the ornaments, turning it over in her hand. Was she being naïve? Was this more than just a couple of Buddhas? She examined the head for signs that it had been stuffed with something, like money or drugs. But the lines were smooth: no plugs or holes. They felt weighty in her hands too, good quality. Solid wood. 'I'd be willing to take one or two but no more.' She could feel Derreck's eyes on her as she sat on the edge of the bed with the heavy object in her hands. She experienced a little thrill when his whole face lit up.

'That's great,' he said, rushing over to her and pulling her into a hug. It was awkward because she was sitting down, but being so near to him was intoxicating. He smelt of lemon-scented laundry and summer days, chlorine and coconut oil, and her stomach swooped. She laughed to hide her embarrassment and desire, pushing him playfully away. 'All right. I'm only doing it for the money.' Even though she knew it wasn't strictly true.

Derreck laughed too, then straightened, turning to John-Paul. 'JP? What about you?'

'If Stace is okay with it then why not?' he said miserably. 'But we'll only take one each. If we take any more it'll be harder to play the innocent tourist card if we're caught.'

The elation Derreck had exhibited only moments before ebbed away, like the sand running out of a timer. 'Ah, well, actually that's a bit problematic. My mate will pay well but only if they're all taken back to England. All eight of them. They're worth quite a bit of money but not enough on their own to make it worthwhile. So . . .' He eyed the door where Griff, Trevor and Martin had made a hasty exit. 'You'll need to convince your mates. If you all take one each there's a lot of money in it. They might not look much, but these ornaments are antique – my mate's contact back in the UK is willing to pay big bucks for them.'

And that was when Stace's suspicions were confirmed. This was the reason they had been invited on this trip. Eight friends. Eight Buddhas. Job done.

34

Olivia

OLIVIA'S HEAD IS GROGGY. SHE CAN'T WORK OUT WHERE SHE is and why she's so cold. The air smells of wet soil and something else, a kind of incense. Like someone has been burning joss sticks. Has she stumbled on some kind of ritual? Dampness seeps through her jodhpurs and her back is resting against something hard. She's sitting on grass. She blinks as her eyes adjust to the darkness surrounding her and it dawns on her where she is. She's at the standing stones. What is she doing here? The last thing she remembers is walking home alone. She knows she had a bit to drink at Jenna's but not enough to black out. So how has she ended up here?

She struggles to her feet, holding on to the large stone she's been slumped against. She can just about see the reassuring glow of the lampposts in the high street up ahead although the Christmas lights have been switched off. It must be late. An icy shard pierces her heart. She remembers being afraid. That someone was following her. A hand on her shoulder, the scream stuck in her throat. She spins around, suddenly terrified. Is that person here now? Did they bring her here to . . . What? Abduct her? Murder her? Use her as a sacrifice? She needs to get away. She needs to get out of this field right now. She stumbles forwards. Her head is still woozy but she tries to run as best she can, slipping on the wet grass, her boots heavy, slowing her down. She's always hated this place – the eerie atmosphere. She darts between the stones: she half expects someone to leap out from behind one. There is no clear path out of this field and the darkness makes her feel disoriented. She focuses on the streetlights ahead. She just needs to get herself over the stile and then she'll be out of here. She just needs to . . .

And then she sees him. Blocking her path. A figure, tall, hooded. Just like that night. He's come back, this phantom, this ghoul, to take her this time. She screams and falls to her knees. No, no, this can't be happening. She hangs her head, covering her ears with her hands. No, no, no, no.

'Olivia?'

His hands are on her shoulders, heavy as though he's trying to push her into the ground, into the soil, to bury her.

She keeps screaming, and struggling.

'Olivia. Stop. Stop. It's me. It's me.'

She recognizes the voice and stops thrashing around. She lifts her head. A man is staring down at her, familiar hazel eyes, messy hair. It's Dale. Why is he here? Has he been following her since he dropped her off? She moves away from him. Was he the one who brought her here?

'Leave me alone,' she cries. She doesn't trust him. She knows he's a policeman but he lied to Jenna about Tamzin. And she's watched *Line of Duty*. She knows not all policemen are good people.

'Let me help you up,' he says, coming towards her, but she inches backwards on her heels. 'Olivia, I'm not going to hurt you. Please trust me.' He holds out a hand but she doesn't take it. 'I was driving through the high street and I saw you – well, obviously I didn't know it was you. I could just see someone stumbling about. It was your bright coat. Look, my car is just there, on the other side of the stile.'

She stares at him, still confused. 'What time is it?'

'It's nearly a quarter to ten.'

How has she lost the last two hours? She feels frightened and starts to shake, blinking back tears. 'I don't know how I got here,' she mumbles. 'I was walking home after you dropped me off and someone was following me and then the next thing I know I wake up here.'

He retracts his hand and offers his arm instead. She wavers. Can she trust him? She has no choice right now. So she takes it and allows him to help her over the stile and out onto the road. 'I should have made sure to drop you home. You said you were going to Wesley's. What happened? Did you have a row?'

She shakes her head. The movement hurts. 'No, I changed my mind at the last minute.' Wesley. She should have gone to see him after Dale dropped her off. She was stupid to be walking home alone, tonight of all nights. The lights in his flat are still on. Suddenly she wants nothing more than to be with him. To be with someone reassuring, whom she trusts. Dale might be helping her now but she certainly doesn't trust him.

He lets her climb over the stile first and as soon as her feet touch the pavement she crosses the road and heads for Wesley's flat without waiting for him. 'Olivia?' he calls, crossing the road after her, confusion in his voice.

'I'll be fine now, thanks, Dale,' she replies, banging on Wesley's front door. Dale stands on the pavement a hundred yards away, hands on his hips, watching her.

Wesley answers the door, reeling in surprise when he sees it's her. 'Liv? What are you doing here?' He glances past her to Dale and then back at her, his eyes searching her face. 'What's going on?'

'Can I come in?'

'Of course.' He widens the door and she experiences such a rush of relief to be in familiar surroundings that she feels weak. She collapses on the bottom step of his stairs. He shuts the door and turns to look at her. 'My God, are you okay?'

'Oh, Wes, I don't know what happened. I think . . . I think someone attacked me.'

'What?' He looks horrified. 'What do you mean? Are you hurt?'

'No, I think I'm fine. I just don't understand what happened.' She bursts into tears. He rushes over to her and wraps her in his arms. 'I'm so sorry for being a bitch to you earlier,' she cries, onto the shoulder of his hoody. 'I don't know what's going on with me at the moment.'

'Come on, silly,' he says, helping her up the stairs. 'It's okay. You're safe with me now.' He steers her through the door and onto the ugly leather sofa she's always hated but now it feels like a lifeboat. 'Let me get you a cup of tea. Do you want to stay here tonight?'

She nods gratefully. 'I'd better let Mum know.'

'I'll let Ana know, don't worry.'

She's shivering so much her teeth are chattering. Wesley fetches her a blanket. He doesn't quiz her on what happened but patiently makes her a cup of tea with extra sugar and taps out a text to her mum. All the doubts she's had about Wesley over the last few weeks vanish. He might not be perfect, she knows she certainly isn't, but he's always had her best interests at heart.

'Jenna said she was attacked in the forest last night too.' Olivia wipes her nose – her hands are so cold. 'Was it the same person who did this to me?'

Wesley places his phone on the table, then reaches over and tucks the blanket in around her knees. This would usually annoy her and make her feel he was fussing but now she's grateful for it. It makes her feel loved. Would moving in with Wesley really be the worst thing? she wonders. She can't live with her mum for ever. She needs to grow up.

He takes her hand and then his face darkens. 'What did you just say about Jenna? When were you speaking to her?'

Too late she sees her mistake. 'Oh, I . . . um . . . I heard someone talking about it, in the Co-op,' she lies. She doesn't want to tell him about the interview. Not yet. She knows he'll get angry.

'What happened, Liv? You're shaking and your hands are freezing.'

She tells him about walking home and the feeling she had that she was being followed. When she's finished, he says, 'Do you think you'd just had too much to drink and then ended up . . . I don't know . . . stumbling towards the standing stones? And maybe blacking out for a bit? You're not used to drinking.'

'I was sure I was being followed, though.'

He squeezes her hand gently. 'Maybe you freaked yourself out.' He frowns at her as it dawns on him. 'Why were you walking alone anyway? I thought you were seeing a friend?'

'It was only a quick drink . . .'

'So why were you with Dale?' His voice is laced with suspicion.

'He found me at the stones.' She explains it all. He's quiet as she speaks and she can see the disbelief in his eyes.

'Has something happened with you and Dale?'

'What?' She can't believe it.

He stands up and begins pacing. 'Let me rephrase that. Is Dale the friend you were out drinking with tonight? Are you fucking him, Liv?'

She thinks she's going to be sick. 'After everything I've been through tonight and you think . . . you think I'm cheating on you? And with him?' She can feel herself getting hysterical. He must believe her because he suddenly backs down, going to her and wrapping her in his arms and kissing the top of her head, like a father who regrets shouting at his child.

'I'm sorry. Just seeing you two together, it made me feel so – so jealous, and I know we haven't been getting on. You've been so emotionally unbalanced lately.' He's rocking her as he speaks to her and she's so exhausted, so frightened by whatever happened to her tonight that she hasn't the energy to protest. She lets him lead her to bed and tuck her up still clothed in her jodhpurs and jumper. She can barely keep her eyes open – she's utterly exhausted. She falls asleep to the melodic tones of Wesley stroking the hair away from her face and telling her how much he loves her and how much she needs him.

35

Jenna

DALE HAD WANTED TO STAY WHEN WE FOUND THE DEAD
birds and I was so tempted to let him sleep in the spare room
again. The last thing I want is to be in the cabin alone. But I
couldn't let him. There has been a subtle shift in our dynamics –
a lingering look, the brush of his hand on my back, the wink. I
might be separated but I feel very much a married woman, and
even though I can't deny I find Dale attractive, I don't want him
to get the wrong idea. Or maybe I don't trust myself. I don't know.

Dale had looked disappointed when I told him I'd be okay
by myself but he'd made me promise to ring him if I was worried, 'whatever time it is. I'm only at my dad's so I'm not far away.'
I'm grateful to him. He's made my stay in Stafferbury much more
bearable and I know he's been kind to me.

I've double-locked the front door and made myself another
cup of tea. I reassure myself with the knowledge that nobody can

get in. If the worst they can do is leave dead animal carcasses outside then so be it. The curtains are closed too, which gives me a safe, cocooned feeling. I throw another log onto the fire and sit next to it, stoking it with the metal poker. Then I sit on the sofa, the sheepskin covering my legs and my phone in my lap.

One thing I've realized is that I've been living in limbo these last four months. It's not fair of Gavin to keep me hanging like this. I don't know if it's the wine, or being away from Manchester, but for the first time I wonder if I'm letting Gavin walk over me like I see Wesley walk over Olivia.

Before I lose my nerve I pick up my mobile, adrenalin coursing through me. I need to do it. I need to confront Gavin. It's time. I haven't spoken to him properly for weeks – most of the childcare arrangements are made through my mum, like she's our very own negotiator.

I check the time. It's nearly ten. Gavin never goes to bed before midnight. He's one of those people who try to drain every last moment of the day before giving in to sleep. Most nights, especially since Finn, I'd go up to bed first and be asleep by the time he crawled in beside me, usually gone 2 a.m. The only time he would ever come to bed early was when he wanted sex. And over the last year that had become less and less frequent.

Still, the phone rings and rings. I picture him sitting up watching football or some documentary on TV, his mobile on the arm of the sofa, seeing my name flashing up and ignoring it. But just when I think it will ring out or go to voicemail I hear his voice at the other end of the line, gruff, familiar, and my heart tugs.

'Jenna? Is everything okay?'

'I'm fine,' I say. 'I just . . . I thought we should have a chat.'

'What? Now?'

'It's been four months, Gav. I've given you your space but I need to know. I can't keep on in this – this kind of limbo.'

'Have you been drinking?' I hear the touch of disapproval in his voice.

'Only a few glasses. I'm working. I'm not on a jolly.'

There's an awkward pause. Then he says, 'We do need to chat. You're right. Maybe when you get back we should talk. Are you back Friday?'

'I hope so, yes.'

'You hope so?' He has that same irritability in his voice, like every word I utter annoys him. Now I think about it that's the way he's been with me for a while – months before he announced he needed a break.

I swallow. 'Well, it's a bit complicated, really. The story I'm covering has taken a bit of a turn. A man has been murdered.'

'What?'

'A local man. I don't know if it's linked but he was involved in the case I'm working on so it could be important. Anyway, Friday should still be fine. I'm just thinking out loud.' I miss talking to him, about work, about our ambitions and dreams. He doesn't even know much about the podcast, how big a deal it is for me to be allowed to do it, to go from writing press releases part-time to undertaking something like this, being taken seriously for probably the first time since I went on maternity leave back in 2008.

But then my job always did take a back seat to his. It was understandable, him being the bigger earner, but he never knew how small it made me feel at times, how unimportant. He never appreciated how much I had to juggle, and when I complained he'd throw in a comment like 'Well, you wanted to go back to work.' As if our son was my responsibility, not his, and that it was down to me and me alone to make a success of working and raising a child.

'Right. Well, I hope you're being careful,' he says curtly, and I wonder how it got to this. How *we'd* got to this. What had happened to us, to the fun, young, free-and-easy couple we once were before resentment started to set in, the bickering about who did the most around the house, who was busier, more stressed, like it was a competition? Where were the couple who laughed at the same jokes, who snuggled in front of the TV to watch reruns of *Frasier*, who went to gigs together? Where was the man who used to love me so much that when I was pregnant he treated me like a princess and wouldn't let me lift a finger, as if I was made of precious stone? Where had the warm, loving, kind, fun Gavin gone? The man talking to me now is like a stranger. Had the cracks started to show after we had Finn? Had I transferred all the love I'd bestowed on Gavin to my son instead? Had our love been slowly draining away, like a leaky tap, for the last ten years?

A tear seeps down my cheek and the heaviness on my chest intensifies so much that I can't speak for a few seconds. I move the phone away from my ear and suppress a sob. I don't want him to know I'm crying.

'. . . can discuss all this when we see each other face to face,' he's saying, when I return the phone to my ear.

'Yep,' I say, trying to sound brisk.

'And if you're delayed on Friday I need to know. I'm . . .' He sounds uncomfortable. 'Well, I've made plans on Saturday.' I think about the woman's laugh I heard. But I can't bring myself to ask him because I'm too scared of the answer.

'Mum can look after Finn for the weekend if I'm stuck here, don't worry, but I think I'll be home on Friday.'

'Right, well, Gloria's done a lot for us.'

More than your own mother, I want to say, but don't. The subject of his parents and the fact I've always felt they looked down on me has been a contentious issue over the years so I've avoided it. And the truth is, I don't care if Sidney and Cassandra like me or not. I just wish they were better grandparents to Finn. As it is they spend all their time with Gavin's sister, Marcie, and her three kids, only seeing Finn on special occasions and for the odd Sunday lunch at their big, pristine house where Finn and I feel too scared to touch anything. Saying that, though, I do like Marcie and her adorable children, and if we end up splitting I hope she'll still want to be my friend.

'Are you still there?'

Gavin's been talking and I've zoned out. I blink, trying to gather my thoughts. 'I'm still here,' I say quietly.

He sighs. And then he says softly, 'I'm sorry, Jen.'

'For what?'

'For all of this. For the disruption. For splitting our family up.'

The tears are back. The end of a marriage – because that is what it is, I can't delude myself any more – feels like a death. 'I'm sorry too.'

'People change,' he says. 'I've changed.'

'I know. Me too.' And perhaps that's the problem: we don't much like the person the other has changed into.

He clears his throat. 'Anyway. We can talk properly when you get back. And, Jenna . . .'

I nod even though he can't see me.

'Look after yourself, won't you? Don't do anything stupid. If there is a murderer on the loose . . .'

'I'm fine. Don't worry.'

'Well, bye, then.'

'Bye.'

I hear him breathing for a few seconds at the other end of the line, both of us connected, each not wanting to be the first to put the phone down, just like it used to be at the beginning.

I end the call first and then I burst into tears.

I go and wash my face, splashing away the tears. I have to pull myself together and put thoughts of Gavin to the side for now and concentrate on why I'm here. I get undressed, go back into the living room and make myself a hot chocolate. The fire is almost dying now. I'll sit until it's burnt itself out. I'm in no hurry to go to bed. For some reason I feel safer sitting here, with all the lights on and my phone within reach.

I glance towards the fireplace, deep in thought, and then my eye lands on a piece of paper resting near the grate, not yet burnt but curling at the edges. I get up, then kneel down at the hearth. The flames have engulfed most of the writing but I can just make out the last two words: BE NEXT. It was the note from my car. I'd left it on the counter, by the laptop, under the book I was reading. How did it get into the fireplace?

It must have been Dale or Olivia. But which one? And why?

36

Olivia

WHEN OLIVIA WAKES UP SHE NOTICES THAT WESLEY ISN'T in bed with her although the room is dark. She leans over for her phone to check the time. It's just gone midnight. She's been asleep for less than two hours.

The euphoria she'd initially felt after arriving at Wesley's flat, knowing she was safe, has dissipated and now she just feels deflated. She has a banging headache too. She's never been a big drinker but she had a few glasses of wine. Not enough to induce this strange sensation inside her, surely. Her leg also aches, more than usual. She reaches down and touches it. She's still wearing her jodhpurs but she can feel a bump. She peels back the duvet and shines the light from her mobile onto it. There is a hole in her jodhpurs and when she pulls them down she can see a bruise on her thigh. It looks almost like an injection site: a spot of red in the middle and a faint bruise fanning out around it. Was she drugged? It would explain how she'd blacked out, the wooziness. She's never taken drugs in her life so doesn't know how she'd feel but she imagines it's how she feels now. She swings her legs out of bed and stands up, groping around her for the light switch, her panic increasing. What the hell happened to her? And where is Wesley? She presses the switch and the room is flooded with light. She wonders if he's in the bathroom but a quick check shows he's not there either. He's gone out. She can't believe it. After everything she's been through tonight he's just left her in the flat by herself.

Her fingers tremble as she scrolls down to his number. A phone on Wesley's bedside table pulsates, on silent. She grabs it and sees her own number flashing up. What the fuck? Her mind is racing. Why would Wesley go out and leave his phone? She slumps onto the bed, her mobile in one hand and his in the other. She tosses hers angrily aside – it lands with a thump on the duvet – and concentrates on getting into Wesley's. But he has a passcode and even though she tries three combinations none is right and it won't let her in. In frustration she replaces his on the pine nightstand. What is going on? Wesley always has his phone attached to him. Unless . . . She goes to the window and pulls aside the ugly brown curtains. She has a view of the high street but it's empty. Has he got another phone? She gulps. She's heard of burner phones, has seen them used in crime dramas on TV. Maybe he's cheating on her after all and uses a different phone to call his other girlfriend. No. No, she's being paranoid. He's probably popped out to get some milk or something at the all-night petrol station and forgot his phone. Nothing more sinister than that.

The light is too bright, one of those cheap paper lanterns that was once white and has yellowed with age. Olivia stands up and flicks the switch so that she is plunged back into darkness. It feels symbolic somehow. Isn't she always the one left in the dark? She continues to sit on the arm of the sofa, with the curtains not quite closed, a chink of muted night sky reflecting on her thigh. She doesn't want to go back to bed until Wesley gets home.

She can hear the far-off wails of an ambulance and she's reminded again of that night twenty years ago. They would still have been in the club on this day in 1998 with no clue of how their lives were about to change. Unless the others knew? And planned to leave her behind.

It had been such a strange time after the accident. She'd been so ill, so worried about her leg and not knowing if she'd ever walk again that those first few months after her friends vanished had gone by in a blur. But something else had made her reluctant to look back on the hours before they went missing. Guilt. Because in the club that night, at approximately this time, Olivia had been thinking bad thoughts.

It had been a normal Saturday night out with the girls. Sally was excited about Mal, the boy she fancied and who, she felt, was close to asking her out. And Tamzin and Katie were on a mission to get drunk. Did Tamzin flash the cash a bit more than usual? Olivia couldn't remember. They did leave the club earlier than they normally would, she recalls that much, and even though Katie and Tamzin had argued they'd seemed fine with each other on the drive home. She has an image of Tamzin staggering over to where Olivia had been standing at the bar by herself while Sally was snogging Mal, and Katie was dancing with a group of strangers. She'd been feeling melancholy, nursing her one glass of wine while the Chemical Brothers boomed overhead, thinking of Wesley and how she wished he'd been there and she'd felt a little – she feels bad for this now – resentful towards Sally for her obvious hostility towards him. She'd been worrying about how her relationship with Wesley was going to work if her best friend couldn't stand her boyfriend. And she'd also felt a twinge of jealousy, as Sally tossed her glossy dark mane back over her shoulder while she snogged and flirted with Mal, that boys seemed to fall at her feet and Olivia had been Wesley's second choice.

'Mate,' Tamzin had said, slinging an arm around Olivia's shoulders, 'don't let me drink too much tonight. I have a booty call.'

'A booty call?'

She'd put her finger to her lips and tried to make a shushing sound, although her hand kept moving away from her face because she was so unsteady on her feet. She gave up and sank onto a bar stool instead.

Who had Tamzin been planning on meeting up with? Olivia shakes her head trying to remember more clearly. Has she remembered this before? She's never really allowed herself to examine that night in forensic detail because it was too painful and, after months in hospital undergoing multiple operations, she had been woozy with morphine. Is she now imagining that conversation with Tamzin? That's the problem with memory. Especially after twenty years. How can you be sure of what is true and what your mind has made up? Looking back at that night is like trying to watch an old VHS movie that's been played too many times so that part of the tape is worn away.

A movement – a flash of clothing – in the field opposite brings her back to the present. She opens the curtains wider, her heart picking up speed. Is it Wesley? But, no, the gait is wrong. This person is tall and wiry. He's climbing over the stile and steps down onto the pavement, his face illuminated by the streetlight. She stiffens in surprise. It's Dale. What is he doing by the stones at this time of night? Subconsciously she touches the spot on her thigh where the bruise is forming. Dale had found her but had he been the one to take her there in the first place? Had he drugged her? No: that makes no sense. Why would he do that to her? *To punish you for telling Jenna about Tamzin.* She pushes away the thought. It's ridiculous. Dale wouldn't do that. He had his own reasons for not disclosing to Jenna that he'd been Tamzin's boyfriend the night she went missing. Unless . . . Her thoughts begin to run away with her. A booty call. That was what Tamzin had said. Who was she going to meet? Could it have been Dale? Had he lied about being away from Stafferbury? Who would have checked? He hadn't been a suspect, had he?

The sound of a key in the lock makes her jump off the sofa. Wesley's back. Had he gone out to meet Dale? She contemplates getting back into bed and pretending to be asleep, but no. She won't. She's going to confront him. She stands in the middle of the room in the dark. He doesn't notice her at first. He's carrying what looks like a shoebox, which he sets down on the kitchen counter. He does everything quietly, like he's in a mime show.

She waits, watching him as he places his keys gently on top of the box and slips off his trainers. And then he takes something from the inside of his coat pocket. It lights up in his hand and her heart sinks. It's a phone. So he does have two. She can't believe he still hasn't noticed her standing there. He opens the cupboard above the fridge, which he knows she finds hard to reach, then slips the box and the phone into it. While his back is turned she makes a decision. She'll go back to bed and pretend to have been asleep. He'll only lie if she confronts him. Or get nasty. Or blame her for being paranoid. This way he won't know she's seen where he's put the box. She can snoop tomorrow.

He turns just as she's getting into bed. She pretends to be stretching in sleep, squeezing her eyes tightly shut, but she senses him walking over to her. 'Liv?' he says quietly, stroking back her hair, the bed dipping under his weight. 'Are you awake?'

She makes a groaning noise but doesn't open her eyes. Let him think she's still out of it. She'll confront him when she knows more about what she's dealing with. She feels him sliding into bed, his back to her. It's not long before he begins to snore. She'll wait until he's gone to work in the morning and then she'll see what he's up to. Her phone next to her flashes, briefly lighting up her corner of the room. She tenses, wondering if Wesley will notice, but he doesn't stir. She reaches for her mobile. Who would be texting at this time of night?

It's from her mum. She opens it, and as her eye sweeps over the sentence, her blood runs cold. It's just one line. Something she thought her mother would never say.

We need to talk about your father.

37

Jenna

I'VE NOT BEEN ABLE TO SLEEP SINCE I SAW THE NOTE IN THE fireplace. Only two people were here tonight, Dale and Olivia. One of them must have thrown the note away. I think of how Dale helped me earlier, offering to drive Olivia home for me and bringing me fish and chips. It was kind of him. But now I'm wondering if he had an ulterior motive. Could he have taken the note when he was preparing the plates and cutlery? Or was it already gone by then? Had Olivia found it when I was in the toilet and tried to dispose of it? I frown and turn over in bed, feeling frustrated.

Suddenly I hear a noise, like a car door banging. I jump out of bed and grab my dressing-gown, wrapping it around myself as I pull aside my curtains. It's dark outside with just the outline of the trees in the distance. Even the little lights in the branches opposite have been turned off. I take a deep breath, trying to calm down. I must have dreamt it. It's nothing. I'm about to turn and go back to bed when I hear a bark, then see movement. It looks like two shadows moving as one, and as I blink, trying to adjust to the dark, I see that they're in the shape of a man and a dog. A big dog. Like a German Shepherd. My heart races as I watch. They're moving towards the cabin opposite and it's not my imagination: a light is flickering beyond the narrow rectangular window. I'm convinced it's the man I saw when I first arrived although it's too dark to tell. I'm not sure if he's alone. Is someone waiting inside for him to return? I check the time on my mobile. It's gone midnight. I contemplate trying to take a photo but it's too dark so I scroll through my contacts until I get to Dale's number. And then I hesitate. Can I trust him? I shake my head, angry with myself. I have to trust him. He's a detective. He's a good guy. And I have no choice.

He picks up immediately. 'Hey,' he says, his voice soft. 'Are you okay?'

'The man I was telling you about? The one with the German Shepherd? He's back,' I blurt out. 'I can see him now. He's going into the cabin opposite.'

'Okay, I'm coming over.' He ends the call and I keep watch at the window. The man is going into the cabin now but as he does so he turns to look towards me. He's wearing a hooded coat, but even if he wasn't, he's too far away for me to distinguish his features. I close the curtains and wrap my arms around my body feeling chilled to the bone. Is that the person responsible for killing Ralph, the person who attacked me, who left animal carcasses on my front porch? What have I stumbled into here? I pad into the living room, feeling safer there, and pace the length of it while I wait for Dale. I'm suddenly wide awake, adrenalin pumping through my body. I go back into the bedroom and pull jeans and a jumper over my nightwear. Then I hurry back into the kitchen, just in case I've missed something in the two minutes I've been away, but from the window I can no longer see any lights on or any activity from the cabin opposite. Everything outside feels unnaturally black. Not like Manchester. Here the darkness feels thick and never ending. Stifling.

Suddenly, two round headlights penetrate the darkness, bouncing over the bumps in the track, illuminating a fine rain. It's Dale, thank God. He pulls up behind my car and steps out. He has a heavy-duty torch and the beam is bright. He sweeps it around, landing on the cabin opposite. I run to the door and wrench it open just as he's by the hood of my car. He lowers the torch.

'Did you say that cabin there?' he asks, pointing his torch towards Foxglove without even stopping to say hello.

'Yes. Wait, let me grab my coat.'

'No. Stay here. It might not be safe.'

I ignore him, pulling on my wellies, but he's stalked off in the direction of the cabin, the light from his torch turning everything in front of him a dull, hazy brown. I close the door and hurry after him, almost slipping on the wet mud as I shoulder on my coat.

'I told you to stay inside,' he mutters, when I've caught up with him. 'For fuck's sake, Jenna. This isn't a game. Don't you ever do as you're told?'

I don't reply. Instead I hang back behind him and thrust my hands into my pockets, feeling for the mace and relaxing when my fingers find it. I bring it out and hold it by my side. A faint slant of light is visible around the curtains at the front window. My heart is beating fast and I tighten my grip on the spray. The door is flung open by a man with a halo of dark wiry hair tinged with grey and a cross expression. He's in his sixties with weath-ered skin and very dark brown eyes that flash with annoyance. He's not what I expected.

'Sorry to disturb you so late. I'm Detective Sergeant Dale Crawford,' he says, holding up his badge.

'It's gone twelve thirty in the morning,' says the man, rubbing a hand across the stubble on his chin. 'Is something wrong?'

'We've had a report that someone has been staying in this cabin illegally,' explains Dale. The man frowns. From behind him I hear a woman's voice. Then she appears at the doorway in a velour tracksuit tucked into Ugg boots, her blonde hair piled on top of her head in a topknot.

'What's going on?' She has a European accent I can't quite place.

'The officer seems to think we're staying here illegally,' he says, turning to her. 'José, get the printout, will you?'

She disappears from view.

'Can I take your name?' Dale asks, lowering his torch and pulling out his notebook from his inside pocket. He must carry that around with him everywhere.

I hear a dog bark and a yellow Labrador pokes its head from around the man's legs. A Labrador. Not a German Shepherd, after all. I oscillate between feeling relieved and embarrassed.

'It's Samuel and Josephine Molina,' says the man, folding his arms across a heavy jumper. He's tall and attractive in a rugged older-man kind of way. 'We've only just arrived. But we're booked in until Sunday.'

Josephine is back and thrusts a piece of paper into Dale's hand. 'We were both working today so came late,' she explains. She glances past Dale as though noticing me for the first time. 'We didn't mean to cause any disturbance.'

I can feel myself blush but, hopefully, it's too dark for her to notice. 'Not at all,' I say, waving a hand in her direction. 'There's just been a little mistake, that's all.'

'Okay,' she says, but her expression is still puzzled and her blue eyes flit back to Dale.

Dale returns the paper to her. 'It all looks in order. Sorry to disturb you,' he says. 'But I do feel I should make you aware that a man was found dead in this forest on Tuesday evening.'

The woman's face is a picture of horror. 'What? We weren't told about this. How?'

'We're still looking into it. So, please, if you see anyone acting suspiciously let me or one of my colleagues know.' He hands her a card with his details on. She takes it.

'Who – who was the man?' she asks, throwing a worried glance at her husband before fastening her eyes back on us.

'A Ralph Middleton. Did you know him at all?'

Their relief is almost palpable. 'No, I've not heard of him,' says Samuel. Did they expect it to be someone else? Josephine nods in agreement and her husband places a reassuring arm around her shoulders.

'And if you need anything I'm just in that cabin over there. Bluebell,' I say, pointing in the direction of where I'm staying. 'I'm Jenna.'

They nod tersely and shut the door on us.

'That's odd,' I say, in a low voice, as we head back, Dale lighting the way with his cumbersome torch. 'Jay didn't mention anyone booked in here when I saw him this afternoon.'

'It all appears above board.'

'Why would Jay put them in that cabin when he knows that's where I suspected someone was dossing down?'

'I have no idea. Maybe it was the only one available.'

'They're all available.'

'Jenna.' He sounds cross. 'Stop trying to see things that aren't there. Jay doesn't have to run it past you every time someone is booked in.'

I feel a stab of hurt. 'I didn't mean that.'

By now we've reached the front door. I hesitate, wondering whether to invite him in. But the note that found its way into the fireplace makes me decide against it.

I turn the key in the lock and step over the threshold. I turn to assess him. He looks freezing, clutching his torch, and I feel a pang of sympathy for him. 'Thank you for coming over,' I say. 'I'm sorry it turned out to be a mistake.'

He smiles wryly. 'A good mistake,' he says. 'I'm glad it's nothing more sinister.'

'I guess we'll never find out who was dossing there and why.'

'It's not like in books, Jenna. Not everything gets explained and tied up nicely in a neat little bow. This world is messy, complicated . . .' He sighs. 'It's fine. I'm happy to help.' He hesitates. And there it is again. Something unspoken between us. 'Go. Go and get some sleep, it's late.'

Reluctantly I close the door on him. It's for the best, I tell myself, as I head back to my bed. I think of Ralph being murdered in his caravan, of being followed through the forest, and of the mystery squatter lurking around the cabins with his German Shepherd.

It's best to trust nobody in this town.

38

No Going Back

AS THE DAYS PASSED STACE FELT JOHN-PAUL WAS SLIPPING further and further away from her. Every time she tried to talk to him he'd reply with a monosyllable, like a stroppy teenager. She'd sit and read most of the day, next to Maggie, laid out on sun-loungers. Sometimes Derreck would lie next to them, although it was always her, rather than Maggie, he sought out to talk to. He listened when she told him her regret at not staying on at school and how she'd felt obliged to help out in her parents' business instead, but that she was a ferocious reader, practically inhaling the books she might have been able to read had she been allowed to do A levels. He had a similar experience, telling her he had dropped out of high school to go travelling. But the more she chatted with Derreck the more withdrawn John-Paul became.

'I don't understand what's going on with him,' Stace said to Maggie, after they'd been in Thailand nearly a week.

'Is it the Buddha thing?' Despite Stace trying to persuade the others to take the Buddhas out of the country they had, so far, refused. It infuriated Stace. What harm could it do? But the others didn't need the money as much as she and John-Paul did. Trevor, Martin and Griff all had good jobs in accountancy or engineering. Maggie was doing well as a beauty therapist, Hannah was a bookkeeper and Leonie worked in a nursing home.

'It's not happening anyway,' she replied, slathering factor fifty over her shins. 'Derreck said it had to be all of us or none.'

'I'm sorry.' Maggie blushed beneath her tan. 'I just don't feel comfortable . . .'

'It's fine. The money would have been nice, but I do understand.'

'I'm surprised you were willing to do it. You've always been so – so careful.'

What could she say? That they needed the money? That she was fed up of never taking any risks? That she wanted to please Derreck and make him think she was a lot more than just a provincial girl from the sticks?

Maggie hesitated as though wanting to say something else. Eventually she said, 'I don't trust Derreck.'

'What do you mean?'

'I can't put my finger on it. I think . . . I think the Buddha thing is more dodgy than he's trying to make out. And how has he got all this money? I'd steer clear if I were you. John-Paul has the right idea.'

Stace frowned and adjusted her straw hat. 'Has he said something?'

Maggie pulled her legs up and fanned her face with a hand. A trickle of sweat was running down her thigh. 'No. It's just a feeling I get. He seems keen on you.'

Stace's heart thumped. 'What? Who?'

'You know who. Just be careful there, Stace. That's all I'm saying.'

Excitement rippled through Stace. So it wasn't her imagination? There was something between her and Derreck. Chemistry. Desire. Could John-Paul feel it too? Was that why he was withdrawing from her?

'I don't know what you mean,' she lied, pulling The Great Gatsby from her bag so she could hide her smile.

They made a habit of meeting up at night when everyone else was asleep and talked about everything, their childhoods, their dreams and ambitions. She felt like she knew more about Derreck than she did about her own boyfriend and she already knew she'd miss him when she returned to England in four days' time. This, she realized, was her favourite part of the holiday, sitting beside him over a drink, with the musky scent of exotic flowers she didn't know the names of, the dying embers of the barbecue and the sound of the crickets. They'd stay up until the sun started to rise and turned the sky a patchwork of pink and yellow.

'I always thought I was happy,' she told him that night, after her talk with Maggie. They were lying, as always, on adjacent sunloungers but, unlike that first night, they were close together, so close that she could feel the heat from Derreck's body. 'I thought I was a homebody, not particularly ambitious, but now it feels like everything's changed.' Including her feelings for John-Paul, although she didn't say that. If she was honest with herself, her relationship with John-Paul had been going downhill for months, even before he lost his job. She'd been taken in with the romance of him, a handsome stranger to their town, but he was miserable. And it had taken this holiday to make her see that so was she.

'I hardly know anything about him,' she said now. 'He refuses to tell me what happened in Goa.'

Derreck sighed softly. 'I don't want to cross any line. JP is my mate. But on the other hand . . .' Their bodies were turned in to each other, their faces inches apart. God, he was beautiful. '. . . I've come to feel . . .' he placed his hand over his linen shirt, lowering his eyes '. . . well, you know.'

She swallowed as her heart burst with emotions. Did she know it the first time she clapped eyes on him standing, like Gatsby, in front of his villa? Their instant attraction? She probably did.

Derreck moved his hand and touched her fingers lightly sending shock waves of desire through her. His voice was low and husky. 'The thing you need to know about JP is that he has a lot of sides to his character. He's been in trouble with the police, back in Spain. Stupid things. Burglary. Stealing cars. And then when we went travelling he got in with some dodgy people.' Why had John-Paul never told her any of this? She'd believed he was a gentle, innocent soul. How naïve she'd been. Derreck continued softly, 'I took him under my wing a bit. He was just . . . misguided, I suppose. He had a terrible relationship with his father, who I think was a bit of a brute.' This was all news to Stace. 'We travelled around together for a while and then . . . then Goa happened. I was his alibi but it freaked him out and that was why he ran off to Britain.'

A cold sensation swept over Stace and she drew her knees up to her chest so that she was in a foetal position, her hand still in Derreck's. Waiting, knowing that at last she was about to find out what had happened.

He was whispering now and she had to inch forward to hear him. 'He was at a beach party with a group of tourists. Young – teenagers and twenty-somethings. JP said he just gave one of them something – a pill. I'm not even sure what.'

'You mean . . . like drugs?' she whispered back.

Derreck nodded and held her hand firmer as though to comfort her, his thumb stroking her skin. 'So he's never told you any of this?'

'No,' she admitted. 'The first I knew about it was when I heard you both talking about Goa on our first night here. I asked John-Paul about it, but he tried to palm me off.'

'He should have told you. I can't bear that he's lying to you.'

'And what happened after that?'

'The guy overdosed. He was only eighteen. The drugs had been cut with something dodgy . . . Like I say, I don't know all the details. Except JP came to the hostel where I was staying, panicked, crying. He made me promise that if anyone asked I'd say he was with me the whole time. And . . .' he dipped his head '. . . to my shame I did. He told me he never knew the drugs were bad. It was that crowd he was in with. They weren't a good influence on him. The next thing I knew, he'd left me a note to say he'd gone away. And later he wrote to me to tell me he had settled in England, had met a nice local girl and . . .'

She retracted her hand. She didn't know what to think. John-Paul wasn't the man she'd thought he was. But, then, hadn't she always suspected that deep down? He'd presented to her a version of himself he knew she'd like. A romantic lead in a movie. The exotic hero who swept into a young woman's boring life and made it temporarily exciting until real life encroached upon them, turning their fantasy to dust.

She groaned. 'I feel so stupid. John-Paul was always so cagey about his travelling days but I thought it was because he wanted them back. I didn't realize he was hiding out with me, running away.' She turned back to him. 'Do you think that's why he's so miserable now? Because being back here has reminded him of that time?'

'Nobody ever came looking for JP. He was being paranoid, flee-ing like that,' said Derreck. 'He told me he was broke and had lost his job. I paid for your tickets to fly out here.'

'John-Paul said he had savings.' Her whole body flashed hot with embarrassment.

'He had nothing, Stace,' he said gently. 'He regretted running away from India. So that's why I invited him here – I thought the Buddha thing could help you both out. But . . .' he reached over and stroked her cheek '. . . I'm just glad I got to meet you. I'm sorry if I'm talking out of turn, but I think . . .' His eyes locked with hers. 'I hope you feel the same.' Desire crackled between them and Stace realized she was holding her breath.

She knew what was going to happen next and she did nothing to stop it as he led her upstairs to his room at the top of the villa. They didn't speak as they peeled off each other's clothes, holding eye con-tact, the only light spilling from the French windows that led onto a balcony and were slightly ajar. She knew she had crossed a line: her future was not set out like she'd thought. And there was no going back.

Day Four

39

Jenna

I SURVIVED ANOTHER NIGHT, ALTHOUGH AS THE DAYS PASS I've got more questions than answers. Who was the man staying illegally in the cabin opposite? Who wrote the note with the flowers and on my car? And who threw it into the fire? Not to mention who killed Ralph and who attacked me in the forest? I can't wait to leave this town – but I know Olivia and her friends will follow me.

The next morning I decide to speak to Madame Tovey. I know Jay and Dale have described her as a charlatan but she's a local institution and was living in Stafferbury when the girls disappeared. She'd be a good interviewee for the podcast.

It's another cold morning, the sky a blanket of white. There is a light dusting of frost on the pavement. I've got my collar turned up against the wind, and as I'm crossing the high street I see Olivia outside Madame Tovey's. She looks harassed, her face pale and tired. She has a maroon beanie pressed down on her head, which does nothing for her sickly pallor.

'Olivia,' I call, speeding up but careful not to slip on the icy pavement. 'Are you okay?'

'No, not really,' she says, glancing up at the window above Madame Tovey's, which I assume is Wesley's flat. She looks like she's barely slept.

'Can I give you a lift home?' I can drop her off and come back to see Madame Tovey. It's not like I have an appointment anyway. 'My car is only over there,' I say, pointing to where I've parked it on a two-hour bay at the end of the high street.

She hesitates. A shadow moves behind the glass. I realize she's worried about Wesley's disapproval. But a defiant expression passes over her face. She sets her chin and nods, thanking me. We walk to the car and don't speak until we are warm inside.

I start the engine. 'Is everything okay between you and Wesley?' I ask, remembering the conversation we had last night.

She tugs off her hat and the static causes her hair to stand on end. She runs her hands over it absently. 'Something strange happened last night,' she begins, as I pull away from the kerb and fall behind a passing Vauxhall. There isn't much traffic; there never seems to be around here.

'Oh, yes?' I want to ask her about the note and whether she had put it into the fire but I can't work out a way to phrase it without sounding confrontational. And if Olivia is guilty of something it might give me the upper hand if I don't reveal I know about the burnt note.

Horror washes over me when she's finished telling me what

happened to her last night. 'Are you saying you think you might have been injected with drugs?'

She blinks and I can see she's close to tears. 'Yes.'

As a journalist I've reported on this before, usually young women in nightclubs. 'God, Olivia. Have you gone to the police?'

'I don't know what to do,' she wails. 'I was in such a state when Dale found me.'

'Dale found you?' My voice comes out strangled.

She explains about him finding her at the stones and I grip the steering wheel, my mind racing.

And then, just when I think it can't get any worse, she tells me about Wesley disappearing, then returning later with a cardboard box and another phone. 'I just know,' she says, with a sob, 'that he's up to no good. And I was hoping he'd go to work first so that I could find the box and see what was inside but he couldn't get rid of me quickly enough this morning. When I suggested going into work late and letting myself out, he wouldn't hear of it. It was obvious he didn't want me alone in his flat.'

'But he left you last night?'

'Yeah, because he thought I'd be out for the count. But still . . . to leave me like that at night after what I'd been through.'

Is she beginning to see what I could all along? That the only person Wesley really cares about is himself?

I turn left off the high street, drive past The Raven and the buildings fall away, everything more countrified.

'It was round about here,' she says, pointing to a stretch of pavement. There are no houses along here, just hedgerows and fields on either side until you reach the riding stables. 'The last thing I remember is walking along here and then I felt a hand, across my face, and that must have been when the person injected me. I remember . . .' she frowns '. . . I remember stumbling into someone's arms. But I can't . . . I can't catch the memory.'

Her voice sounds small and vulnerable, and my heart aches for her. Sometimes I forget she's my age – she just seems so much younger. So naïve and innocent. And then I remember the note. Maybe not that innocent, after all. Have I got her wrong? Is this just a manipulative game she plays to make everyone underestimate her?

'It's all so confusing,' she says, as I manoeuvre into her driveway and pull up alongside her mother's Land Rover. 'And now,' she lowers her voice, 'my mum has suddenly announced – by text, no less – that we need to talk about my father.'

I turn to her in surprise. 'What?'

'She's never told me much about him except to say she was going out with him for a while but they split up when she fell pregnant. Nobody ever talked about him. Like once I remember asking Sally's mum – she was really good friends with my mum, at least she was until the accident – but she just told me he was a "bad egg" and that I was better off without him in my life. I began to wonder if maybe Mum was lying, that there had been no boyfriend and she'd been raped or something awful.'

'Oh, my God, do you think that's the case?'

'I honestly don't know.' She looks down at the bobble hat sitting in her lap. 'I'm almost scared to find out.' She doesn't move from the passenger seat.

'It'll be okay,' I say, trying to reassure her even though I have no idea if that's true.

'I just wonder why she wants to tell me all this now,' she says, almost to herself. She sighs heavily. 'Right. I'd better go and find out.' She flashes me a pained smile and pulls on her hat. 'I was supposed to feed the horses this morning so she'll be pissed off at me about that.'

'God, Olivia. You've been attacked. You should be going to the police. Do you want me to come with you?'

'No. It's okay. I'll do it later.'

'Take care,' I say, as she gets out. 'If you ever need to talk, and I mean confidentially, as a friend . . .'

'Thanks.'

I watch her walk towards the stables, her shoulders slumped, dragging her feet. She looks like a condemned woman.

I'm thinking about Olivia and what happened to her, and how Dale was the one to find her, as I head to Madame Tovey's place. Something really odd is going on around here. I don't believe it's mystical or supernatural, whatever some of the locals think. But I do believe it's calculated and linked to the events surrounding Olivia's three missing friends.

Madame Tovey's is painted in a garish purple that stands out against the muted tones of the other buildings. A bell tinkles as I push open the door into the shop. It's small and smells musty, of incense and ageing fabric and overly brewed tea. The shelves are lined with tarot cards and baroque jewellery. Tasselled bags in crushed velvet hang from a rack by the window. In the corner, at the end of the room, a table covered with a dark green satin fabric and a large crystal ball stands between two high-backed chairs. I stare at my surroundings, wondering how many customers Madame Tovey actually gets.

An internal door opens and a woman dressed in a long floaty garment, with a stack of bracelets halfway up her arms, waltzes through. She must be in her sixties at least, with thick dark hair piled on her head. She's holding a tray with a teapot and two cups, which she sets down next to the crystal ball. I'm not sure whether she plans to use it to read my tea leaves or just to drink the contents.

'Hello, dear,' she says, smiling at me. She has on too-red lipstick that has settled in the lines around her mouth. 'Can I help you?'

I explain who I am and why I'm here and she stares at me the whole time, her dark eyes unblinking. It's actually quite unnerving.

'I knew you were coming,' she says, when I've finished. I resist rolling my eyes. Easy for her to say that when I'm standing in front of her. 'Take a seat.' She sits in the chair behind the table and I perch on the one opposite. 'Tea?' She places a bone-china cup and saucer in front of me and begins pouring from the pretty silver teapot before I've had the chance to say anything.

I stare at the brown liquid dubiously. She takes a sip and watches me over the rim. 'So you want to interview me now?'

'If you have time.'

'Of course.' She goes to the door, her skirts rustling as she walks, and turns the sign to CLOSED. 'And now we have privacy.' She flashes her teeth at me and returns to her seat opposite. I take out my phone and go to the app to record the interview. My mobile looks strange on its little stand next to her giant crystal ball.

I ask her a few warm-up questions, like how long she's lived in Stafferbury – 'Thirty years, my love' – and how long she's been a 'medium': 'Since I was a child and I heard my dead aunt talking to me.'

'So you were living here at the time of the three girls' disappearance?'

'I certainly was.' She blows on her tea. 'I even gave a statement to the police.'

'Really?'

'Yes. I felt it was my moral duty. It came up in the cards, you see. Not that they took any notice of me.'

'What did you tell the police?'

'Oh, lots of things.' She grins and moves her delicate china cup to her lips and sips gingerly.

I wait, irritation mounting, as she swallows her tea and places the cup carefully back on its saucer. 'But they're blind, you see.'

'Blind?'

'To what's going on in this town.'

I move forwards in my seat expectantly. 'And what is going on, exactly?'

'There are forces at work. Unseen forces. Those stones were built on ley lines and they evoke a very powerful energy. Bad things throughout history have taken place at those stones. Sacrifices, rituals.'

I swallow my disappointment. I thought she was going to tell me something factual, not a load of mumbo-jumbo about ley lines and bad energy.

'Drink up, dear,' she says, waving her arms in my direction, her bracelets clinking.

For a wild moment I wonder if she's drugged my tea, then tell myself not to be so ridiculous. This isn't a TV drama and she's not some badly disguised villain. I take a sip. It tastes of aniseed and isn't entirely unpleasant.

'So what did you tell the police back then?' I ask, trying to get her back on track. 'What exactly was in the cards?'

'A man with a scar.'

I sit up, adrenalin pumping. 'What about a man with a scar?' Had Olivia told this woman about him or had Madame Tovey really 'seen it' in the cards?

'He's still here. I can feel his presence.' She touches a ruby brooch on her chest. 'He's the key to why those girls went missing.'

'And this is what you told the police?'

'Yes. Just after the accident.'

'Do you know his name?'

'Sadly not.'

'And did you ever see him yourself, around town?'

She shakes her head. A tendril comes away from her bun and hangs over her high cheekbone.

'And . . . the girls,' I say, dreading the answer. 'Do you know what happened to them?'

'Only that they are here. They are still here.' She tucks the loose hair behind her ear.

I inhale sharply. 'Are you sure?'

'It's what the cards have told me.'

'Do you mean they're still here on this earth? Or here in Stafferbury?'

'Why, in Stafferbury, of course. They've always been here.'

She sips her tea. Is she mad? Or a fantasist? Or a bit of both? Or – the tea is hot at the back of my throat – does she mean they're dead and buried here? 'And what about the man with the scar?'

'He's still here too, like I said. And, as I've said before, everyone just needs to open their eyes.' She places the teacup back in its saucer. 'Do you understand what I'm saying?'

'Not really. The man with the scar was apparently following Olivia before the accident.'

'Yes, he was. She wasn't lying about that.'

I feel a thud of disappointment. So she has spoken to Olivia. Have they concocted this tale between them? Did Olivia hope that if she told Madame Tovey she was being followed and asked her to back it up to the police she might be believed? How well did they know each other back then?

I ask this question. 'Oh, not very well. Not then. Obviously now I see her a lot because her boyfriend lives above this place. Not that he's there much.'

I remember what Olivia told me last night about the shoebox. 'What do you mean?'

'Aye, it's none of my business. Just that he comes and goes at all hours.'

'Do you live here, then? In the shop?'

'In the back there,' she says. 'Nice little studio. Suits me perfectly. Here,' she reaches over and takes my hand, 'let me read your cards. I'll do it for free.'

My heart sinks. I don't want to be rude so I go along with it. She drops my hand, picks up the stack of tarot cards and deals them out in front of her. The Death card comes up first. Of course it does. She sees me looking at it. 'It's not what you think it is,' she says, smiling widely and showing all her teeth. 'The Death card isn't a bad thing. It means new beginnings. Renewal.' I think of Gavin and the end of our marriage, and a lump forms in my throat. 'You're going through something painful right now but it will be okay, my dear. You'll come out the other end and things will be better.' She pats my hand before pulling out another card. The Lovers. 'Ooh, this is interesting,' she says. 'New relationships. You have a choice to make.'

I swallow. I don't know if I want to be doing this any more. I push back my chair and get up. 'Thanks,' I say, gathering up my bag. 'It's really kind of you but I need to be going now.'

'You're afraid,' she says calmly. 'And that's fine, Jenna. But you need to face your fears. You mustn't be scared of change.'

'I'm not here to talk about myself,' I say, backing away from her. 'I'm here to find out about the man with the scar and the missing girls . . .'

'The Lovers,' she says, with a sigh. 'This card isn't just about you.'

I frown. Now this is interesting. 'What do you mean?'

'It's how it all started. It's the crux of the whole thing.'

A swell of frustration rolls through me. I don't want to hear riddles. If she knows something why doesn't she just tell me? 'And what is that?'

'I'm just the vessel, my dear. I don't know what it all means. I'm just telling you what's in the cards. That's all.'

I stare at her, feeling more confused than when I came in. 'Okay, so let's get this right. You're saying the man with the scar is back in Stafferbury and he has something to do with the three missing girls.'

'He has everything to do with the missing three.'

'And the Lovers card. It's important because?'

'They started the whole thing off. But, again, I know nothing more than that. I just know they are intrinsic to this whole sorry affair.'

'Right. Fine. Thanks, you've been very helpful.'

She raises an eyebrow at me. 'Open your mind, Jenna. Allow yourself to believe that there are some things that are just inexplicable.'

I fold my arms across my chest. 'And what about Ralph Middleton? Is his death linked as well?'

'Oh, yes, I should say so.'

As I'm packing up she adds, so quietly I can hardly hear her, 'Don't trust anyone. That's what the cards are warning you, Jenna. Everyone is lying.'

40

Olivia

THE HORSES ARE STILL IN THE FIELD. OLIVIA FROWNS. There is a lesson at 11 a.m. and three of the horses need to be brought in. Her mother should have done it ages ago. She feels a tug of guilt. She should have been here to help. Her mother isn't getting any younger.

She swallows her anxiety. She needs to face whatever her mother will tell her about her father.

Olivia checks the little shed they use for the office but it's empty so she goes to the tack room at the other end of the yard to see if her mother is there. When that's empty too she begins to worry. Her mother's Land Rover is in the driveway. She must be in the house. As she's making her way through the gate her mobile buzzes. She reaches for it, thinking it will be her mum, but Wesley's name flashes up. He never usually calls her from work.

'Hey, Wes. You okay?'

'Not really, no.' His voice sounds subdued, and from the sound of cars whizzing past and the way he's breathing, she gathers he's walking along a busy street.

'Why aren't you at work?'

'I've had to come all the way to fucking Devizes, haven't I?'

'What? Why?'

'I had a phone call just as I was about to leave for work. From the police.'

Olivia's heart speeds up. 'The police. Why?'

'They want me to answer some questions, apparently.'

'You haven't been arrested?'

'Of course I haven't been fucking arrested. Jesus, Liv. They've asked me to come down to the station and that's what I'm doing. I'm being a good boy.' He sounds thoroughly pissed off but Olivia senses a trace of anxiety in his voice too.

'What do they want to talk to you about?'

'I'll let you know.'

Is it about what happened last night? The box he was carrying. The burner phone. The suspicion he's involved in something dodgy intensifies.

'I hope everything's going to be okay.'

'Sure,' he says, but he doesn't sound confident. 'I'll ring you later.'

He ends the call abruptly. Olivia hasn't got time to worry about it. She has more pressing matters to think about.

Her mother is sitting at the pine table in the centre of the kitchen nursing a cup of coffee. She still has her padded jacket on and her riding boots. There is a streak of mud on her cheek and her hair, usually in a sleek grey bob, is dishevelled.

She knows her mother loves this job and being outside with nature. But it's a physically demanding job. Olivia keeps telling her they need to get a yard manager or someone to help out, but her mum insists they can't afford it, that the books are barely ticking over. Not that Olivia would know. She's not allowed to touch the books.

'Mum,' she says, pulling out a chair and sitting opposite her, 'I got your text. Is everything okay?'

Her mother looks up at her with tired, bruised eyes. 'I need to talk to you. Can I get you anything to eat?'

Olivia couldn't possibly eat. She wants to get this over with. Rip off the plaster once and for fucking all. 'Just tell me,' she says, in a low voice.

'I'll make you a coffee,' says her mother, getting up as though unable to contain all her nervous energy and going to the kettle. *She's worried about telling me. Why?* Olivia watches as she opens one of the old-fashioned farmhouse kitchen cupboards to get a mug. The whole place needs updating but her mother has never been that bothered with fancy things. 'Wholesome', 'unpretentious', 'capable' and 'earthy' are words people use to describe her. She watches her straight, proud back, the horse hair still clinging to her padded vest, and Olivia feels a lump in her throat. She wants to savour this moment because after their conversation she knows everything will change.

It's true what they say. Ignorance is bliss.

Her mother hands her a coffee and sits down at the table. She already has one in front of her, growing cold, as though she's been sitting in the kitchen for ages just waiting for Olivia to get home.

'Go on, then, tell me,' says Olivia, bracing herself. This is the moment she's going to hear that her father is some kind of monster, a rapist, a psychopath.

'I think your father might be in town,' she says, and Olivia is so surprised she nearly knocks over her mug. 'He was seen.'

'What? Who saw him?'

She waves a hand dismissively. 'It doesn't matter. And I'm sorry I never told you much about him. The truth is I loved your father. Once, I thought I loved him very much. But there was an . . . incident and we split up. Then I found out I was pregnant with you.' A shadow passes behind her eyes and, for a moment, Olivia knows her mother is recalling the pain that was inflicted on her.

'Why have you decided to tell me this now?'

'Because I think he wants to meet you. I've been told he's here, in Stafferbury, and the only reason he would want to come here is to see you.' There is a desperation about her that Olivia's never witnessed before. She's usually so composed.

'Why would he want to see me now when he didn't bother for years? When he left you pregnant?' Her head pounds. This is all too much.

'Well, he was away for a long time.' Her mother pushes her fringe from her eyes. Olivia notices her hand is trembling.

Olivia fidgets in her seat. 'Where was he?'

'This is the thing . . . This is why I didn't tell you.' She laces her fingers around her mug. 'He's been in prison. For a long time.'

'What did he do?'

Her mother's next words make Olivia go cold all over.

'He killed someone.'

41

Jenna

MY MIND IS STILL FULL OF MY CONVERSATION WITH MADAME Tovey as I pull up outside the cabin. I climb out of the car, slightly distracted, and start when I see a figure standing by my front door. I put my hand to my chest, my heart in my throat, then relax when I realize it's the man, Samuel, from Foxglove.

He blows on his hands and stamps his feet. The ground is covered with patchy frost. 'I didn't mean to startle you. I'm sorry if José and I were rude last night. We arrived late and we were tired and grumpy,' he says, smiling broadly.

'Oh, no, not at all. It was totally my fault.' As I explain my mistake, his expression grows more sombre.

'So, let's get this straight,' he says, when I've finished. 'You came over last night because you previously saw a man staying in the cabin who shouldn't have been there and thought he was back?'

I nod. I pull my bag more firmly over my shoulder.

'What did the man look like?'

'Um . . .' I cast my mind back to that first night. 'He was wearing a long raincoat with a hood – you know the ones, like fishermen wear. And I didn't get the chance to see his face. Not properly. He was tall. I'm assuming it was a man but I suppose it could equally have been a tall woman.'

'Can I ask you to take a look at this?' I notice then that he's holding a photograph, which he passes to me with an unsteady hand. It's of him when he was younger with another man. They both have the same dark hair and eyes but the other man looks thinner. Samuel has his arm around the man's shoulder and he's in profile. 'Could it have been this man? He'd be older now. Mid-sixties.'

'I don't know. I mean, perhaps. I didn't see the man's face closely enough to tell. Who is this?'

'He's my brother – well, half-brother. We had the same father but we've lost touch. And then I heard he was in Stafferbury so we travelled down from where we're living now in Cumbria to see him. I've had someone looking into his whereabouts, and there was a booking made here in Stafferbury under his name, a few days ago at the local B-and-B. But when I went there to ask they said he didn't turn up.'

I try to imagine the man older with a long waxed coat on. I hand him back the photo. 'Is your brother tall?'

'He's just over six foot.'

It could have been the same man. But why would he be hiding out here if he'd booked a B-and-B? Maybe he didn't have any money and thought these cabins were empty so decided to use one. Another thought hits me. Could this be the person who attacked me on the night of Ralph's death?

'If he was here he was probably just passing through,' says Samuel. 'I've been so close the odd time over the years but he's elusive. It's almost,' he glances down at his feet and looks slightly ashamed, 'as if he doesn't want to be found. I wasn't the best brother to him, in the end.'

He reaches into his back pocket for his wallet. 'I also have this. This was taken on the same day and was the last time we saw each other, twenty years ago now. It isn't such a good photo of him, though.' He hands it to me. It's crumpled, and this time the man is sitting alone on an old stone wall, sadness in his eyes. He has a cigarette hanging out of his mouth. I don't recognize him at all. I'm about to return the photograph when I notice something about the man's face. I peer more closely.

'What's that there?' I ask, pointing to something dark and puckered on the left cheek. It wasn't apparent in the first photo because of the way the man was standing.

'Oh, that. Yes, he got into a fight a few years before. It's a scar. It was pretty nasty too – he could have lost his eye.'

A scar.

'What's your brother's name?' I ask. I don't know how it links together but this could be important.

'John-Paul,' he says. 'His name is John-Paul Molina.'

42

Jenna

I'VE ONLY BEEN BACK TO THE CABIN FOR TEN MINUTES when there is a knock at the door. I open it, expecting it to be Samuel again, but Dale is standing there. His hair is tousled and he smiles at me, his warm hazel eyes softening, and my stomach does a strange little dance. Urgh, Jenna, don't even go there, I tell myself. I know it's just a reaction to my pride being hurt by Gavin and our conversation last night, the finality in his words. And, anyway, Madame Tovey's words are still playing on my mind. *Everyone is lying.*

I resist smiling back. 'Dale,' I say crisply. 'Everything okay?'

Confusion flickers on his face. 'I wanted to check on you after last night. First the dead birds. And then the mix-up with the man in the cabin.'

'I'm fine,' I say. 'But I saw Olivia this morning.' I recount what she told me. 'She said you'd found her at the stones. What had you been doing there? And why didn't you tell me last night that you'd found her in such a state?'

He folds his arms against the cold. The tip of his nose is red. 'I was just walking past. Following up a lead. I didn't tell you last night as I was worried about you and wanted to get to the bottom of who was in the other cabin. You called me, remember. I had just accompanied Olivia to Wesley's when I received your call.'

'Olivia thinks she might have been drugged.'

His expression hardens. 'That's what I was afraid of. Look, can I come in? It's freezing out here.'

He must notice my hesitation because he puts up his hands, as though he's overstepped a mark I didn't even know I'd drawn. 'That's fine. Maybe we should meet somewhere instead.' I'm giving him mixed messages. One minute ringing him up asking him to help me, the next pushing him away. I'm being ridiculous to believe anything Madame Tovey said. She's a bloody con artist. Dale has been kind to me, I remind myself. I've worked with other detectives on past stories and none of them was as forthcoming at sharing information with me as Dale has been.

'No, sorry, of course, come in.' I stand aside to let him into the hallway. He smells of cold air and lemon shampoo. I have to trust him. Who else have I got?

He follows me into the kitchen and perches on one of the bar stools while I make us both a coffee. I pass the milk to Dale, who pours it into his mug. 'There's a lot that's been going on,' he says. He has a little black notebook in front of him and he flips it open. I move a bit closer on the pretence of reaching for the milk to get a better look at his handwriting, thinking of the note, and almost fall into his lap as I do so. He looks taken aback. 'What are you doing?'

'Sorry, I slipped. Just need the milk,' I garble, my cheeks hot when I return to my stool.

He frowns and passes it to me and I pretend to add it to my coffee, even though I always take it black.

'I know I've been a bit cagey,' he says regretfully, 'but I'm working in close contact with my colleagues on the Drugs Squad. They're investigating county-lines stuff. And for a long time now they've been watching Stafferbury.'

I sit up, forgetting about trying to read Dale's notes. 'What? This little town?'

'It's usually little towns like this,' he says drily. 'Not always big cities. There's a drugs ring here, supplying crack cocaine. Ralph was found with a large supply of drugs in his system and the money we found in his caravan means we think his death might have been drug-related.'

'You mean he died of drugs and not the blow to the head?'

'No. It was the blow to the head that killed him. I mean he was being used as a dealer. He was a vulnerable man. An easy target. We don't know all the details yet but we think he was murdered by another member of the gang.'

I remember what Olivia told me this morning about Wesley coming home with a shoebox and a burner phone. I repeat this to Dale. 'Do you think he could be involved?'

He takes a deep breath. 'He's definitely a person of interest.'

My heart goes out to Olivia. She's been through so much.

'Another thing,' he says, looking down at his little black book. I glance at it again. This time it's easier to see the handwriting. It doesn't look like the writing on the notes, which makes me think it's more likely to have been Olivia who tried to dispose of it in the fire. It still doesn't make sense, though. If she wrote the note for me to find why would she then dispose of it? She must know I would have taken a photo of it. Unless she didn't write it herself. But she knows who did?

I tune back in to what Dale is saying, realizing I missed the beginning of his sentence. '. . . received a phone call this morning from the man staying in the cabin opposite. His name is Samuel Molina and he's here looking for his brother.'

'Why did he phone you?'

'Because he had my card from last night. He must have thought I'd be able to help him find his brother.'

I recount my conversation with Samuel this morning and tell him about the photograph. 'He had a scar. He must have been the man who Olivia said was following her before the accident.'

'Yes. When Samuel described him to me I did some digging.' He closes his notebook and reaches into his coat pocket for his mobile. He swipes the screen and shows me a photo of what looks like some kind of lease. He stabs at it with his finger. 'It's a copy of a lease agreement signed in 1979 by a Miss Anastacia Rutherford and a Mr John-Paul Molina.'

I frown. Rutherford. 'Is Anastacia related to Olivia?'

'Yes. She's her mother. And I suspect, although I don't know for certain but just based on the fact she was born in August 1980, that John-Paul is her father.' He doesn't speak for a few seconds, allowing me to digest this information.

'Does Anastacia know that Samuel is in town looking for his brother?'

'Hmm. Well, when I asked Samuel about Anastacia Rutherford he hadn't heard of her. He didn't know she was once his brother's girlfriend. According to this, they leased the flat above what used to be the launderette in the high street, but it's now a jewellery shop. Anyway, back in 1980 John-Paul was convicted of drug-smuggling.'

'What?' I'm reeling. First that the man with the scar might be Olivia's father and now the drugs conviction. 'Does Olivia know?' That must have been why he was following her, back in 1998. But why not tell her who he was? Why disappear and make her wonder all these years?

'I'm not sure. It's still very murky.'

'So what happened to him after he was seen in Stafferbury in 1998? Olivia never mentioned seeing him since.'

Dale tucks his notebook back into his coat. 'I checked and there is no record of John-Paul Molina going back to prison and it doesn't look like he left the UK.' He takes a sip of his coffee. Mine sits, untouched, in front of me. 'That's what we're trying to piece together. Why disappear for so long and why come back now?'

'We need to speak to Olivia again,' I say. 'Her dad is back and he's a known drugs felon. Olivia reckons she was drugged last night. Ralph had drugs in his body and money hidden in his caravan, and then there's Wesley and the burner phone. Are they all in it together? Is Olivia making up being drugged?'

'Something doesn't add up about it all,' he agrees, his eyes focused on the middle distance. 'I have my theories but . . .' He shrugs and looks at me. 'I think Olivia must know more about all this than she's letting on.'

I feel jittery, like I've drunk too much caffeine, and I can't stop my leg jigging up and down.

Everyone is lying.

Has Olivia been lying to me the whole time?

'She could have given Ralph the drugs when she went to see him the afternoon he died,' I say, remembering. 'Or the money. Did they argue about that? Is that why she was crying? She could be part of this whole drugs ring.' I jump off my stool. 'I'm going to pay her a visit. See what I can find out.'

Dale shakes his head. 'No, Jenna, that's not a good idea. I was planning to go there myself after seeing you. I told her last night I'd pop over and talk to her about the night of the accident.'

'She's hardly going to admit anything to you, but she might to me.'

Dale looks concerned. 'I don't know . . .'

'Come on, Dale. She wouldn't tell you anything. She'd clam up. You know she would.'

He hangs his head, defeated.

'And I'm good at getting people to open up. It's my job.' I hesitate. I really want to trust Dale and it's been niggling at me since Olivia told me Dale had found her. 'Why were you at the stones last night? Why didn't you go home after seeing me?'

He sighs. 'I told you. I was following up a lead. I work crazy hours.' But he breaks eye contact and picks up his mug, draining the remains of his coffee. The feeling returns that he's not telling me everything. 'Right, well.' He gets up too and takes our mugs to the sink. 'I'd better get going.'

He follows me into the hallway and watches as I pull on my boots.

'Jenna,' he says softly, when I've opened the door. Our eyes lock and his gaze is intense. 'Just be careful. We don't know Olivia's full involvement in this.'

I dip my head, my cheeks hot. 'I'll be careful, I promise.'

I close the front door behind us and watch as Dale walks swiftly to his car, his overcoat flowing out behind him. As I get into my Audi I see in my rear-view mirror that he's sitting behind the wheel, his mobile pressed to his ear. He's talking intently to someone and glances in my direction before averting his eyes. He ends the call and pulls away from my drive.

43

Olivia

OLIVIA STARES AT HER MUM, AGHAST, AS SHE LISTENS TO her describing her father's attributes, their relationship, but she can't stop thinking about the one fact that overrides everything else.

'My dad killed someone?'

Her mother stops talking and nods, glancing down at the pine table.

'And you never thought to tell me before?' The room tilts. Another secret. Another lie. 'Who . . . who did he kill?'

'Does that matter?' her mother replies sadly.

'How? I mean, why? I just . . .' Olivia pushes back her chair. She can't breathe. A pain shoots from her knee to her hip. She'd forgotten to take her medication this morning after everything that happened last night. 'I need to get out of here,' she says, stumbling towards the door. She grabs her coat from the porch and rushes out into the cold winter air. Mel's car is pulling up on the driveway and she steps out, waving to Olivia. Olivia plasters a smile on her face to cover her true feelings. The horses aren't even ready. Three adults are booked into the 11 a.m. class. Mel will be annoyed.

'We're running a bit behind schedule today,' Olivia calls, her voice carrying on the wind. 'I won't be long.'

She doesn't wait for Mel to reply. Instead she heads to the tack room to retrieve the saddles and bridles required for Roxie and Prince. She'll come back for Petal's. She can't think of anything but her father. He's back in town. He's a murderer. A convict. She saddles up Prince first, a fifteen-hand bay gelding. She feels calmer as she goes through the motions of slipping the bridle over his head by pushing her fingers into the corner of his mouth to insert the bit between his teeth. She hears footsteps outside the yard and sees her mother coming out of the tack room carrying the saddle for Petal, the piebald. She has so many questions she wants to ask about her father. He'd always been a faceless entity, someone with no name, no personality. A spectre, really. A heartless bastard who'd left her mum while pregnant. But now – now he has a name. John-Paul. And a personality – gentle, her mother had said, kind but also troubled. Secretive. It must be a family trait.

And he'd killed someone.

She moves on to Roxie. As she does up her girth Mel arrives. 'I'll take her. Laurie's waiting,' she says, grabbing the reins from Olivia. She already has hold of Prince with the other hand. Olivia nods and watches her walking off, leading both horses, then hides in Roxie's stable until the clients and their horses have followed Mel into the arena.

'Darling?' She looks up to see her mother poking her head over the door. 'We need to talk.'

'I can't right now. We've got work to do,' Olivia snaps, ignoring the guilt she feels at being mean to her mum.

'I'm so sorry to lay this on you. Please, for the moment, don't tell Wesley or anyone else.'

Olivia murmurs her agreement, then turns her back on the pretence of raking Roxie's bed. She waits until she hears her mother's retreating footsteps before leaving the safety of the stable.

Mel's loud, posh voice instructing the clients to do a rising trot carries on the wind as Olivia heads to the office. She's just in time to see her mother's old Land Rover pulling out of the driveway. Something sad and melancholy opens inside her as she sits behind the desk with the diary spread in front of her. She should feel . . . not happy exactly. How can she be happy when she's just found out she has a criminal for a father? But intrigued, certainly. Yet she feels apathetic to the notion she has a father who's living and breathing and in the vicinity, wanting to meet her. It just feels like another piece of armour weighing her down.

The sound of tyres over gravel makes her sit up straighter, expectantly. Is that him? She feels sick. She doesn't know if she's ready for this. But it's Jenna who appears in the doorway, her cheeks red, her beautiful copper-coloured hair windswept.

Despite everything Olivia is pleased to see her and can't stop the smile spreading across her face. Her first genuine smile since she heard the news about her dad.

'Have you got time for a coffee?' Jenna asks, as she strides into the office with a confidence that Olivia envies.

Olivia tries not to look too delighted to have this welcome interruption to her relentless negative thoughts. Mel will be at least another forty-five minutes with her class. 'Sure.' She collects the two ugly red Nescafé mugs from the side and pours them both an instant coffee. She remembers that Jenna likes hers black.

Jenna takes it gratefully and sits opposite Olivia, blowing on the coffee. There's a fan in the corner chugging out warm air but it doesn't do much to heat the room. 'How are you feeling now?'

'A bit more human, thanks to this,' Olivia says raising her coffee mug, which is a lie. Tears well up every time she thinks about her father.

Jenna suddenly looks uncomfortable and keeps fidgeting on the chair. 'I do need to tell you something, though,' she says, making Olivia's heart sink. 'I've . . . I've . . . God, I don't know how to say this.'

'What?'

Olivia listens intently as Jenna tells her about Samuel Molina and John-Paul. 'This John-Paul has a scar down the side of his face, Olivia. I think the man with the scar you saw in the days leading up to the accident is him. I think John-Paul could be your father.'

Terror rises in Olivia, making her feel hot and cold at the same time.

The man with the scar is John-Paul Molina? Her father?

And then, despite promising her mother she wouldn't, she tells Jenna everything she's learnt today.

'Wow,' says Jenna, after she's finished.

'I wonder if my mum knows his brother is looking for him.'

Jenna appears to think about this. 'Maybe,' she says eventually. 'It does seem strange that he arrived last night and she chooses this time to tell you all about your father.'

'But how did she find out he's back?' Olivia sighs. So many more questions. She shouldn't have run out on her mum. She should have stayed and listened to what she had to say. 'And why was he following me in the days leading up to the accident? Why didn't he just come over and tell me who he was? Urgh.' She pushes the diary away from her in a sudden burst of anger. 'I'm so fucked off with this.'

Jenna casts her eyes down. 'I'm sorry,' she says.

'It's not your fault. Thank you for telling me.' Tears spring again to Olivia's eyes. 'I'm worried my dad has something to do with the accident. If he's the man with the scar I saw in the white van . . .' She swallows. She almost said too much. She tries to remember the details of her conversation with her mother earlier. 'Mum said he went to prison. But I'm not sure when.'

'It was in 1980,' says Jenna, gently. 'Dale told me earlier. For possession of class-A drugs. I think he was there for eighteen years.'

Olivia sits up straighter, confused. 'No, that's not what my mum said. She said he went to prison for killing someone.'

'Killing someone?' There is alarm in Jenna's voice. 'Who? Who did he kill?'

Before Olivia can answer she sees a shadow at the door and her mother is standing there, her arms crossed in front of her chest and a strange expression on her face.

'You might as well know,' she says, and Olivia almost wants to laugh at the shock on Jenna's face as she swivels towards the figure in the doorway.

'He killed Derreck, the man I loved.'

44

The Lovers

THEY'D FALLEN ASLEEP, WRAPPED IN EACH OTHER'S ARMS, NA-
ked, with just a sheet draped over their bottom halves. She'd barely
had time to open her eyes, to stretch, to realize where she was when
she heard shouting from below Derreck's room. Stace felt Derreck
stir beneath her and her heart twisted when she realized the shouting must be John-Paul. She hadn't wanted him to find out this way.
She felt Derreck's arm tighten around her and she levered herself up
onto her elbow and looked into his deep aquamarine eyes. 'I don't
regret anything,' she whispered. 'Whatever happens next.'

His face was intense, his gaze not leaving hers. 'Neither do I. I've
never felt this way about anyone before. That was the best night of
my life.'

She kissed his face softly. How could it be that she was falling in
love with a man she'd known for just over a week?

And then John-Paul burst into the room, fully dressed, his

hair standing on end and one side of his face creased, as though he'd not long woken up. He was closely followed by Griff and Trevor.

'I fucking knew it!' he yelled. 'I knew something was going on between you two. You,' he pointed at Stace, who cowered in the bed, the sheet up to her chin. 'Do you think I didn't know you were sneaking off every night? And you,' he turned to Derreck, 'you're supposed to be my mate.' He made a sound like a wounded animal that pierced right through Stace's heart. She felt like the worst person in the world. The very worst. She never meant to hurt him. Derreck inched closer to her.

John-Paul covered his face with his arms as though he was trying to protect himself physically from the scene before him and moaned. Griff and Trevor stood awkwardly in the doorway. And then there was the sound of bare feet slapping on marble as the others ran into the room and Maggie gently steered John-Paul away. 'Come on,' she said softly. 'They're not worth it. Let's leave them a moment . . .' She shot Stace such a look of disgust it broke her heart nearly as much as John-Paul's distress. They all trooped out, their bodies surrounding John-Paul like a human shield, Trevor only stopping to glare before slamming the door behind them, their silent disapproval echoing around the room even after they'd left.

Stace's mouth went dry as the horror of what had just happened hit her. 'Oh, God,' she said, scrambling out of bed and pulling on yesterday's dress. 'I shouldn't have fallen asleep. I should have told him rather than him finding out like this . . .'

Derreck's face was sombre. 'I'm sorry too. JP is my mate. Was my mate. But . . . hey, Stace.' He crawled to the end of the bed and held her by the shoulders. She was crying now. Great big tears of guilt every time she remembered the anguish on John-Paul's face and that guttural sound he'd made. 'It will be okay. No regrets, remember? You're worth losing my mate over.' He folded her in his arms and she knew she felt the same. Being without him was more unbearable than hurting John-Paul. That was the truth of it. She had three days left before they returned to the UK and she wanted to spend every minute with Derreck. For that to happen John-Paul had had to find out about them.

He kissed her longingly, hungrily. 'Derreck,' she murmured. 'I can't. I have to talk to John-Paul.' She reluctantly pulled away from him even though it took everything she had.

He sat back on the bed, still naked, his lovely blond hair tousled. She couldn't look at him or her resolve would vanish, and John-Paul needed an explanation.

'I'll wait here for you,' he said. She leant over and kissed him, then ran from the room before she could change her mind.

John-Paul was in the garden under the awning, their friends crowded around him. They looked up at her as she approached, their body language frosty. John-Paul stared ahead at the pool, avoiding her gaze. If only she'd woken earlier she could have spoken to John-Paul before everyone else had got up, could have explained it. Yes, he'd have been gutted, but for him to see her in bed with another man, his mate, God, she felt sick.

Stace stood in front of them all, like she was facing a trial. Leonie was practically sitting on John-Paul's lap, her boobs in his face. Maggie was perched on the arm of the sun-lounger and Hannah was standing behind him, rubbing his shoulders. The men knelt by his side, like he was some kind of emperor.

'He doesn't want to talk to you,' hissed Leonie, her eyes narrowed. 'How could you? What's wrong with you? Are you some kind of animal?'

Stace hung her head. Was she? What was wrong with her? How could she do this to the man she'd thought she loved?

'I thought you'd have more respect for me,' said John-Paul, meeting her eyes and speaking to her for the first time.

'I'm so sorry,' she said. 'I really didn't mean to hurt you.'

John-Paul stood up and the others fell away from him. His eyes were red and puffy. He stalked off towards the villa and Stace followed. Thankfully, the others stayed where they were. She shadowed him through the kitchen and into the living room at the front, a room they rarely used. The shutters were closed and it was cool, with dark wooden floorboards and cream sofas. John-Paul shut the door behind them, standing in front of it. She felt a swell of panic. She was trapped.

'Who are you?' He shook his head, his eyes hardening. 'I never thought you'd do this to me. Never in a million years. How could you, Anastacia? How could you? I thought you loved me.'

He started to cry again and the sight of him so broken made her crack. Tears rolled down her own cheeks. She'd never seen him cry in the eighteen months they'd been together.

'I'm sorry. I'm so sorry, John-Paul. I didn't want to hurt you but . . . I can't explain it. I've never felt like it before . . . I just . . .'

'Oh, thanks. So you're saying you feel more for this guy after two minutes than you do for me after nearly two fucking years? What has he got that I haven't? Huh? Oh, yeah, that's right.' He waved his arms in the air as if he'd had the answer all along. 'Money!'

But it wasn't the money. She couldn't have cared less about that. How could she explain that it was chemistry: powerful and intoxicating sexual chemistry. That she was drawn to him in a way she couldn't control. Like he was her soul-mate. She had to be with him even if it hurt everyone else. But she remained silent. Anything she said would be too painful for him to hear.

He assessed her. 'Don't you love me?'

'I – I thought so, I really did. But how can I if I feel this way about Derreck?'

He let out a sound like a yowl. 'Fucking hell. I can't believe this. I mean, I saw the way he was with you. I saw you sneak out every evening when you thought I was asleep. Is that what you were doing every night? Fucking him?'

She blanched. It wasn't like John-Paul to use coarse language. 'No, nothing happened between us until last night. And you!' A sob caught in her throat. 'You pushed me away! You wouldn't tell me about Goa. Derreck had to in the end. You were keeping secrets from me and when I tried to ask you about them you refused to talk to me.' She held up her arms in desperation.

'Oh, I bet he loved telling you that. Painting me as the villain.'

'I just wish you'd told me . . .'

'And has your precious Derreck told you the truth about why he wanted us here, yet?'

'The ornaments . . .'

He expelled a bitter laugh. 'Those fucking ornaments. They're filled with drugs.'

She stared at him in shock. 'Of course they aren't. I checked. They – they're solid wood.' But a part of her had always known, hadn't it? Maybe the others did too.

'Yep. Derreck was going to put us all in danger. Get us all to smuggle them out of the country. Even you, Stace. Even you.'

'You agreed? Even though you knew.'

'I'd never have done it. Not when I knew for certain what they contained.'

She remembered the drugs in Goa. 'But this wouldn't have been the first time. Isn't that right? Is this what you and Derreck did on your "travels"?'

He shook his head. 'Who are you?'

'And who are you?' she shot back angrily. 'We obviously didn't know each other at all.'

His dark eyes flashed and he lunged for her, grabbing hold of her upper arms and shaking her. And then he let go of her so suddenly she lost her balance and collapsed onto the hard wooden floor. She cried out, more from shock than anything else.

Suddenly Derreck burst into the room in his boxer shorts and a T-shirt. 'Leave her alone,' he yelled. 'I could hear you shouting at her from upstairs.'

It all happened in a blur. John-Paul leapt at Derreck, his fist catching the side of Derreck's jaw. Stace jumped back as John-Paul landed another punch to the other side of Derreck's face.

And she screamed in horror as Derreck collapsed to the floor, his head smacking against the hard wood, blood flying from his lips.

'No!' she cried, pushing past John-Paul to kneel beside Derreck's motionless body. 'What have you done?'

45

Jenna

'AND YOU!' SAYS ANASTACIA, STARING AT ME AFTER SHE'S FIN-ished her story, her voice hard, and I wonder why she's even telling me this. 'This is off the record. It happened when we were in Thailand in 1980. I never even knew Derreck's surname.'

'So John-Paul went to prison? In Thailand?' I ask, confused.

'Yes.'

'In 1980?' I clarify. Dale never mentioned he'd gone to a Thai prison. I'd assumed it was in the UK.

'Yes. For eighteen years.' Anastacia crosses her arms.

She's still standing in the doorway and the icy air weaves around my ankles. Something about this doesn't add up. 'I thought John-Paul was imprisoned for possession and smuggling drugs,' I say.

I can feel Olivia's eyes boring into me but I don't look at her. Instead I concentrate on the woman in the doorway.

'Well, you heard wrong.' But she averts her gaze as she says it.

'Mum,' Olivia says, and I turn in her direction. She looks small and scared behind the desk. 'It sounds like John-Paul . . . my father . . . came looking for me in 1998. But where has he been since? Did he go back to prison?'

'I don't know,' says Olivia's mother, irritably. 'He came and then he disappeared again. I can't be answering all these questions now. I don't know much more than you. And you, Jenna,' she fixes her grey eyes on me, 'I've already said too much. You'd better go.'

I glance at Olivia and she inclines her head. I bend down, grab my bag and leave, while they watch me in a tense silence.

As I walk back to my car I'm certain of one thing.

Anastacia Rutherford is lying.

I get behind the wheel, check my mobile and see I have two missed calls and a voicemail from a number I don't recognize. I listen to the message, pleased when I discover it's from Izzy Thorne: 'I'm so sorry I haven't called before. But I wanted to talk to my mum about it first before getting in touch. She'd like to speak to you too. I know it's short notice but it's my day off so if you're free we'd love you to come over.' She reels off an address and then the message ends. I stare at my phone in surprise. With everything that's happened over the last few days I'd almost forgotten I'd passed my number to Izzy. And her mum wants to talk too. It couldn't have come at a better time.

I call back to tell Izzy I'm on my way, then drive straight to the address. Five minutes later I've pulled up outside a 1980s detached house with a double garage at the front. I'm still thinking of Anastacia Rutherford and the inconsistency in her story. Why would she tell me that John-Paul had killed some guy called Derreck in 1980 when that was the year he'd gone to prison for possession of drugs? Not for murder. And if she's lying about it, then why?

I knock at number five and an attractive woman with sharp cheekbones and deep-set dark eyes answers. She must be in her sixties and is slim in dark jeans and a long-sleeved navy and white Breton top. She's an older version of Izzy. And Sally, I think.

'You must be Jenna,' she says warmly, shaking my hand. 'Izzy told me all about you and your podcast.'

Izzy appears behind her mother holding a large fluffy cat, which leaps from her arms and runs upstairs. 'She's not very friendly.' Izzy laughs. 'Come through.'

I go into the living room at the front of the house. It's large and chintzy with pale blue linen sofas, lemon walls and plush curtains at the window. The mantelpiece is crowded with framed photographs of Izzy, when she was younger, and Sally. Izzy's mum sees me looking and picks one up: a photo of teenage Sally with Izzy aged four or five. Izzy has pudgy arms firmly planted around the neck of a giggling Sally. They look so happy. 'This is my favourite,' she says, smiling sadly at the photograph.

'I'm so sorry,' I say, feeling choked.

She shakes her head, her eyes bright with tears. She has a grey streak at the front of her dark hair, like Mrs Robinson in *The Graduate*. She replaces the photo and takes a seat next to a cross-legged Izzy on the sofa by the window. I sit in the armchair by the door.

'Would you like a cup of tea?' she says, about to get up again.

'No, thank you. I've drunk so much today already. Do you mind if I record you for the podcast?'

Mrs Thorne nods. 'Of course not. Go ahead.'

I set up my phone on the coffee-table, then dump my bag by my feet.

Mrs Thorne begins to talk in her slow, deliberate way as though she doesn't want to waste any words and her eyes keep flicking to my phone as though she's self-conscious. I hope she'll forget it's there after a while and be more natural. Izzy sits beside her, listening quietly and nodding every now and again. Mrs Thorne talks about Sally, what she was like, how funny she was, how studious. 'She would never have run off without telling us where she was going,' she says adamantly. 'Tamzin, maybe. But not Katie and definitely not my Sally.'

'What do you think happened to them?' I ask gently.

Mrs Thorne presses a tissue to her eyes and Izzy reaches over and squeezes her mum's hand. 'I think something bad must have happened. It's just been so long now without a word. But, also, there's that little bit of hope, you know? We've kept her bedroom the same. All her . . .' her voice catches '. . . all her things are still there.'

'I go in there sometimes,' says Izzy. 'I can pretend I'm eight again and that my big sister is just out for the evening.'

A beat of silence before I ask, 'Does the name John-Paul Molina mean anything to you?'

Mrs Thorne frowns. 'Gosh, I haven't heard that name in years. He used to go out with Olivia's mum.'

'Do you know what happened to him?'

'Why are you asking?' She doesn't sound angry, more intrigued.

I explain everything that Dale told me, plus my conversation with Anastacia and Olivia.

She exhales. 'So John-Paul is back in town? After all these years?'

'It sounds like it. When was the last time you saw him?'

'In Thailand in early 1980.'

46

I STARE AT MRS THORNE IN SURPRISE. 'IN THAILAND?'

'Yes. January 1980. We were all on holiday as a group.'

I shift in my seat. 'The holiday where Anastacia met Derreck?'

'Yes.' She tucks a lock of hair behind an ear. 'We all went to stay with him, although we hardly knew him, but things weren't great between Anastacia and John-Paul. They were already having problems and Derreck was so charming. So handsome. That hair. Like a young Robert Redford. Stace – that's what we all called her – fell hard for him. Poor John-Paul didn't stand a chance. I did feel sorry for him. And then there was that whole horrendous business at the airport on the way home.'

'Is that where John-Paul got arrested?'

She nods and glances at her daughter. Izzy is staring at her mother as though she's never heard this story before – she probably hasn't. It happened long before she was born. 'He tried to smuggle drugs out of the country. It was such a stupid, stupid thing to do.'

I flinch when I imagine John-Paul getting arrested and having to spend eighteen years in a Thai jail. 'Anastacia said something strange to me. She didn't say John-Paul went to prison for drugs. She said he'd killed someone.'

Mrs Thorne looks puzzled, but then it seems to dawn on her. 'Ah, yes, there was a bit of bad business. I remember Stace telling me on the plane home. Apparently John-Paul had caused the death of one of his friends while he was travelling in Goa by selling him a dodgy batch of drugs. He used to be a bit of a dealer, although obviously we didn't know that at the time. But,' she pulls a confused face, 'as far as I was aware he never went to prison for that.'

'She said he killed this Derreck in a jealous rage?'

'What?' She gives a disbelieving laugh. 'Derreck? Not that I'm aware of. John-Paul did beat him up after he found Stace in bed with him – it was awful. But Derreck was very much alive when we all left Thailand. He didn't even come to the airport with us to say goodbye. There was too much bad feeling between him and John-Paul. We were at the airport about to fly home but drugs were found in John-Paul's backpack while we were waiting to board our flight. It was all very dramatic and . . .' she puts a hand to the necklace at her throat '. . . scary, really. He was dragged off. We had no choice but to fly home without him. Stace was distraught. Totally distraught. It was awful, really awful.'

I frown, my head spinning. 'Why would she tell her daughter that John-Paul had killed Derreck? Unless it happened later? I'm sure she said in 1980, though.'

'I never heard from or saw Derreck again so he could be dead for all I know. But I do know that back in 1980 John-Paul went to prison for drugs. Not murder. It's strange Anastacia told you that.' She turns to Izzy who shrugs.

We're interrupted by the phone ringing beside the TV. 'Excuse me, I'd better get that,' she says, standing up. 'I'll make us a cup of tea afterwards. I've a feeling this is going to be a long interview. We've only just got started.'

'That would be great, thanks, Mrs Thorne.'

'Please,' she says, reaching for the phone. 'Call me Maggie.'

Maggie moves out of the room to talk to whoever is on the phone and Izzy stretches her legs. 'Wow,' she says. 'I never knew anything about Thailand or this John-Paul person. I was so young when Sally went missing. I remember all the business with Wesley and his obsessive behaviour, putting notes on my sister's car and bombarding her with flowers and teddies. I was only nine so I thought it was very romantic, although now . . .' She shudders. 'It was all a bit much. He was properly obsessed. I remember one night my dad going outside to have a stern word with him and tell him Sally wasn't interested and if he kept hanging around he'd call the police.' She plays with her ponytail. She has sparkly gel nails, big hoop earrings and high-waisted jeans. She's very beautiful, and I can only imagine how Sally must have been.

'And did he get the message after that?'

'Yep. He never bothered her again. A few months later he was going out with Olivia. I remember Sally telling Tamzin about it up in her bedroom.' She laughed. 'I used to eavesdrop on their conversations. But my sister was worried about Olivia. She thought Wesley was a creep.'

Maggie comes back into the room with a tea tray and a plate

of custard creams. 'Sorry about that. It was Martin, my husband,' she says, setting the tray on the table. 'He's a bit of a worrier. Since Sally . . . Well, he likes to check up on us regularly while he's at work, bless him. Milk?'

'Just a little. Thanks.'

She hands me the tea and offers me a biscuit. I resist the urge to dunk it.

'So,' I begin again, when she's sitting down. 'Did Anastacia get pregnant in Thailand?'

'No, she was already pregnant before she went. She didn't know it at the time, though. It wasn't until she was nearly sixteen weeks gone that she found out, because she was still getting her periods. Anyway, the baby was definitely John-Paul's with those dates,' she clarifies, as though reading my mind. 'But poor Stace was heartbroken. Here she was back in Stafferbury, broken-hearted over having to leave Derreck behind, guilty about what had happened to John-Paul and how he ended up in prison. She had to move back in with her parents.'

'And you all still stayed friends?'

'Yes. I found out I was pregnant with Sally around the same time so that bonded us. Leonie and Hannah already had kids – they'd started young. They'd left them with grandparents when they went to Thailand, which I was shocked about because Tamzin and Katie were not yet a year old and –'

'Wait,' I say, frowning, as my brain plays catch-up. 'So your other friends who stayed with Derreck in Thailand were . . . ?'

'Hannah and Trevor Burke and Griffin and Leonie Cole. The parents of Katie and Tamzin.'

47

THEY WERE ALL IN THAILAND TOGETHER.

'You were friends?' I ask.

'That's right. Great friends. Not so much with John-Paul as he hadn't been going out with Stace that long, but the rest of us, definitely. I think you've already met Katie's mum, Hannah, haven't you? She told me you went to see her. Sadly her husband, Trev, died a few years back. Prostate. And Leonie and Griff split up. They've both moved away and we don't keep in touch.' She looks wistfully towards the fireplace. 'Stace and I were best friends. We were very close when the girls were small and remained that way until . . . well, the accident. After that Stace seemed to retreat and cut off me, Leonie and Hannah. Olivia was so badly hurt in the crash and Stace had her hands full, being her carer and looking after the riding stables and . . . I had no bad feeling towards them. I knew Olivia wouldn't have done anything to hurt my Sal. But it was like Stace couldn't face me, or Hannah and Leonie.' She looks down at her hands and twiddles one of her rings. 'I think she felt guilty because her daughter was still here while ours . . . weren't.' She sighs and Izzy moves closer to her. 'Anyway,' Maggie lifts her head, 'I'm shocked that John-Paul's back in town.'

'Apparently before the accident Olivia said she saw a man with a scar following her. I've just found out that John-Paul had a scar after some fight.'

Maggie clutches her throat. 'So you're saying that could have been him?'

'It's sounding that way now.'

'So where has he been since then?'

I lean forward to place my teacup on the coffee-table. 'Well, that's the thing. Nobody seems to know. It sounds like his brother has been trying to find him for years. But the trail has led back here.'

'I wonder if he ever tried to contact Stace,' she says, nursing her mug. 'She did tell me that she wrote to John-Paul once, in prison, to tell him about Olivia but she never heard anything back. She wasn't even sure he'd received the letter.'

'And what happened between Stace and Derreck? Did she ever see him again?'

Maggie sips her tea and offers me another biscuit, which I gratefully take. 'Actually she was very cagey about him but I got the sense they kept in touch. She'd disappear every now and again for the weekend, without Olivia, to meet up with some mystery man. She told me she wanted to compartmentalize her life now that she was a mum, and I respected that. But she was so smitten with Derreck. I'd never seen her like that with anyone before, so I have wondered if it was him she was still seeing. I remember on the last day of our holiday in Thailand she and Derreck disappeared for the day. You can just imagine the atmosphere in the villa – poor John-Paul. The lads were great with him, though, took him out drinking. Anyway, when Stace and Derreck came back she told me that they'd got matching tattoos and asked me not to tell the others. They both had it done in the same place, here.' She points to her upper arm. 'A Chinese symbol to remind them to take chances, not to settle. To be brave. So they were serious about each other. It was more than just a holiday romance.'

A Chinese symbol. It rings a bell and I try to remember who I've seen recently with a tattoo like that. And then, with a jolt, I remember. It was Jay. I noticed it when I was in his office and he was reaching for the blind. It was also on his upper arm. What did he say it meant again? Courage.

An image of Jay and Anastacia arguing on the side of the road pops into my mind. He made out he hardly knew her. Something shifts and settles.

'Dale, can I ask you a favour?' I say, into the phone, as soon as I'm back in the car. 'What do you know about Jay Knapton?'

'Why do you ask?' He sounds bemused.

'They were all together in Thailand.'

'Who?'

I fill him in on everything Maggie has just told me. 'They were all friends. Katie, Tamzin, Sally and Olivia's parents. And they were all in Thailand when John-Paul got arrested at the airport.' I explain about Anastacia and Derreck betraying John-Paul and then getting matching tattoos. 'I don't know how Jay Knapton fits into all this but I saw he had the same kind of tattoo –'

'Hold on. I'm at the station right now. Let me just see if he's in our system. Right . . .' I can hear him tapping away at a keyboard. It sounds busy in the background with the murmur of voices and phones ringing. 'Yes. So he's sixty-five. Born 1953 in Australia. Oh, interesting. It looks like he was arrested and charged with possession of a class-B drug with intent to supply back in 1982 in Dover. He escaped a custodial sentence.'

'What's his full name?' I ask.

'Um . . . let's have a look. It says here that his full name is Derreck Jason Knapton.'

Derreck.

'I knew it! I don't quite understand what's going on but Anastacia Rutherford is a liar. She told me and Olivia that John-Paul killed a man called Derreck in Thailand. But then the tattoos . . . Derreck from Thailand and Jay Knapton surely have to be the same person. He must just have dropped his first name, shortened Jason to Jay. Apparently Anastacia was infatuated with him. And when I spoke to Jay he told me he didn't know Anastacia but then I saw them arguing by the side of the road.' I take a deep breath.

'Okay. Hold on. I need to speak to my colleagues about this and I'll call you back.' He hangs up before I've had a chance to ask any more questions.

My heart quickens. I turn on the ignition, my head spinning. I don't know how, or even why, but I think this leads back to Olivia and her missing friends.

The sky darkens and it begins to hail, hammering down so fast that my wipers can't work quickly enough. I stay put, waiting for the hailstones to ease, watching as they ping off the windscreen, cocooned in the warm car with the wipers swishing back and forth, the hail drumming on the hood and roof. I run through everything I've learnt since I've been here. How does it all tie together?

When the hail slows I pull out of Maggie's road. I drive along the high street and then down the Devil's Corridor. It really is a sinister, lonely road. The type of road you'd get in TV dramas where people pull over and bury a body. I shudder. I turn left onto the dirt track that leads to the cabins and pull up outside mine. At least I'll be going home tomorrow. On one hand I'm glad, I'm desperate to see Finn again, but on the other things are beginning to come together and I hope Dale keeps me informed. As I'm getting out of my car I see Samuel with his dog. I call a friendly hello and ask if there's any more news about John-Paul.

He shakes his head. 'I went into town earlier and asked around but nobody seems to know much.'

I hesitate, wondering if I should tell him about the connection with Anastacia Rutherford, then think better of it.

'Actually,' he says, reaching into the pocket of his coat, 'I found this in the cabin.' He shows me a bright orange card. 'It says "A. Rutherford" on it. Do you know who it belongs to?'

My blood runs cold. 'Yes,' I say, taking it. It looks like a loyalty card for some kind of equestrian warehouse. Why would Anastacia's card end up in the cabin? Unless . . . Bile rises in my throat. I'd assumed it was a man hiding there but could it have been her all along? 'Can I take this? I know who it belongs to.'

'Sure. I found it under the bed.' He gives a little salute before his dog drags him away. I stand and watch as he heads further into the forest, his collar up against the weather.

It starts to rain heavily again so I dart into my cabin, shutting the door hurriedly against the gathering winds. My mind is full of Anastacia. What is going on? I slip the loyalty card into my pocket.

I take off my boots. I have mud on the hems of my jeans and they feel damp with rain. I'm freezing and little balls of ice fall from my coat as I hang it up. My mind feels fractured, like looking at my reflection in a broken mirror. I can see different parts but can't understand where they all fit.

It's dark in the cabin and, for a moment, I can't work out why. Then I realize that all the curtains are drawn. That's weird. I'd opened them this morning when I got up.

I'm halfway into the living room when I see I'm not alone.

'Hello, Jenna,' says a deep male voice I recognize.

It's Jay.

48

Olivia

IT TAKES OLIVIA TWENTY MINUTES TO WALK THROUGH town to the forest. She cuts through the standing stones and the fields at the back. Her leg aches and she's soaked through by the time she finds herself outside Jenna's cabin. She hopes she's in. She tried phoning her but it went through to voicemail.

After Jenna left earlier she'd tried to ask her mum about Derreck and John-Paul but her mother's mobile rang and she left to answer it. Olivia had sat there, in the freezing cold office, with just her dark thoughts for company. She was going to confront her mother once and for all about the bright lights she saw after the accident. And the one thing she's always been scared to ask: *Were you there?*

She wonders if her mother will lie about it. After all, she's been lying to Olivia her whole life. Ralph told her that. And now there's this business with John-Paul being her father and the man with the scar, and she suspects her mother's lying about him going to prison for murder too.

She needs to talk again to Jenna, this time without her mother being there. So that's why she's here now, trekking through mud with an aching leg and a heavy heart.

She's relieved when she sees Jenna's car in the driveway. Jenna is the only one who has been honest with her. It doesn't escape her notice that the only person she trusts is a journalist she's known for a few days. What does that say about her life and the people in it?

Olivia knocks on the door and waits. She hears a dog barking from inside the cabin and she feels a flash of unease. Jenna doesn't own a dog. When nobody comes to the door she raps on it again with her knuckles. She tries to peer through the bedroom window but the curtains are closed, and then, another bark. Something is wrong. She tries phoning Jenna but it just rings out.

Olivia creeps around to the back and into the small rear garden with the neat patch of lawn freshly turfed. There is a single patio door but the curtains are closed. Why would all Jenna's curtains be closed during the day? Unless . . . She blushes at the thought. Is Jenna in there with a man? Maybe Dale? She can see he has a thing for her. Is that why she's not answering the phone? But that doesn't explain the dog.

She's just about to turn away when she spots a man's ankle through the gap in the curtains: the trouser leg of a navy blue suit and smart black shoes. Whoever it is looks like they're pacing and, yes, yes, it looks like a dog. A big dog.

'Olivia?'

She turns at the voice behind her. Her mother is standing in the garden. She must have followed her here. 'What's going on?'

Her mother's face is crinkled with worry. 'I think he's lost the plot. He's been backed into a corner.' She clutches Olivia's hand and tries to pull her away from the door. 'It's not safe. Please, we need to leave.'

'What?' Who is her mother talking about?

'It's Jay. He's lost it.'

Olivia stares at her mother in horror. 'Jay Knapton? What's going on? Is he hurting Jenna? Please, Mum. You can't let this happen.'

Suddenly the patio door is thrust open and Jay is standing there. Her mum drops Olivia's hand.

'About time,' says Jay, coldly, addressing her mother. 'Why don't you come in and explain yourself, Stace!'

Stace? Only Maggie ever called her that. Everyone else, including Wesley, shortens her name to Ana.

Olivia watches, frozen to the spot, as her mother steps reluctantly into the cabin. And then she sees Jenna sitting wide-eyed and terrified on the sofa, her arms crossed as though for protection.

Jay turns to her mother with a malevolent look. 'Do you want to tell them about the night of the accident? Or shall I?'

49

The Night of the Accident

IT WAS LATE. WAY PAST HER BEDTIME. STACE LIKED TO WAIT UP *for Olivia to get home. She was only just eighteen and had never been a particularly outgoing girl. She had only got into drinking and partying in the last few months. She was sure that was Tamzin's influence. Since Leonie and Griff had split up their only daughter had become even wilder.*

Things were never quite the same between her old gang of friends after Thailand. They rallied around her, of course – probably because they felt sorry for her being alone and pregnant, with John-Paul banged up in a Thai prison. But she always felt like she was hiding a part of herself from them.

Or, rather, someone.

Derreck Jason Knapton. Her Jay. The love of her life.

After the night they slept together and John-Paul had beaten him up, Derreck had told her everything: the drugs that were in the ornaments, the business he was in, the real reason he had so much money. 'I'm so sorry I didn't tell you before,' he had said, in the bedroom, as she attended to his wounds. 'I never expected to fall for you in such a big way.' At least he was being honest with her, she had reasoned. She insisted he tell her everything and he did. He had smuggled drugs for years, mostly cocaine. He didn't deal it, he said. That had been John-Paul's role and that was how they had met. He had asked John-Paul to come to Thailand so they could carry on working together – but John-Paul had resisted. Kept changing his mind. The Goa episode had knocked his confidence. So Derreck had tried to persuade him to get into smuggling instead. He'd wanted to use Stace and her friends too, thinking it would be less risky if they each had just the one ornament: a token of their holiday.

Before she'd met Derreck her knowledge of drugs was limited to TV dramas and films. But Derreck made her see it wasn't necessarily like that, and normal everyday people could make a lot of money from what he called 'distribution'.

The money was more than she could ever have earned working for her parents in their riding stables, but she knew it was more than that. She was so infatuated with Derreck she'd have done anything he asked.

When she returned to England, pining for Derreck and guilt-ridden at what had happened with John-Paul, she found out she was pregnant. When she broke the news to Derreck over the phone he assured her that it made no difference: he still wanted to be with her. That he loved her. Not long afterwards he moved his 'distribution services' to the UK so they could be together and they met up regularly in different seaside bed-and-breakfasts around the country. She wanted to keep Derreck and his distribution business away from Olivia so he became her secret. She never even told Maggie and *the others about him, and in the end she could almost convince her-self Derreck was just doing a bit of courier work on the side, a well-paid delivery man. After he got arrested in Dover in 1982 he started going by his middle name, Jason. Until she suggested shortening it to Jay. Like her hero, Gatsby. She loved him so much she closed her ears to his dodgy deals and the many businesses he'd set up to clean the money he'd made through drugs.*

In the last eight months he'd even begun visiting her in Stafferbury on the odd occasion – although they were very careful never to be seen together, usually holed up in the little Airbnb apartment he rented under a false name. She was looking forward to seeing him tomorrow night as he was in Stafferbury on 'business'. At first, she'd been terrified one of her old friends would recognize him but it had been nearly eighteen years since Thailand and he had changed a lot, losing most of his lovely blond hair and growing a beard. He was still sexy to her, though. He always would be.

Just as she was turning off the TV the headlights of a vehicle swept across the room. Olivia was home later than usual. Stace loitered in the hallway, expecting to hear the key in the front door. She waited but there was no sound. She didn't want Olivia to think she was waiting up for her so she tiptoed to the front porch to see what her daughter was doing. Maybe she had a boy in the car with her – perhaps that Wesley Tucker she'd been hanging around with. Stace didn't want to pry but when she cupped her hands around her face and peered through the glass, instead of Olivia's little Peugeot she saw a white van. She wondered if it was Derreck but he'd never just turn up because of Olivia. Maybe she would tell Olivia about him one day but she knew he – like her – preferred to keep their relationship separate from everyone else. Derreck wasn't the marrying kind and that was fine by her as long as he was in her life. Other couples lost their heat, their lust for one another, but not them and that was, at least in part, because she didn't have to pick up after him and wash his dirty pants. Theirs was a love that took place inside luxury hotel rooms and quiet little Airbnbs, having sex in bath tubs with champagne on the side.

Someone was getting out of the van. It was a man she didn't immediately recognize, although there was something familiar about the way he walked, the curve of his back, the arms hanging limply at his sides. And then he stopped and looked directly at her, with haunted brown eyes, and she knew straight away who it was. A ghost from her past.

She grabbed her coat from the peg and rushed outside, still in her slippers. The ground was wet although the rain was slowing.

Why was he here?

'John-Paul? Is that you?'

'Stace . . .' His voice was thick, like he was dehydrated. As he stepped closer the light from the porch illuminated his ravaged face, his hollow cheeks, his closely cropped hair and wild beard. She hadn't seen him since that terrible afternoon when he was arrested at the airport. Nearly nineteen years ago.

'What . . . what are you doing here?' She couldn't keep the shock out of her voice.

'I'm sorry . . . I've done something stupid. So, so stupid. I didn't know where else to come.'

A coldness washed over her. 'What do you mean? Where's Olivia?'

'She's my daughter and you never told me,' he sobbed. 'I've been watching her for the last few days. I took photos.' He tapped his pocket. 'I know she's mine. The same chin, the same nose.'

'I did tell you. I wrote to you in prison when I found out,' she

said, trying to speak calmly despite the panic rising within her. After everything that happened in Thailand she owed him that at least. 'What's happened, John-Paul? Where is Olivia?'

'I never got a letter.' He gave a strange kind of howl, his breath blooming out and dissipating into the damp air. 'I blamed you. I blamed you all. I came back here for an explanation and then I saw her. Found out her name. Olivia . . .'

'Where is she, John-Paul? Where is Olivia?' she cried. She felt more scared than she ever had in her life. John-Paul looked deranged standing there with his puckered scar and his unkempt appearance.

'There's been an accident. It was my fault . . .'

'Where? Where is she?' Stace felt for her car keys, which were in her waxed jacket.

'The Devil's Corridor. She's hurt, Stace. I couldn't get her out of the car but I've got the others.'

She pushed past him to her jeep and started the engine, veering away from the drive so vigorously that her tyres screeched on the gravel. From her rear-view mirror she could see him standing there, looking after her car. But she couldn't think about him now. She had to get to her daughter. She drove as fast as she could through the dark lanes, along the high street until she was out on the Devil's Corridor. A low fog made it hard to see clearly but then her headlights picked out Olivia's car on the opposite side of the road, which was otherwise empty. She swung the car into the other lane so that she pulled up in front of Olivia's Peugeot. She could see her daughter in the passenger seat, conscious and blinking, blinded by her headlights. There was a man with her. It was the oddball, Ralph, who lived in the caravan, she was sure of it. Where were the others, though? Olivia had told her she was going out with Sally, Tamzin and Katie. But she could see they weren't in the car.

And then she remembered John-Paul's words. I've got the others. *What did he mean? Why did he have the others? It wasn't like he was taking them to a hospital.*

Her blood turned cold as she recalled his other words. About blaming them all. About revenge.

And then she heard the far-off sounds of a police siren. Help was coming. Olivia would be okay. She looked like she was conversing with Ralph, that he was helping her.

She hesitated. All her instincts screamed at her to go to her daughter but what about the others? What had John-Paul done with them? She had to make a decision, and quickly. So she reversed, did a U-turn and put her foot down. As she drove back towards the stables she rang Jay on her car phone. 'It's urgent. I need you to come to the farm. As quickly as you can. John-Paul is back. I think he's done something . . . something awful.'

She was home within five minutes. John-Paul was standing exactly where she'd left him. As though no time had passed at all.

'Where are the other three girls, John-Paul?'

He turned to look at her, his face full of anguish. 'I didn't mean to hurt them. I just wanted to take them . . . for a little bit. I thought if I took them for a few hours, a day at the most, it would scare you. It would scare all of you and then you'd come clean. One of you would admit what you'd done. It was a moment of insanity.'

'I don't . . . I don't understand. You're making no sense.'

'One of you set me up back in Thailand. I know it wasn't Derreck because he wasn't at the airport. And there were no drugs in my bag when I left the villa. I'd made sure. I hadn't trusted the bastard after what he did with you. So someone slipped those ornaments into my bag at the airport.'

'Please, John-Paul. Where are they? Where are the girls?'

He threw her an odd look before walking calmly to his van. 'In here,' he said opening the rear doors. 'I didn't realize ... I didn't realize how injured they were ...'

Stace couldn't take it in at first. The sight that befell her. Tamzin, Katie and Sally. They were unconscious.

She pushed past him. 'You stupid, stupid man. What have you done? Are they alive?'

'I ... I don't know.' He looked sick. 'It was a stupid spur-of-the-moment thing. I was following Olivia from the club and I was behind her but it was raining so heavily and I had to slow down but I figured she'd be coming back here and then ... I came upon her crashed car. She must have been just a minute or two in front of me. I pulled up behind her and saw them all, unconscious, and it was a stupid wild plan.' He clutches his head. 'I don't know what I was thinking. They were alive when I took them from the car, I promise they were. Unconscious but alive.'

Stace climbed into the back of the van, kneeling beside each girl, horror washing over her when she couldn't feel a pulse for any of them.

'You need to call an ambulance, John-Paul. Now!'

'I can't. How am I going to explain why I took them? How can I explain that I didn't call an ambulance at the scene? They were alive then. Maybe the paramedics could have saved them. They'd say I killed them. I can't ...' He rocked back on his feet, anguish and fear on his face. 'I can't go back to prison.'

Stace was gripped by fear. This wasn't the man she'd left behind in Thailand. That John-Paul wouldn't have hurt a fly. And then she remembered how he'd pummelled Derreck in the face. How he'd stormed out and left him bloodied and bruised on the cold wooden floor. How he'd been dealing drugs before she met him, had caused a teenage boy to die in Goa. And he'd spent eighteen years in a Thai jail, facing horrors she couldn't even comprehend.

She stared at him now, sickened. There were three dead girls in the back of his van because of some spur-of-the-moment revenge plan for the actions of one of their parents.

And it had all been for nothing. Hannah and Trev, Leonie and Griff, Maggie and Martin. They were innocent. All innocent.

'John-Paul, you stupid fucking fool,' she sobbed, getting out of the van. She wanted to scream into the cold night air. 'I was the one who set you up. I put the drugs in your bag! Not them. Me!'

She saw too late what a terrible mistake she had made by admitting it was her fault he'd spent nearly twenty years in a Bangkok prison. His face changed. His once warm eyes grew cold and hard and furious.

And then he lunged for her.

50

Jenna

I'M FROZEN TO THE SOFA AS I WATCH THE EVENTS UNFOLD-
ing in front of me, like I'm the only audience member in a warped
stage play. When I found Jay sitting in the armchair with a German Shepherd at his side everything began to slot into place as he
ranted at me about Olivia's mother and how this was all her fault.
He was acting deranged, not like the cool and collected businessman he'd appeared when I'd first met him. And all I could think
about was trying to find a way to escape. I'd been relieved when
Olivia and her mother had turned up. But now, after listening to
Anastacia's story, I realize I'll be lucky to get out of this situation
alive. They're telling me too much.

Olivia slumps into the armchair by the fire as though her
legs can no longer keep her upright. She covers her face with her
hands. Anastacia is pacing my living room as she tells her version

of events, and Jay is standing by the fireplace, the dog on the floor by his side.

'So they're dead?' Olivia says, removing her hands and staring up at Jay with her pale face. She looks a mixture of terrified and furious.

'Of course they're dead,' snaps Jay. 'If they'd had any chance of survival the idiot John-Paul put paid to any of that.'

'Then why didn't you just go to the police?' Olivia wails. 'It's not like it was Mum's fault. John-Paul was the one who'd taken them.'

Anastacia stops pacing and exchanges a glance with Jay. 'He wasn't in his right mind,' she says quietly to Olivia. 'And I wouldn't have put it past him to hurt you. That night . . . I don't know if he would have taken you as well if you hadn't been trapped.'

'So that's why you didn't ring the police? Because you thought he'd hurt me? Then what? You just let him go?'

Guilt is written all over Anastacia's face. I watch as she locks eyes with Jay and, from the fury in his expression and the infinitesimal shake of his head, I can tell he's silently communicating with her. And suddenly I know exactly why she didn't go to the police.

'You killed him, didn't you?'

'No!' Olivia cries. 'That can't be right. He's back. He's been seen in Stafferbury.'

The look that passes between Jay and Anastacia tells me I'm right.

'It was self-defence,' cuts in Jay. 'He went for her after she told him it was her fault he'd been caught with drugs in Bangkok.'

A sob escapes Anastacia's lips. 'I was terrified. He was deranged.' I can tell from her face that she's actually telling the truth. 'In Thailand I was so angry with John-Paul, so angry, for the way he beat up Jay.' The look she gives Jay is tender, but there is something else behind it too. Guilt, perhaps. 'And I wanted to impress you,' she says now to Jay, 'so I agreed to take three of the Buddhas.' She turns back to Olivia with a stricken expression. A confession between mother and daughter. 'I knew it wasn't the exact requirements of the customer. That was all eight of them. But it would be some money and it would be a way for me to prove to Jay how much I loved him. But then, at the last minute, in the minivan on the way to the airport I lost my nerve. So, as we were getting out of the van I shoved the ornaments into John-Paul's bag. I never thought for a minute he'd get caught. And I thought even if he did the drugs were so well sealed . . .' She groans. 'But then . . . he was pulled out of the queue and his bag searched. And that was when . . . I didn't mean for it to happen,' she wails. 'Please believe me, love,' she says to Olivia. 'It was just bad luck . . .'

Nobody speaks, not even Jay, although by his expression I can tell he's heard this before. We're all frozen in that moment until Anastacia speaks again. I know what she's going to say and bile rises in my throat.

'After I told him . . . that night . . . he went for me. I had to run for my life. He chased me into the stables, screaming that he was going to kill me. He wasn't in his right mind, I knew that. And I . . .' she pales '. . . I grabbed the first thing I could find, a pitch fork, and I – I drove it into him. It wasn't premeditated. It was about survival. And then . . . Jay . . .' I can see she's trembling '. . . Jay turned up and . . .' She looks at Olivia imploringly. 'It was wrong to cover it up. But I was so scared of losing you. You had nobody else. If I'd called the police I could have gone to prison, and then what?'

Olivia shakes her head in confusion. 'So John-Paul isn't back in Stafferbury? Then why did you say he was? Why did you say he was looking for me?'

'I . . . we . . .' Her eyes flick to Jay and then back to her daughter. 'We wanted people to think John-Paul was still alive. So over the years we would book things under his name. Just in case anyone was looking for him. We hadn't done it for a while and then –'

'Is that why you hid in the cabin opposite mine?' I interject. 'To make me think it might be John-Paul dossing down?' I take the card Samuel gave me from my coat pocket and hold it up. 'This was found in the cabin.'

Anastacia snatches it, turning it over in her hand. Then she hangs her head.

So she had been going in and out of the cabin with the dog. Jay must have been in on it too, gave her the key, then pretended not to know what I was talking about when he came to meet me that day.

'But you ruined it all when you stupidly booked that B-and-B in the high street under his name,' snaps Jay, 'which led his brother here.'

'I didn't even know he had a brother!' wails Anastacia, rounding on Jay. 'How could I know that this would happen?'

'So you panicked,' says Olivia, in a strangled voice, 'and told me that he was back.'

Anastacia looks shame-faced. 'I had to go along with it when I found out his brother had arrived.'

'So why did you tell me he'd killed Derreck?'

'It was stupid . . . I was worried you'd find out that Derreck was really Jay. And . . .'

I remember Dale's comments about the county-lines stuff, a Stafferbury drugs ring and Jay's previous conviction. I've no doubt Jay – Derreck, whatever he wants to call himself these days – is involved.

Olivia's eyes narrow. 'Your friends . . . Maggie . . . they deserve to know the truth about what really happened.' She turns to Jay. 'This is all your fault,' she spits. 'I bet it was you who helped cover it all up.'

'Yes. And I've been clearing up her fucking mess ever since.' His tanned face is contorted with fury. 'You,' he snarls at me. 'If you hadn't come here, poking around, none of this would have happened. Thanks to you I've had the police sniffing around, looking into my affairs. My businesses.'

'It has nothing to do with me,' I say, trying to remain calm. 'It sounds like they've been looking into you and the drugs ring for a while.'

Anastacia shoots Jay a scathing look. 'Like I haven't been covering for you too. Your drug deals. Getting Wesley involved. I told you not to do that. And then there's Ralph . . .'

'Shut up. You've already said too much.'

'Stop!' Olivia stands up. 'Stop it. This ends here. It all ends here . . .' She lets out an anguished sob. 'Please, Mum. Just tell the police what you did. It was self-defence with John-Paul. And the others . . .' A tear trickles down her face. 'Their deaths weren't your fault.'

Anastacia rushes to Olivia and takes her hand. 'I'm so sorry.'

'Tell them, please. For me.'

I stand up, too, and then I hear it. A laugh. Cruel and deep and guttural. It's coming from Jay.

'Oh, I don't think so,' he says to me. 'Do you really believe I can let you leave now? You know too much.'

He slowly reaches into his pocket and that's when I see he's got a knife.

Olivia screams. 'Run! Jenna, run!'

I hesitate for a split second. I don't want to leave Olivia but I have to get out of here if I want to live. He makes a grab for me as I dart towards the door, but I'm younger and quicker and manage to duck under his arm. I run from the cabin, sensing he's right behind me. My heart is pounding: Jay knows the forest well – he'll find me there in minutes. Samuel's car isn't in the driveway, I have no choice but to run towards the Devil's Corridor in the hope I can stop a passing car, if Jay, or his dog, doesn't catch up with me first. He might be twenty-odd years older than me but he's stronger and more powerful and clearly psychotic. If he kills me he won't get away with it, but that's of little comfort to me.

I run like I've never run before, like I did as a child. It feels as though my legs won't be able to keep up with me. My lungs are burning with the effort. I can hear Jay behind me, the bark of a dog. He's gaining on me. It's raining again and the weight of the water seeping through my clothes is slowing me down. I'm nearly at the end of the dirt track. I just need to get to the main road. I make the mistake of looking back. Jay is within reach and Anastacia is running behind him, her arms windmilling in the air. Is she trying to stop him or is she urging him on? Olivia is standing at the cabin and she's bravely grabbed the collar of the dog, thank goodness, phone pressed to her ear.

I dart across the road. I'm so blinded by fear I only notice the pick-up truck heading out of town as I sprint past it. I collapse and roll into the grass verge on the other side, shaking at the near miss, but then I hear the screech of brakes and a thud. The truck has stopped and a man is getting out on the passenger side and another guy – the driver – is standing over a figure lying prostrate in the road.

51

Olivia

DALE HANDS MUGS OF TEA TO HER AND JENNA. THEY ARE sitting side by side on the sofa in Jenna's living room and Dale takes the armchair by the patio door. Olivia feels like she's gone into shock. She can't stop shaking and she feels she might throw up. By the look on Jenna's face she must be feeling the same.

Jay was taken off in an ambulance and her mother went with him, along with a police officer. Olivia and Jenna stayed behind to give their statements to the baby-faced constable DC Stirling, and now they're in Jenna's cabin, alone with Dale.

'What will happen to my mum?' she asks Dale now. Her voice sounds small even to her own ears. She laces her fingers around the mug, trying to steady her trembling hands.

'We'll need to interview her formally.'

'She might deny it.'

'If she does we'll just have to gather all the evidence we can and hope it's enough. But don't think about that now. You've been through so much,' he says kindly. There is sadness in his eyes too and she remembers how fond he'd once been of Tamzin.

To her horror she begins to cry and Jenna reaches over and rubs her arm.

'I suspected they must have died . . .' she sobs '. . . but to have it confirmed, it feels . . . well, it feels . . .' Her chest is so heavy with grief she can't breathe. 'Do you think they would have survived the accident if it hadn't been for John-Paul?'

'We'll never know,' says Dale. 'You were lucky to survive it, Olivia. I know it doesn't feel that way after what you've lived with but . . .'

She remembers Katie and Tamzin weren't wearing seatbelts. She can't bear the thought of them in the back of that van, in pain, denied hospital treatment because of her psychopath of a father. If he hadn't moved them they might have survived their injuries.

'All these years. My mother knew and never told me. No wonder she didn't see Maggie and the others again. How could she face them knowing the truth?'

'It would have been difficult for her,' pipes up Jenna, who had, until now, remained quiet. 'She did say she was trying to protect you. I like to think I'd have done the right thing, if it had been me, but having to leave my son . . .' Pain flashes in her face. 'I'm not excusing her, just saying it must have been a hard decision.'

'But it was self-defence, wasn't it? He was chasing her,' says Olivia. 'She might not have gone to prison.'

Dale places his mug on the coffee-table. 'She must have be- lieved everything was stacked against her and didn't want to take the chance. Maybe she was worried the police would find out about the drugs and her role in it all.'

'I bet Jay didn't help,' says Olivia, her voice bitter. 'He's had a hold over her all these years. It was so manipulative,' she turns to Jenna, 'the way they pretended John-Paul was still alive by hiding out in the cabin opposite. Scaring you like that.'

'Jay borrowed the dog from one of his dealer mates,' explains Dale. He crosses his legs and Olivia notices he has novelty penguin socks on. 'I don't know if you're aware, Olivia, but Jay is currently being investigated for his role in a drugs ring here in Stafferbury.'

Olivia isn't surprised. 'My mum said something about Wesley. Is he involved too?'

'It's looking that way. I'm sorry,' says Dale. 'There's something else about Wesley.' He grows uncomfortable and fidgets in his chair. He glances at Jenna, then back at Olivia. 'I'm happy to tell you about it in private.'

'I don't care about Wesley,' she blurts out. 'After everything else that's happened he's the last thing on my mind. And Jenna,' she turns and smiles at the journalist, 'I have no secrets from her.' She swallows the lie with a gulp of the hot tea.

Dale fidgets in his seat. 'I went back to the stones last night, after I found you. I had my suspicions about what happened to you. And I found a needle and had it tested. Your theory was right. Someone injected you with a date-rape drug.'

Olivia sits up in her chair, her hands gripping her mug. 'But . . . I wasn't raped. There'd be signs, wouldn't there?'

'I don't think the plan was rape,' he says softly. 'I'm not sure what it was. I'm afraid for that you'd have to ask Wesley.'

Nausea rises in Olivia's throat. 'Why?' she asks. Her whole body goes hot and then cold, like she's been doused with a bucket of water.

'I went to The Raven and asked to look through their CCTV footage. I saw you with Wesley, around seven thirty p.m. He was carrying you along the high street, away from his flat and towards the standing stones. There was a witness too. A woman in the pizza place saw him carrying you across the road to the field.'

She recalls the fear she'd felt last night as she walked home, the neck-tingling sensation that someone was behind her, following her. A hand. A hand had clasped her mouth. And the pain she'd felt in her leg all day. That pin prick in her thigh, the tear in her jodhpurs. He'd injected her. She can hardly believe it.

'Why? Why would he do this to you, Olivia? That's . . . I just can't comprehend it.' Jenna shakes her head.

But Olivia knows why. 'Because he's been gaslighting me for years. I suspected it but I lacked self-esteem so I was just grateful to have someone. He knew I was moving away from him. He wanted me scared. And it almost worked. I went running to him like an idiot. Hoping he'd keep me safe from the monsters. But he is the monster.'

Dale and Jenna remain silent, just staring at her. Is that admiration on their faces?

'God, you're so brave, you know that,' says Jenna. 'I wish I had half your courage.'

It's one of the nicest things anyone has ever said to her. And despite this being one of the most horrific weeks of her life she allows herself a moment to glow, until she remembers and her world comes crashing down again.

Later that afternoon Jenna decides they should go for a walk to clear their heads. Dale has promised to keep them updated but Jay is in a critical condition in hospital and her mother and Wesley are in custody. Olivia wonders if her mum will backtrack on her confession when faced with the police. She wants to see her as soon as she's able, but Wesley, as far as she's concerned, can rot in Hell. He'll be looking at a prison sentence, Dale reckons. They might not be able to prove what he did to her with the injection and the drugging – it horrifies her every time she thinks of him doing that to her, then leaving her alone among the stones in the dead of night – but a raid on his flat found enough cocaine and MDMA to prove it was much more than recreational. Dale believes he'll buckle under questioning and Olivia hopes he's right. She never wants to see Wesley again.

'I need to tell you the truth about something,' Olivia says now, as they make their way through the thicket of trees. The sky has cleared and sunlight glints through the leaves, casting dappled shadows on the ground. Olivia thrusts her hands into her pockets to keep them warm.

'What's that?' says Jenna, stepping carefully over tree roots. They are walking towards the clearing to where Ralph's caravan is.

'Those notes. In the flowers and on your car. My mum wrote them. I recognized her handwriting straight away. For so many years I wondered about the night of the accident and those bright lights. I was in and out of consciousness but Ralph also saw the lights – although he thought it was alien-related.' She gives a small laugh. 'Poor Ralph. I was blinded by those lights, so couldn't see who was in the car. But when the car turned and drove away, I was sure I saw the number-plate. Our number-plate. I told myself, over the years, that I imagined it. But when I saw the notes . . . I realized my mum must have known something more about that night.' She wipes a tear away from her eye. She's been crying, on and off, all day. 'I was selfish. I knew that to ask her could change everything.'

Jenna turns back to look at her, eyebrow raised. 'Oh, Olivia.'

'I was worried you'd realize my mum wrote the notes. So when I saw that one from your car in your kitchen I threw it on the fire just in case it had her fingerprints on or someone else recognized her writing. It was stupid of me. I shouldn't have tried to protect her. I never knew the extent of it all, I promise.'

'I know,' says Jenna.

'I didn't know she'd hurt anyone. I just thought she . . .' She sighs. Her breath blooms out in front of her before dissipating into the cold air. 'I thought maybe Mum knew more about what had happened to Sally, Tamzin and Katie.'

Jenna stops and squeezes her hand in sympathy.

Olivia hadn't even begun to process how her father – this John-Paul – fitted into all this. Was he the figure she saw standing in the road? He'd told her mum that he had been following them in his van and was behind them when the accident happened, so it couldn't have been him. Maybe it had been Ralph and he'd lied to her. Or perhaps the rumours about strange goings-on in Stafferbury had some truth to them after all.

They begin walking again, both deep in thought.

They've reached the clearing and Olivia stops at the sight of Ralph's caravan, overcome with emotion as she remembers their last meeting. She shivers. She doesn't want to be out here in the forest, so near to where Ralph died.

'Who do you think killed him?' asks Jenna, as if reading her mind.

'I don't know.'

'Do you think it was Jay? Something to do with the drugs?' She glances at Olivia and must see the pain in her expression. 'I'm sorry, let's not think about it now. Come on.' She links her arm through Olivia's. 'Let's go and sort those horses of yours. I can help. And if you don't fancy being on your own tonight you can stay at the cabin with me.'

Olivia swells with gratitude. She suddenly yearns to be back with her beloved horses.

After all, they don't lie and cheat and manipulate or let you down, like people do.

Day Five

52

Jenna

*THE DEVIL'S CORRIDOR HAS TAKEN A FURTHER VICTIM.
This time Derreck Jason Knapton – also known as Jay. He
died in the early hours of this morning. I came here to cover a
story about the disappearance of three young women. I never
imagined I'd be at the epicentre when the truth was revealed.
It might not have been a mystical or supernatural phenomenon
but Madame Tovey had been right about one thing. It had all
started with the lovers.*

Izzy is in Bea's Tearoom when we arrive for breakfast. I stayed
at the stables with Olivia last night, both of us not wanting to
be alone. We drank wine and sat up for hours, just talking and
thinking out loud. About Wesley and her mother, Jay and the
drugs ring. 'I think Wesley was so desperate to move in with

me to clean this dodgy money he had made,' she'd said sadly. 'I thought it was odd after so long. I think he's been working for Jay for a while. At least two or three years.'

'You should speak to him, really. Get some answers.'

She'd sighed. 'Why? He'd only lie. I don't think that man has ever been straight with me.'

Now she stands next to me, pale-faced and baggy-eyed. The tearoom is packed and there is only one table free. When Izzy spots us she rushes over and grabs hold of Olivia's arm. 'Is it true? Did you know?'

Olivia backs away. 'Of course I didn't.'

Izzy doesn't look convinced. Her dark eyes flash but then she seems to remember where she is and plasters a professional smile onto her face. 'Sit down and I'll fetch you some menus.'

I can feel many pairs of eyes on us as we walk to our table by the window. Maybe this wasn't such a good idea, after all. We've just sat down when a woman approaches us. It's Hannah Burke, Katie's mum. 'How can you show your face around here? Your parents are responsible for killing my child . . .'

'I'm so sorry, Mrs Burke,' Olivia begins, her chin wobbling.

'Hey, she doesn't have anything to apologize for,' I butt in. 'I'm sorry about your daughter but it's not Olivia's fault. She's just as much a victim in this as her friends.'

Mrs Burke slumps onto the seat opposite us and her shoulders droop in defeat. I notice the other customers staring in our direction, expectation on their faces. 'My Trevor died never knowing . . .' A sob escapes her lips.

Another woman appears at the table. Short and round with blonde hair. 'Come on, Hannah, love,' she says, putting an arm around Mrs Burke and almost lifting her from her chair. 'It's not Olivia's fault. None of this is her fault.'

I watch as the woman leads Mrs Burke back to the table.

'God,' mumbles Olivia. 'I feel awful. Can we go?'

'Sure,' I say, getting up. But as we leave, aware that our every movement is being scrutinized, I want to tell Olivia this is what it will be like for her, if she stays in this town. But then I remember: it's always been like this for her. Ever since the accident. She's used to it.

I drive Olivia back to the safety of the riding stables but run into the garage on the way to pick us up some croissants. Thankfully, there are no lessons booked in today so she doesn't have to face anyone.

'Do all these horses belong to you?' I say, as I follow her into the yard after we've sat in the cold office and eaten a croissant, although Olivia picked at hers.

'No, only Sabrina. The rest are livery. It means that we look after them for their owners, some on a reduced rate if they let us use their horse for the riding school,' she explains, when she notices my blank expression. She sets about sorting out the horses as though on auto-pilot. I help her as best I can even though horses terrify me.

'I'm not going to be able to keep this going by myself,' she says, as she stuffs some hay into a large net.

'Maybe cancel all lessons and close for a few days,' I suggest. 'Then you can have a think about it. You could get someone in to help you?'

She doesn't say anything but presses her lips together so that they turn white. And then I realize what she's not saying. There is nobody to help her.

I'm standing uselessly in the middle of the yard watching Olivia hauling horse dung and wet straw into a wheelbarrow, trying not to feel sick at the strong smell of ammonia, when I hear a car pull up. Dale strides through the five-bar gate, his shoes clipping the concrete as he makes his way over to us.

'Thought I'd find you here when I saw you weren't at the cabin. For a moment I thought you'd left without saying goodbye. Hi, Olivia,' he adds, when he notices her next to me.

'Is everything okay? Have you seen my mum?'

'I haven't but she's been charged with manslaughter and perverting the course of justice. She'll go before a magistrates' court later. She's pleading not guilty so it looks like her case will be referred to the Crown Court.'

'When will I be able to see her?'

Dale's eyes soften. 'Soon. I'll arrange it.'

'And Wesley?' I ask.

'Well, he's pinned everything on Jay, which is easy to do now that Jay is dead. But he's agreed to help us with information concerning other members of this drugs ring for a more lenient sentence. Jay Knapton, it appears, was only one cog in a large wheel.'

Olivia doesn't say anything. She just looks at her feet.

'Who would have thought a small town like Stafferbury had such a massive drug problem?' I say. 'How long was Wesley involved?'

'A long time by the sound of it. Different scams and ways of making money. He's got a charge sheet as long as my arm.' He looks like he wants to say more but doesn't. He meets my eyes, then looks at the ground, a flush creeping up his neck. What is he not saying?

'Did my mum have a part to play in that too?' asks Olivia, raising her head and fixing her gaze on Dale.

'I'm afraid so, yes. To what extent is still unclear.'

There's more he's not saying. I can sense it.

Olivia's shoulders slump but she remains silent.

'So what time are you leaving?' Dale says to me.

I glance at my watch. I still need to get back to the cabin and gather the rest of my things. 'Soon,' I say regretfully. I feel bad about leaving Olivia.

'Reporters are already beginning to descend.' He folds his arms across his chest. 'Just be careful what you tell them,' he says to Olivia, 'and if there are any problems, give me a call.'

I feel a swell of gratitude towards him.

'I'll see you back at the cabin,' he says to me, then walks off towards his car.

I turn to Olivia. Her eyes have filled with tears. 'It's silly,' she says, brushing them away.

'Come here,' I say, and I hug her close. 'You'll be okay,' I say, into her hair. 'You're strong. You've endured a lot and you can get through this. And remember, if you ever fancy a change of scene you're always welcome to come and stay with me in Manchester.'

As I drive away I see her in my rear-view mirror standing by the gate, looking small and lost, and my heart breaks.

53

DALE IS WAITING FOR ME BACK AT THE CABIN.

'So come on, then, Mr Detective Sergeant CID, what is it you couldn't say in front of Olivia?' I say, as I step out of the car.

'Nothing gets past you, does it?' He laughs, falling in beside me.

'Nope.'

I let us into the cabin. 'It's about Tamzin,' he says, taking a seat at the kitchen table. He's wearing black socks today. For some reason it makes me feel sad, like it's symbolic. 'Wesley was black-mailing her. He told her to steal the petty cash from her work or he'd tell me and her friends that she'd slept with him.'

'What a fucking toad,' I say, shocked. 'Was he sleeping with her?'

'He says so. Before he started going out with Olivia, but while she was with me.' He shrugs. 'He could be lying, of course. A way to goad me, no doubt. Why else would he admit that now?'

'And what about Ralph? Do you know who killed him?'

'Wesley says it was Jay. That Ralph didn't want to be a dealer any more. They could no longer trust him, apparently. But, well, Wesley would say that, wouldn't he? I wouldn't be surprised if it was Wesley who'd killed him. But, of course, we can't prove that.'

'And the photos that were in Ralph's caravan?'

'Anastacia said Jay had taken them from John-Paul's coat and hidden them in Ralph's caravan because he didn't know where else to put them. He was worried about burying them with John-Paul's body because he didn't want there to be a link between him and Olivia if his body was ever found. He could have burnt them, of course, which makes me think he kept them at Ralph's to set him up if it ever came to it.'

'Where did Jay bury John-Paul and . . . the girls?'

Dale grimaces. 'He would have had people to call upon. His drug-dealing mates. The police will put pressure on them to reveal it. And Anastacia too. I'm sure she knows.'

I think of Madame Tovey's words about John-Paul, Katie, Tamzin and Sally still being here, in Stafferbury, and a shiver runs down my spine. She was right. Maybe she isn't a charlatan after all.

'Wesley said Jay was so worried about the tourism going down, and nobody visiting Stafferbury, that he perpetuated the myths about the strange goings-on around here,' says Dale. 'There were recordings on Jay's phone of a child crying.'

'Wait! So that child crying I heard? That was just some kind of recording?'

Dale purses his mouth and nods.

'I heard it on the night I was attacked.'

'Wesley has admitted to attacking you and playing the recording. He said he never meant to hurt you. Jay wanted him to scare you away so that you'd talk about the supernatural elements of Stafferbury in your podcast. I think he was hoping you'd not focus so much on the crash. Jay always got someone else to do his dirty work. He was a bit of a father figure to Wesley by all accounts, especially in the last few years. He admitted to the dead birds too.'

'God.' I let this information digest and curdle in my stomach.

'I think on one hand Jay wanted you around to report on the myths and legends in order to boost tourism, but on the other he didn't want you to find out what was really going on with the drugs ring and the girls' disappearance.'

I touch the back of my head where I was struck. I'd had a lucky escape.

Dale rubs his stubble. He looks exhausted with shadows under his eyes, his hair even messier than usual. 'God, this has been a case and a half. I need a holiday.'

I suddenly think of something. 'Can I be the one to tell Brenda?'

He chuckles. 'Sure. I need to get back to work anyway. Another day, another caseload.' He stands up and I follow suit. There is a moment of awkwardness and our eyes lock. 'Thank you, Jenna. I've enjoyed you being here, having someone to chat to about all this.' He pulls me into his arms and hugs me tightly. I'm so surprised I inhale sharply, breathing in his musky scent. I hug him back.

We stay like that for a moment before I pull away. 'You'll keep an eye on Olivia, won't you? I'm worried about her.'

'I promise,' he says.

I follow him to the door and watch as he walks to his car. Before getting in he turns to me, his expression pensive, and then he folds himself into the driver's seat.

As I wave him off a lump forms in my throat.

An hour and a half later, my bags are packed into the boot of my Audi and the keys posted through the letter box. I wonder what will happen to Knapton Developments. I stand outside, looking up at the cabin, my heart heavy. I've updated my editor, Layla, who was beyond excited when she heard I'd have a conclusion to the podcast after all. After Dale left earlier I'd gone to see Brenda and told her everything. She'd stared at me in wide-eyed surprise as I recounted it all, her hands to her face as I told her about how Jay chased me with a knife.

'I can die happy now,' Brenda had said, as she showed me out. 'I was worried I'd never find out what happened to them.'

It's a relief to be leaving even if I will miss Olivia and, if I'm honest with myself, Dale too. As I get behind the wheel and drive slowly away I bid a silent farewell to the cabin in the forest where so much has happened.

As I turn onto the Devil's Corridor and away from Stafferbury, the heavens open. And I don't know if it's the misty rain causing my mind to see things that aren't there, but in my rearview mirror I'm sure I see the shape of a hooded figure standing in the road.

Three months later

THE ROOM IS NOISY WITH THE HUM OF EXCITABLE CHATTER and it smells of vegetables and bad breath. The guard shows Olivia to where her mother is sitting behind a table and gives her instructions on not touching or getting too close.

'Thank you for coming.' Her mother looks up with haunted eyes. Olivia thinks she seems well, considering. Her grey hair is longer and is tied back at the base of her neck, making her appear older but her eyes tell a different story. They are mirrors of grief and horror and loneliness. 'I didn't think you would visit,' she says.

It had taken her a while to agree to her mother's request. But now she feels ready, although she avoids her gaze as she pulls out a plastic chair. She can't start feeling sorry for her now. As she sits down she casts her eye around the room where more than a dozen other interactions between the female inmates and their loved ones are taking place.

'I'm so sorry.' Her mother's voice cracks. 'I'm sorry for what I did and for never telling you, for letting you wonder about your friends for all these years. I hid it all, the business with Jay, the drugs, everything because I didn't want to implicate you or drag you into the murky world I found myself in. I was angry that Jay had recruited Wesley.'

But Olivia doesn't want to talk about that. She doesn't want to hear excuses. She's tried to get on with her life in Stafferbury. It hasn't been easy but she's getting through it. She's finally grown up and is standing on her own two feet.

They fall silent, although Olivia can see the barely suppressed emotion behind her mother's rictus smile.

'The stables are doing well,' Olivia says, to break the tension. 'Jay got what he wanted with the tourism. It's thriving since the truth came out.'

At the mention of Jay her mother's face falls and she looks down at her hands.

'I've employed a yard manager,' Olivia continues. 'A woman around my age called Violet. She's a bit of a loner too. No husband or kids. She's been a lifeline, and has become a good friend. And I have a proper accountant now to do the books. And two part-time helpers who come and muck out the horses.'

Her mother looks up. 'How did you find the money?'

Thankfully, the riding stables had been run legitimately, so the police didn't seize it after the drugs ring was broken. 'I've begun renting one of the outbuildings as an Airbnb. Borrowed some money from the bank.'

'I'm proud of you,' she says softly, her eyes sparkling.

Olivia swallows the lump in her throat. She hardens herself. 'Have you heard about Wesley?'

Her mother shakes her head.

'He's got twelve years. He admitted to theft and drug-dealing and possession of class-A substances. He's got away with what he did to me, though.'

'I'm sorry I got him so wrong. I thought he was your Gatsby.'

'Oh, for fuck's sake, Mum,' Olivia hisses, causing her mother to shrink back in her seat, like she's been slapped. 'Why do you still hold on to all these ridiculous romantic notions? You do know what happened to Gatsby, don't you?'

'Of course I do. I've read the book enough times.'

Olivia gives a hollow laugh. 'It sounds like John-Paul was more your Gatsby. Look what you did to him.'

'Please don't be bitter, Olivia. I want you to find love.'

'Well, I don't want it, thanks very much.' She takes a deep breath. She doesn't want to argue. She's getting on with her life and she's happy. Sort of. She's got a new friend in Violet and she keeps in touch with Jenna. It's more than she deserves. She tries not to resent her mother. She still loves her, despite everything.

'Will you come and see me again?' her mother asks, when their session has ended.

Olivia stands up. 'Of course I will,' she says briskly.

This is what their relationship will be like now, she sees, snatched conversations across tables in prison visiting rooms. Her mother has an eight-year sentence for manslaughter. She changed her plea to guilty in the end in exchange for a lighter sentence but she'll still be in her early seventies by the time she's allowed out.

She can feel her mother's eyes on her as she leaves the room. It's not until she's outside, away from people, that she lets the tears flow freely down her cheeks.

* * *

On the train home she calls Jenna. They speak once every few weeks. Olivia is hoping to get up to Manchester soon.

'Still not driving, then?' Jenna asks now.

'I will. I promise. I need to do a refresher course or something. It's been a long time.'

Jenna's voice softens. 'And how did it go today?'

Olivia glances out of the window at the countryside rushing past. 'As well as could be expected. Mum looked okay, though, so that's good. She hasn't been beaten up or anything. How are you?'

Jenna lets out a deep breath. 'I'm okay. The house is on the market. I'm staying in it with Finn until it's sold. Anyway, eventually Gavin will have Finn every other weekend.'

'So the divorce is definitely going ahead?'

'Yes. Finding out about Clara has moved things along.' She gives a bitter laugh. Olivia wasn't surprised to hear that Gavin had fallen for another woman, a work colleague ten years his junior. She could hear Jenna fighting back tears when she first told her not long after returning home. 'It's not a surprise and I actually feel okay about it.' She laughs. 'Well, no, that's a lie. I'm fucking furious about it but I'll get over it. At least I have Finn and, on the occasion I do need to stay overnight somewhere, my mum looks after him. Finding out about Clara gave me the ammunition I needed. Gavin has no choice but to be reasonable now.'

'And what about Dale?'

'Oh, we keep in contact.' She hears the smile in Jenna's voice. 'I think maybe . . . in the future something could happen. But it's too soon right now. I need to be on my own for a while first. It's going to take me a while to trust a man again.'

'I definitely get that,' agrees Olivia, snuggling back in her seat. And in that moment, despite everything, she feels contentment wash over her.

She asks the taxi driver to drop her off at the Devil's Corridor. She hasn't been to the forest in weeks and has tried to avoid it since the bodies were recovered. But now she feels a macabre desperation to visit the place where they were found. To say goodbye.

Dale had called her just after Christmas to tell her where Jay – or one of his cronies – had buried them. Their remains have now been removed, funerals held. She went to them all, standing at the back with Dale, trying to make herself invisible, although Izzy and Maggie hugged her at the end of the service. 'We don't blame you,' Maggie had whispered in her ear, as she embraced her. And it had been a huge weight off Olivia's shoulders.

She heads to the cabin where Jenna had been staying, blissfully unaware that the victims lay in a patch of the forest just beyond the garden. She wonders if Jay had chosen that cabin especially for Jenna, as though he enjoyed toying with her. With all of them.

She barely knew the man. But she hates him with every fibre of her being.

The cabin is still intact but at the foot of the garden there is a massive hole. It took the police a long time to discover where the bodies were buried because her mother professed to not knowing where they were. Olivia hopes she was telling the truth because the least she could do was put her former friends out of their misery.

Olivia steps over upended soil and rocks until she reaches the bottom of the garden. Darkness washes over her as she remembers everything that happened in Jenna's living room: her mother's confession, Jenna's terror, Jay's psychotic behaviour. He'd acted like a wild animal who knew he was backed into a corner. She kneels down on the hard, uneven ground and bows her head, offering up a prayer to a God she's no longer sure she believes in.

It's a cold February afternoon and frost has formed over the soil so that it crunches underfoot. Olivia gets up and pulls her hat more firmly onto her head, blowing on her gloved hands. She half expects to turn around and see Jay standing behind her, with that evil glint in his eye. How could her mother have fallen for a guy like that? But then again, didn't she do the same thing, not noticing Wesley's flaws at first?

She whispers a goodbye to her three friends, in particular to Sally, who she'll miss for the rest of her life. And then she walks away, heading for the field of standing stones that will lead her back in the direction of the stables. Her leg has started to ache but she has enough energy to make a detour past the clearing to where Ralph's caravan still stands, now empty, the windows cracked.

She bows her head. If only she had some flowers to put there, the place where he died. But that would look weird.

She had been so grateful for Ralph's help on the night of the accident. Her gratitude had blinded her to his flaws. When he found the money in the footwell of her car – the money she later realized Tamzin had stolen – he'd kept it and told her about it when he came to visit her in hospital a few weeks later. It was the missing two hundred pounds and she'd said he should keep it. She did it to protect Tamzin so she wouldn't get into trouble for stealing. And she was sure, at that point, that her friends would come back.

When she went to visit him on the night he died she was unaware of the hand grenade he was about to throw her way.

He had been in the forest earlier that day, he said. And he'd heard her mother arguing with Jay Knapton. Olivia had been confused. 'Why were they arguing? They don't know each other,' she'd said.

And then he'd told her about how he sometimes worked for Jay dealing drugs and that her mother was also involved. She refused to believe it, telling him her mother would never do anything like that.

'They were arguing about the night of the accident. It sounded like they'd covered something up. About what happened to your friends. I think you need to tell the police,' Ralph had said. And in that moment Olivia knew her worst fears were confirmed. The lights on the night of the accident. The number-plate. It *had* been her mother's car. She didn't know how or why, but it sounded like her mother was somehow involved.

He was unusually firm with her. Agitated, almost. 'The police have been sniffing around. I'm fed up with always being the one they point the finger at. They still think I had something to do with your friends going missing. They saw me with Jade the next morning but I know they think it was Tamzin. It wasn't. I was buying some weed from Jade. The missing girls was nothing to do with me. It's unfair. And all the time the real culprits are under our noses.'

'I can't grass on my own mother,' she'd replied, aghast. 'And if she is part of some drugs ring with Jay Knapton, won't they come looking for you too?'

But Ralph hadn't been so sure. He'd started ranting about

endless police questions, about his involvement with Jay Knapton and what he actually did for him. He told her the net was closing and something had to be done, the focus needed to be on something else. *Someone else.* Like her mother.

Olivia had left the caravan crying. She'd hung around the forest, trying to gather her thoughts. What was she going to do? She needed to go back and persuade Ralph not to say anything. Convince him he'd heard it wrong. Her mother would never be involved with Jay. If he wanted to blame someone then let him blame Jay Knapton, not her mother. It wasn't fair to use her as a scapegoat. But he'd been unusually aggressive and high when she returned, and he'd rounded on her when she challenged him. She hadn't set out to kill him. Picking up the rock and striking him as he walked away had been a reflex.

'I'm so sorry,' she says now, tears staining her cheeks. She'll feel guilty for the rest of her life.

It had all been for nothing. Her mother was arrested and charged anyway.

She'd only seen Wesley once after he was arrested. He rang her, begging her to visit him in prison, and she'd relented. He'd looked surprisingly well, sitting opposite her, and she was shocked when he apologized to her for everything. 'I did love you, you know,' he'd said sadly, hanging his head. 'I still do. I always will. I know I didn't always show it in the right way but I wanted a better life for us. That's why I got involved with Jay. I'd lost my job at the bank and I didn't want you to be disappointed in me.' He then explained how he'd been getting up every day and putting on a tie and driving to the next town to pretend to go to work. No wonder he'd told her never to call him at the bank and always seemed to be taking sickies. 'When Jay came up with another way to make money I thought it was so easy. I didn't mean to hurt you. I was scared I was losing you.' She appreciated his words, not that she'd ever forgive him. She never wanted to see him again. Just before their time was up he'd leant across the table and quietly, so that only she could hear, mouthed, 'I told the police Jay killed Ralph.' She'd stared after his retreating back, too shocked to move.

Did he suspect? She'll never know for certain. Secrets. She'd kept so many and now she had another to take to the grave.

She thrusts her hands into the pockets of her yellow raincoat and, with one last regretful look towards Ralph's caravan, she trudges out of the forest towards home.

Acknowledgements

THE GIRLS WHO DISAPPEARED WAS ONE OF MY MORE COM-plex books to write and I'd spent months alone with it until I'd finished the first draft and sent it to my wonderful editor Maxine Hitchcock. I knew it was a messy, out-of-control beast and I am so grateful that Maxine saw exactly what I was hoping to achieve with this book and whipped it into shape, along with the brilliant Clare Bowron. Once I had their notes back I could see more clearly what I needed to do to make the book sharper, pacier and tighter, and I ended up cutting out nearly fifteen thousand words. The book is so much better for their edits and I can't thank them enough for their wisdom, intelligence and advice.

Also a huge thank-you to the rest of the brilliant Michael Joseph team: Rebecca Hilsdon, Ellie Morley, Vicky Photiou, Ella Watkins, Beatrix McIntyre, Deirdre O'Connell, Hannah Padgham and Katie Corcoran. A special mention to Lee Motley for the beautiful and striking book jackets, and to Hazel Orme for her meticulous copy-edits, as well as her enthusiasm and kind words. I'm so grateful to you all.

I am so lucky to have Juliet Mushens as my agent. Her advice, determination and talent has meant my books are published in more than twenty countries and I can't thank her enough for all her support and friendship over the years (and the shared love of floofy – and sometimes naughty – cats!), for making me laugh, for keeping me sane and for being simply the best! I'm also indebted to Liza DeBlock, Kiya Evans and Rachel Neely – the rest of the wonderful team at Mushens Entertainment.

Thank you to my foreign publishers, particularly Penguin Verlag in Germany, and Sarah Stein, Kristin Cipolla and the rest of the Harper team in the US and Canada.

A special thank-you to my fellow West Country writer friends, Tim Weaver, Gilly Macmillan and Cally Taylor, for their support, advice, meet-ups and laughs. I wrote this book at the same time Cally was writing her recent thriller, *The Guilty Couple,* so we decided to work in tandem, supporting each other every day with word races and encouragement, and it was so motivational.

Thank you, as always, to my wonderful family, especially to my mum, Linda, and sister, Samantha, for reading my drafts before they are published, and to my dad, step-parents, step-siblings and in-laws.

To my husband, Ty, and children, Claudia and Isaac, who have to put up with me droning on about plots and deadlines. Love you so much.

A massive thank-you to all the bloggers and reviewers who have been so supportive to me over the years. I'm so grateful for everything you do. You are amazing.

And finally, this book is dedicated to you, my readers here in the UK and abroad. Without your support I wouldn't be able to do this job, which – messy first drafts aside – is my dream job. So thank you. Thank you for buying, borrowing and recommending my books. It means the world.

About the Author

CLAIRE DOUGLAS HAS WORKED AS A JOURNALIST FOR FIF-
teen years, writing features for women's magazines and national
newspapers. She wanted to be a novelist since the age of seven, a
dream that came true with the publication of her first novel, *The
Sisters*, which won *Marie Claire's* Debut Novel Award. She lives
in Bath, England, with her husband and two children.

DON'T MISS THESE OTHER NAIL-BITING THRILLERS!

"Douglas is a true must-read thriller author."
—POPSUGAR